The Lost Women of Lost Lake

The Lost Women of Lost Lake

ELLEN HART

MINOTAUR BOOKS ✻ NEW YORK

THE LOST WOMEN OF LOST LAKE. Copyright © 2011 by Ellen Hart. All rights reserved. Printed in the United States of America. For information, address St. Martin's Press, 175 Fifth Avenue, New York, N.Y. 10010.

Library of Congress Cataloging-in-Publication Data

Hart, Ellen.
    The lost women of lost lake / Ellen Hart.—1st ed.
        p. cm.
    ISBN 978-0-312-61477-5
    1. Lawless, Jane (Fictitious character)—Fiction.   2. Women
detectives—Minnesota—Minneapolis—Fiction.   3. Restaurateurs—
Fiction.   4. Minneapolis (Minn.)—Fiction.   I. Title.
    PS3558.A6775L67 2011
    813'.54—dc22

                                                                2011020348

First Edition: October 2011

10   9   8   7   6   5   4   3   2   1

Cast of Characters

Jane Lawless: owner of the Lyme House restaurant and
                 the Xanadu Club in Minneapolis

Cordelia Thorn: artist director at the Allen Grimby Reper-
                 tory Theater in St. Paul; Jane's best friend

Lyndie LaVasser: owner of the LaVasser Gift Emporium &
                 Soda Fountain in Lost Lake; Kenny Moon's
                 grandmother

Tessa Cornell: playwright; Jill's wife; Jonah's aunt

Jill Ivorsen: owner of Thunderhook Lodge in Lost
                 Lake; Tessa's wife; Jonah's aunt

Fontaine Littlewolf: stage manager and janitor at the Lost Lake
                 Community Center

Jonah Ivorsen: high school student; Tessa and Jill's nephew

Emily Jensen: housekeeper at Fisherman's Cove

Kenny Moon: Jonah's best friend; Lyndie LaVasser's grandson

Helen Merland: elderly resident of Lost Lake

Wendell Hammond: Helen's houseguest; photographer

Steve Feigenbaumer: visitor to Lost Lake

A. J. Nolan: ex–homicide cop turned PI

What can the England of 1940 have in common with the England of 1840? But then, what have you in common with the child of five whose photograph your mother keeps on the mantelpiece? Nothing, except that you happen to be the same person.

—George Orwell,
The Lion and the Unicorn: Socialism and the English Genius

Conviction is a good motive, but a bad judge.

—Albert Einstein

The Lost Women of Lost Lake

A crimson sun sat low in the sky over the blue waters of Lost Lake when the stranger walked into the LaVasser Soda Fountain & Gift Emporium on Main Street. Lyndie LaVasser, the owner, happened to be standing behind the cash register at the time, hiding the cigarette she was smoking by keeping her hand tucked under the counter. She'd been watching her grandson, Kenny, hustle a girl who'd graduated from high school with him last spring. She was seated on one of the old-fashioned chrome and red Naugahyde stools. The girl's name was Emily Jensen, a vapid but pretty little flirt. Kenny was ignoring the rest of the customers, which concerned Lyndie because, with the bad economy, the soda fountain was keeping the emporium afloat.

She cleared her throat.

Her grandson glanced up and grinned.

She nodded to the man waving his hand, trying to get his attention.

"Be back in a flash," Kenny said to Emily.

The boy might look like a linebacker for a pro football team, yet he was still a child, in Lyndie's opinion—happy one minute, down in the dumps the next. Emily, with that ethereal look in her eyes, overdone makeup, and long, golden, naturally curly tresses, was a diva in training, not the kind of girl who would ever understand a difficult personality like Kenny. The boy needed someone down-to-earth, someone who could watch a Vikings game with him and then go outside during halftime and enjoy watching him blow stuff up in the backyard. In her experience, men rarely picked wives for the right reasons. They went for looks. Legs. Breasts. Hips. Mouths. Eyes. Smiles. Damn the torpedoes and anything else that got between them and their favorite body part.

Lyndie made a mental note to talk to Kenny about this Emily kid, and yet as she watched the stranger move around the store, the thought drifted out of her mind.

Dipping down to take another quick drag, Lyndie eased onto a stool. At sixty-two, she was still slim and attractive, although she also fit quite easily into the grandmother category, which annoyed the heck out of her because inside she felt a tad divalike herself. Outward appearances, as she well knew, could be deceiving. Lyndie had a past, and that past told her the man eyeing the books by Minnesota authors along the back wall was a cop.

Working his way up to the front, the man smiled at her as he touched the black brim of his Chicago White Sox cap. "Evening."

"Can I help you?"

"I hope so. I'm looking for a woman named Judy Clark." He planted a pair of hairy hands on the glass countertop. "She'd be in her sixties now. About your age, I would guess. I have a photo, although it's old. And it's not very good." He reached into the inner pocket of his light cotton jacket, drew it out.

Lyndie stubbed out the cigarette and slipped on her reading glasses. "You say this person lives in Lost Lake?"

"That's what I've been told."

The photo showed a waiflike young woman in jeans and a navy peacoat standing next to a handsome, sandy-haired guy in a ripped army jacket. Both were wearing bulky scarves that partially obscured their faces. "Have you tried the phone book?"

"She's not listed."

Handing the snapshot back, Lyndie shrugged. "Sorry. I've never seen either of these people before. As you said, the picture's kind of old. Where was it taken?"

"Chicago. November, nineteen sixty-eight."

"A long time ago."

He didn't respond, just nodded.

"Who's the guy?"

"Name was Jeff Briere."

"Was?"

"He's dead."

"I'm sorry. Was he a friend?"

"I never met him."

"So . . . it's the woman you're interested in?"

"Correct."

"If you don't mind my asking, who is she to you?"

His thick eyebrows drew down over penetrating dark eyes. He reminded her of a crow—sleek, watchful, clever. "Just a person I need to talk to. I'll find her. One way or the other." He turned, looked up at the old tin ceiling. "You've got quite a place here. A piece of history, something from the early part of the last century." Glancing over at the soda fountain, he added, "That almost looks real."

"It is real. My ex-husband and I had it removed, piece by piece, from a drugstore that was going out of business in a small town in South Dakota. It's a big attraction around here,

3

especially in the summer when the fishermen arrive and the resorts fill up."

He gazed around him a moment more, then faced her. "I take it you're a lifelong resident."

"That's right."

He repositioned his cap, clearly not ready to end the conversation. "The guy over at the hardware store told me about a woman in town who might be able to help me. Her name's Helen Merland. Apparently she and her husband own the Lost Lake Brewing Company."

"Used to. Helen's husband died many years ago. She's in her late eighties now."

"The guy said she knows everybody. That's what I'm looking for. Someone with connections and a good memory."

"Well, then, I think you're out of luck. Helen was diagnosed with Alzheimer's last year."

"Oh. Sorry."

He didn't look the least bit sorry, just disgruntled.

"How bad off is she?"

Helen was forgetful. She became mixed up easily, would occasionally move back and forth in time, and yet, for the most part, was still able to take care of herself and live in her own home. Lyndie had never considered that Helen's growing affliction would have any bearing on her life, other than the sadness that came from slowly, inexorably losing a dear friend to a terrible disease. "I wouldn't bother her if I were you."

He returned the snapshot to the pocket of his jacket.

"Are you planning to stick around?"

"For a while." He took out a card. "If you think of anything that might help me, that's my cell."

4

She waited until the front door closed behind him before she picked up the card and read the name.

STEVEN FEIGENBAUMER
CELL: 984-555-8291

With a last name like that, he had to be related.

"What's wrong?" called Kenny, still hovering near Emily.

Lyndie forced a smile. "Nothing. Everything's fine."

Except that it wasn't. She did know a woman named Judy Clark. She saw her every morning when she looked in the mirror.

2

"What if he's out for revenge? Or wants to turn us over to the police? We've got to *do* something!"

Tessa Cornell held the phone away from her ear and could still hear Lyndie's braying voice through the phone line. "I agree," she said, setting her briefcase down on the kitchen island. "But what?"

"You're the one with all the ideas," said Lyndie, all but hyperventilating. "If it weren't for you, I wouldn't be in this mess."

"That's bullshit and you know it."

"Don't use that kind of language around me."

So it was finally here, thought Tessa. She was about to face the adversary she'd always known would come. Now that he had, she felt a strange calm settle over her, though she knew it wouldn't last.

"Once upon a time," began Tessa, about to deliver a history lesson.

"Just stop it," said Lyndie. "I've changed. I'm not the same person I was back in Chicago."

Tessa felt the gulf, too, between the woman she'd been and the woman she was now.

"If that man knows we're here—"

"You said that all he had was an old picture of you and Jeff that barely showed your faces."

"Yeah, but—"

"So how does he get from a bad photo to us?"

"I don't know, but I'm scared. I mean, why, of all places, did he choose to come into the emporium? Maybe he knows more than he's letting on."

Tessa was furious with Lyndie for not grilling the guy harder to find out what he knew. Bad luck had tied Tessa's fate to Lyndie's, though there was little she could do about it now. Lyndie was a lightweight. She was also a chameleon. Her usual MO was to let the men in her life fill in the blank space between her ears.

"He wants to talk to Helen," said Lyndie.

"He won't get anything out of her."

"What about the Alzheimer's?"

The last time Tessa had talked to Helen she'd seemed almost normal. Still, it was something to consider. "Just keep your mouth shut. You haven't said anything to George, have you?"

George was Lyndie's fiancé and the pastor of Lost Lake Lutheran. To think that Lyndie, alias Judy Clark, with her past, had ended up engaged to a minister might have been hilarious if it weren't so absurdly ironic.

"If George ever finds out what we did—"

"Call me tomorrow," said Tessa. "And relax. If the guy had more, we'd already be in jail."

"Or dead."

"I can always count on you to be Miss Sunshine, right, Judy?"

"Don't call me that. They might be tapping our phones."

"Who's *they*?"

"You know. People who tap phones."

"Just be careful."

"A little late for that." She hung up.

Tessa was glad now that she'd called the rehearsal early. She was directing an Alan Ayckbourn farce, *Relatively Speaking*, for the Lost Lake Community Theater, but as the evening went on, she found herself growing increasingly annoyed by the playwright's babbling dialogue. Dialogue was supposed to be an Ayckbourn speciality. She usually found the riffs and charming misunderstandings entertaining. Perhaps it was the leaden way the actors were delivering their lines. For the past four weeks she'd done her best with them. Summer audiences expected humor, light entertainment. The show opened next Friday. She had work to do before then, but couldn't deal with it tonight. Ultimately, the play would be what it would be. She laughed, somewhat bitterly, to think that her youthful idealism had turned into such aging fatalism. Cozy bromides aside, " 'Twas ever thus" still seemed an accurate statement of human affairs.

Early on, Tessa had chosen to keep her partner, Jill, in the dark about her past, although she often wondered if she'd made the right decision. Unbelievable as it seemed to her now, the kid who had once wandered the streets of a small town in Nebraska wondering if there was anyone like her anywhere else on earth had ended up in a twenty-six-year relationship with a woman she adored. Dreams did come true.

Jill's family had owned Thunderhook Lodge, Lost Lake's premier resort, ever since Lars Anders Ivorsen, Jill's great-grandfather, had built the main lodge in the early nineteen twenties. For Jill, Thunderhook was a connection to her childhood and a job she loved. For Tessa, Lost Lake suited her needs because it was about as remote as a person could get and still find some semblance of civilization.

Unlike Lyndie, who never saw a cocktail she didn't like, Tessa rarely drank anything stronger than a glass of wine with dinner. Back in the day, she remembered thinking that people who did drugs were weak-minded. She refused to partake, even when most of her friends, people she trusted and admired, frequently got wasted on booze or stoned on pot. After the phone call from Lyndie, however, she felt the urge for something stronger than chardonnay.

Tessa held the tequila bottle over the blender jar. Several long glugs later, she added the Rose's lime juice and the triple sec, then a bunch of ice cubes. In a matter of seconds she had herself a pitcher of margaritas. Not that she bothered to find an actual pitcher.

Stepping out on the deck overlooking the lake, feeling the breeze off the water ruffle her short, dyed blond hair, she drank straight from the blender jar as she stood at the railing. The burn in her throat felt good, centering. In the blue twilight, lights dotted the far shoreline. She assumed that Jill was still up at the main lodge working the reception desk, which meant she had some time to tuck her emotions safely back inside. She hated all the lies, although in the years she and Jill had been together, she had found no way around them. To tell Jill the truth would have made her an accomplice.

It was possible, Tessa supposed, that Steve Feigenbaumer would find nothing concrete and go away quietly. If all he had was a faded snapshot, he didn't have much to go on. Still, the fact that he was even *in* Lost Lake meant that he'd learned something, and that thought acted like acid, eating away at the barriers Tessa had so carefully erected between the woman she used to be and the woman she was now.

What was that famous Faulkner line? "The past is never

dead. It's not even past." That was the best definition of her life she'd ever come across.

Sitting down on a chaise, Tessa continued to sip from the blender jar. Under normal circumstances, the waves lapping against the shore would have provided some sense of calm. Tonight, however, with the restless mood she was in, the waves did nothing but irritate her. She couldn't work on the new play she'd begun writing, didn't want to think. The truth was, she was sick to death of her own nihilism. If Nietzsche and Eugene O'Neill were right, a person needed a heavy set of delusions to find any meaning in life. Her delusions had been burned to the ground long ago.

Hearing the garage door open, Tessa got up and walked over to the stairs leading down to the driveway. Jill was backing the Jeep out into the drive. When Jill cut the motor, Tessa called down, "Didn't expect you home so early."

Jill slid out of the front seat and smiled up at her. "I figured you'd be at the rehearsal until ten." She cocked her head. "What's in your hand?"

"Margaritas."

"Are you planning to share?"

"Possibly."

"Something wrong?"

"What could be wrong?"

Jill leaned partway over the hood. "Thought I'd run up to the store and get us some munchies. I was hoping we could watch a movie tonight."

Tessa took an unsteady step down the stairs. "How do I know you don't have a girlfriend waiting for you at the Piggly Wiggly?"

"If I did, would you be jealous?"

"Damn straight."

Another smile. "I'm a little too old for that kind of hanky-panky." She pointed to her silver hair.

"You look pretty good to me."

"That's because your eyes are aging as fast as my hair."

Tessa had just turned sixty-five. Jill was sixty-eight. Her hair had gone gray in her late forties, so it was nothing new. Tessa thought it was beautiful, thought Jill was beautiful. "Don't forget the chip dip."

"And don't you start the festivities without me." With that, she hopped in the front seat.

Tessa watched the red tail lights disappear up the gravel road, surprised by the tears welling in her eyes. She wasn't sure what she'd do if anything ever happened to Jill.

Tessa lived her life inside her head. She always had. She was clumsy when it came to sports, never did play on a softball team like every other good dyke in the universe. She was chunky and hid it under heavy sweaters in her youth and updated Mexican peasant dresses now. She favored scoop necks to show off her turquoise jewelry and shawls to hide her one too many curves. Given the choice between sitting in a chair and reading a book or going for a walk, the chair and the book would win every time.

Jill was athletic, lived in a body that still water-skied in the summer, skated and cross-country skied in the winter. She ran a couple miles every day, swam in the evenings if the weather permitted. She loved activity and took great pleasure in the simple joy of motion. She liked nothing more than fixing things— cars, motorcycles, boat motors, clocks. To her, everything was a puzzle, and that meant everything had a solution.

What seemed most ironic to Tessa was that Jill, in the eyes

of the world, was a nobody. Tessa was the accomplished one. She'd written twenty-seven plays, most of which had been produced at least once. She had a dozen or more awards to her credit. And yet, without Jill as an anchor, she would have spun off into the cosmos long ago. Jill kept her going, kept her feet firmly planted on the ground. She was strong and centered and kind. In a crazy world, Jill was Tessa's tether to a reality that kept her sane.

Taking another couple of swallows from the blender jar, Tessa continued down the stairs to the garage. She weaved a little, thinking it was funny until she nearly tripped over a crowbar. She kicked it, angry that it had crawled into her path, then bent down to pick it up. The cold, heavy metal felt good in her hand. A solid means of destruction. Swaying out of the drive, past the log pile into the trees that surrounded the cottage, she took a swing at a low-hanging branch. To her amazement, it ripped clean away. She would take this crowbar up to her study to help her hack through the thick weeds of thought.

Forging ahead, with a nearly full moon lighting her way, she continued to sip from the jar. By now there wasn't much left, which was probably why her body felt light and buoyant. In contrast, her ruminations had grown so heavy that she was afraid they would crack her head open.

"Stop it," she ordered, recognizing alcohol-fueled melodrama when she saw it.

"Besides," she grumbled, "it was all Hubey's fault." She took a swipe at another branch. "It was freakin' kindergarten ethics. Always has been. You're either for us or against us."

She walked on, not thinking too much about where she was headed. The night air felt cool against her hot skin. When the blender was empty, she set it down on a rock, intending to come back for it. "Time for a gut check. Gotta keep doing those gut checks. Where are you? What are you thinking? Come on, now. No cop-outs. A cop-out is a mortal sin." She cringed at the jargon of her youth.

Wielding the crowbar as if it were a scythe, she cleared the brush as she went. "Always needed a theory to rationalize my life. Gotta have a good theory. A good theory can take you anywhere you want to go."

Stumbling over a tree root, she righted herself with some difficulty and then turned around, deciding that it might be politic to head back. "Before I get totally lost," she mumbled. "Hell, I am totally lost. With me, it's a state of being." She thrust the crowbar in the air. "Kill the mind-controlling maniacs."

She was halfway up the deck stairs when Jill pulled the Jeep back into the drive. As she got out, she glanced up. "What are you doing with that crowbar?"

"Where's a good dose of healthy doubt when you need it?"

"Huh?"

"Doubt!"

"I don't know what you're talking about."

"My *life*," she shouted. She twisted around to make her point by banging the crowbar on the railing. Instead, she lost her balance and fell forward. She heard Jill's scream as she hit the bottom step.

"Are you all right?" cried Jill, rushing to her. She knelt down, a look of horror on her face.

"I think . . ." said Tessa, arching her body in pain, "I think I just broke something."

3

"Her ankle?" said Jane.

"Gravity isn't always our friend, Janey." Cordelia reapplied her lipstick as she gazed languidly in a compact mirror. "She fell down the deck steps last Thursday. Jill called me last night, told me it was a grade-two sprain—partial tearing of the ligaments. Thank God she didn't break it. The doc wants her to keep it up and apply ice through the weekend. She gets an air splint and a walking boot tomorrow, although it will be a few weeks before she's back to normal." She smacked her lips together, looking satisfied that she'd completed the repair.

Jane pulled out a kitchen chair and sat down, stunned once again at how swiftly accidents could happen. " Can she walk at all?"

"For now she's using crutches. She can't put any weight on it until she's in the walking boot tomorrow. Makes you think twice about being out in the boonies all by yourself."

The comment was directed at Jane. She'd taken the last two weeks of July and the first two weeks of August off from her restaurants in Minneapolis to vacation at her family's summer lodge on Blackberry Lake. She had good managers in place, men and women she trusted—longtime employees. Instead of sticking around to micromanage, her usual MO, she'd decided to give herself the gift of a real vacation. With everyone and his uncle dropping in to say hi, it wasn't exactly the kind of peace she'd been hoping for. Since the lodge was only fifty miles north of the Twin Cities, it was Cordelia's third trip out. "I better call Tessa."

"That's one possibility." Cordelia stood with her back to the kitchen counter, sipping from a tall can of Izze blackberry soda, her current "go-to" beverage. "She's in for a long haul."

"Poor kid."

"Yup. That's why I'm here. Cordelia Thorn to the rescue."

Jane had wondered why her friend had appeared so suddenly on a such a lovely Sunday afternoon. It wasn't as if Cordelia was into the joys of nature. She could easily have phoned with the news. She'd arrived shortly after one in her newest car fetish, a used 2006 cherry red Mercedes CLK350, the top down, the radio blaring. Mouse, Jane's brown lab, had begun barking even before the car purred off the gravel road and stopped in the dirt drive. Again, Cordelia had made her usual flamboyant entrance. When she got out of the car, revealing a faux leopardskin dress with a plunging neckline, shoulder pads, and a wide-brimmed raffia sun hat, Mouse simply sat on his haunches and stared.

Cordelia was a large woman, in every sense of the word. Six feet tall—even taller in the patent leather pumps she was wearing—and well over two hundred pounds. She was a curvaceous giant. Her lipstick matched the car, a small detail that most would never have noticed but would have been central to Cordelia's "idiom," as she called her various fashion statements. She'd even managed to find pantyhose with seams down the back. All clothing was costume to Cordelia. And, of course, all the world a stage.

"So here's the deal." She crushed the empty soda can in her fist and flipped it over her shoulder into the sink, "I want you to drive up to Lost Lake with me."

"Why are you going to Lost Lake?"

"Why not?"

"Is this a philosophical debate?"

"No. Strictly practical. I promised Tessa I'd take over the last week of rehearsals for the play she's directing."

"Is that really necessary? She'll be in a walking boot tomorrow."

"You know Tessa. A hangnail is cause to summon the paramedics."

It was true. Tessa was a world-class hypochondriac.

"I see this as an opportunity to right a wrong. We haven't been up there to see Jill and Tessa in three years. Don't you think we owe them a visit? And beyond that, the last week of rehearsals for any play is crucial. If Tessa misses a day or two, it could be fatal."

Tessa and Cordelia had a lot in common, in Jane's opinion. They were both drama divas.

"It's an Ayckbourn farce," continued Cordelia. "A staple of small community theaters. I've directed it so many times that I can jump in quickly. I don't have anything pressing at the Allen Grimby right now, and Melissa's on assignment in Rochester. Sure, Tessa might be able to find someone to carry her on a bier to the theater for the final rehearsal on Wednesday night, but before that, we have to get through the tech stuff. The preview is scheduled for Thursday. Once the play opens, the director becomes irrelevant. I'm not saying *I* would become irrelevant."

17

"Of course not."

"A few days of my time is all she needs. Jill said they'd give the two of us adjoining rooms. All meals comped. Come on, Janey. What are friends for?" She raised her eyebrows, tilted her head toward the car in the drive. "We'll have a blast. It'll be just like old times. You and me tearing up the backroads. Cruising the lake on the pontoon. Cannonballing off the dock. Playing shuffleboard by flashlight. Remember those caramel rolls they make at the Jacaranda Café in town? Ambrosia." She kissed her fingertips.

Jane and Cordelia had been friends with Tessa and Jill for nearly twenty years, ever since Cordelia had produced and directed one of Tessa's plays at the Blackburn Playhouse. While Jane's partner, Christine, had been alive, they'd visited Thunderhook at least once every summer. And because Tessa was a dedicated foodie, and Jill loved the cross-country ski trails at Lebanon Hills in Apple Valley, they usually came down every winter and stayed for a week. Cordelia was right. They both had great memories.

"And we wouldn't be gone that long," said Cordelia, continuing to make her pitch.

In Jane's opinion, Tessa could be a lot of fun, but she was also a true pain in the ass. "She can't be an easy patient. I'm sure Jill could use some help."

"You could do a few meals. And I could handle the rehearsals."

Jane crossed into the living room, to a picture window overlooking Blackberry Lake. A black man in denim overalls and a canvas boonie hat sat in a rowboat a few hundred yards from shore, his fishing line in the water. Mouse relaxed in the sun at the end of the dock, keeping him company. "I don't know. I'm not sure I can leave him. He's only been here a few days."

18

A. J. Nolan was a retired homicide cop who worked these days as a private investigator. In early May, he'd taken a bullet in the stomach—a bullet that was meant for Jane. She already loved him as a friend, and now she owed him her life.

"He'll be fine," said Cordelia, searching through the refrigerator for another soda. "He's just here to recuperate. He can do that with or without you. Don't you have any more blackberry soda?"

"Try the clementine."

She dug around. "Nolan's got his car, so he can drive himself into town if he needs groceries."

Jane had a couple more weeks before she had to return to work. She'd invited Nolan out to the cabin to stay as long as he liked. His digestion was still giving him problems, as was his back, although he was growing stronger every day. If she did agree to go with Cordelia—and she had to admit that she was tempted—she and Nolan would still have some time together when she got back. He didn't have any pressing reasons to return to the Twin Cities and seemed to be enjoying himself fishing and just hanging out. "Let me talk to him."

"I'll help."

"No. Just me. And if I catch any hesitation from him *at all*, I'm not going."

Several hours—and a stop at a roadhouse for lunch—later, Jane and Cordelia were on their way up Highway 169, driving through a patchwork quilt of small towns, prairie, and corn fields.

"Nolan said he'd enjoy a few days by himself," said Jane, cleaning her sunglasses with the edge of her blue chambray shirt. "He's lived alone since his wife died and said he's grown to like it. Besides, without me around, there'd be more fish for him."

Cordelia roared around a slow-moving truck. "See, what did I tell you? And you'll be back before you know it."

"It'll be fun to see Jill and Tessa again. It's been too long. I would guess that Tessa isn't in the best mood."

"Is she ever? As Bertie Wooster once put it, she's 'experienced some difficulty in detecting the bluebird.'"

"I don't think she trusts many people."

"Why should she? Look at where she lives. Jill and Tessa are the only out lesbians in all of Lost Lake. Small towns are steaming cauldrons of gossip to begin with. If Tessa wasn't a playwright, successful in the eyes of the world, and if Jill's family hadn't built the one truly great resort in the area, they might not find the populace quite so friendly."

"The world is changing."

"Granted. But in small-town America, I wouldn't bet on finding a lot of social ecumenism. That's all I'm saying. Tessa has a right to protect her privacy."

"Then again, it's hard to be private when you lead such a public life."

Cordelia turned to stare. "No it's not. That's the beauty of her chosen profession. If you want to be creative and at the same time fade into the woodwork, become a playwright. It's a nearly invisible career path."

"Seriously?"

"Are you kidding me? The only other writer I can think of who's more invisible is a poet."

"Doesn't say much for our society."

"You mean when teenage blondes with bad attitudes, bad

voices, and brutal boyfriends become entertainment icons? It's our culture, Janey. Love it or leave it."

On their way through Grand Rapids, Cordelia insisted on stopping so they could put the top up on the convertible. It was beginning to look like rain and she wasn't interested in getting her costume wet.

"I wear clothes," said Jane. "Not costumes."

"I know," said Cordelia dryly. "And with all the holes in the knees of your jeans, I'd be more inclined to call them rags."

"I'm on vacation."

"Your point is?"

They sped out of town on Highway 38, heading for the Chippewa National Forest.

"So many lakes up here," said Jane. "Did you know that there are at least a thousand in just this one area?"

"Easy to imagine one of them getting lost," said Cordelia, slipping a Cheryl Wheeler CD into the Harman Kardon CD player and turning up the volume.

Years ago, Jane had found a brochure that detailed the history of the resort and the town. Lost Lake owed its existence, in no small part, to Jill's great-grandparents, Lars and Maj Ivorsen. A black-and-white photo on the brochure's cover showed the two of them in work clothes, sleeves rolled up past their elbows, swinging a hammer along with four others, the partially built three-story log structure in the background. In constructing Thunderhook, they'd created a resort that wasn't just state-of-the-art for the nineteen twenties, but unique in its own right. The artistic influences were various—art deco, Native American, Scandinavian. A vacation resort and fishing lodge in the summer, a cross-country ski lodge and snow playground in the winter, Thunderhook had become *the* destination in the Chippewa National Forest for those who wanted something more than the plain, rough fishing and hunting cabins the smaller resorts offered.

Thunderhook had kept the economy of the town alive through the worst of the Depression, primarily because, even then, there were enough wealthy people around who could pay to get away from the hurly-burly of the city to spend some quality time enjoying nature—as long as nature afforded them a respectable dining experience every morning and evening and had the amenities they considered essential.

Many years later, because of its reputation inside the state, Lost Lake had become what it was today—a picturesque, quaint lakeside town with a jewel of a resort at its center. The downtown featured art galleries stocked with artwork by local artists and artisans, half a dozen gift shops, a local newspaper, and another half dozen excellent restaurants and cafés. "We turn right up ahead," said Jane. "That should be Larson Lake Road."

"You know, Janey, there's something terribly manly about being in the woods." Cordelia puffed out her anything-but-manly chest. "Good thing I brought plenty of plaid with me."

"Seems like you packed for an army." Jane glanced around at the trunk in the backseat.

"I never know what my mood will be on any given day."

Seven miles and three Cheryl Wheeler songs later, they made another right, this time heading through the outskirts of Lost Lake. The closer they got to the center of town, the more FOR SALE signs they saw in front yards.

"This is depressing," said Cordelia, her gaze sliding from one side of the street to the other.

When they reached Main Street, Jane noticed that several of the gift shops, a couple of the galleries, and one of the restaurants had closed their doors. Other businesses were shut down too, with FOR RENT signs displayed prominently inside bare windows. In years past, the central downtown streets had been festooned with large hanging flower baskets. These were also gone, perhaps another victim of the economic downturn.

They drove the rest of the way in silence. As they passed the old painted wood sign for Thunderhook Lodge, dark blue letters on a canary yellow background, Cordelia hung a left toward the lake and parked in the circular drive in front of the building. The lodge, which faced the lake, sat nestled into a broad stretch of tall, straight, white pine.

Trying to work a little something positive back into the gloom, Jane rolled down her window, breathed deeply and said, "Smell that air."

"Ah, yes," sighed Cordelia. "The great outdoors. Pine. Wood smoke. Silage. Cow. The occasional skunk. Can't get enough of it. Let's go in and scare up Jill."

The main lobby featured a stone fireplace, beamed ceilings with log trusses, full round chinked and varnished log walls, and a series of small paned windows that overlooked the lake. The furniture was old and rustic. Even in summer, a fire burned in the fireplace, welcoming guests inside.

Coming through the heavy log door, Jane waved at Jill, who was standing behind the reception desk.

Jill hooted. She disappeared into the back room and came out a side hall a few seconds later.

"You made it before the storm," she said, wrapping them each in a hug. "Where's your luggage?"

"Still in the car," said Jane.

Jill's enthusiasm was as infections as ever. "I've put you on the second floor. Both rooms have a bedroom and a sitting area. One of them has a small kitchenette, the other a Jacuzzi. I'll let you fight it out for who gets what."

"Dibs on the Jacuzzi," said Cordelia.

Jill held their hands. "It's so great to see you two."

Like Dorian Gray, she must have owned a painting of herself in an attic, one that aged for her, because she looked the same as ever.

"How was your drive up?"

"Uneventful," said Cordelia.

"Which means we didn't run in to any moose," said Jane. "Cordelia thinks the woods up here are lousy with them."

"They are," said Jill, directing her gaze at Cordelia's clothing. "They especially like women in leopardskin dresses. I'll help with the bags. We'll get you all settled in your rooms and then we can walk down to the cottage. Tessa's waiting for us."

"I think we may need a forklift for Cordelia's trunk," said Jane on their way outside.

"Ah, yes," said Jill. "The trunk. Not many people travel with them these days."

Cordelia huffed. "If it was good enough for John Jacob Astor, it's good enough for me."

"Astor died on the *Titanic*," said Jane.

"Which is why I never travel by steamship."

4

Jonah Ivorsen ambled along the shoulder of Highway 169 with his thumb out, iBuds planted firmly in his ears and his iPod playing an old Stones CD. He'd been lucky all day, first by catching a semi from Iowa City up to Albert Lee, and then climbing aboard a Mayflower Moving van all the way to Hill City. From where he stood right now to Lost Lake was about sixty-five miles. Too far to walk and yet enticingly close. After a couple of days on the road, he felt totally grody and was looking forward to a shower and some clean clothes.

Jonah had spent the last few days feeling like a traitor for leaving his mom and dad in St. Louis, especially with the mess they were in. Without him around, he figured they could scream at each other 24/7 without needing to censor themselves. Sometimes he thought they should just bag it—get a divorce and move to opposite ends of the universe. All he knew for sure was that he had one year of high school left and he intended to spend it in Lost Lake, not that lame-ass Webster Groves High with its billion students, all of whom knew each other and had no room for a new guy. Family solidarity be damned. This was *his senior year*. If he could somehow get his aunts on his side, he might be able to persuade his parents to let him move back. At least, that was the working theory.

Checking over his shoulder, he saw a black Toyota Camry approaching. He hated Toyotas on principle. There were so many of them on the roads that they were like ants—boring and annoying. Why didn't people look around, try for something a little more unusual? It was just like that song—little boxes, different colors but all the same. Pete Seeger sang it. Jonah liked Rise Against's recording better. Still, it was the words that counted. He wasn't going to live his life that way. He intended to put more thought into his decisions and not spend his life following the masses, drinking the same bullshit Kool-Aid everybody else did.

As the Toyota slowed to a stop, the passenger's window rolled down and the man inside called, "Looking for a ride?"

"Yeah," said Jonah, resting his hand against the roof.

"I'm headed up to Empire."

"Perfect. If you could let me out at Larson Lake Road—do you know where that is?"

"Sure do. Get in."

Jonah slid into the front seat and tucked his duffle between his legs.

"Looks like we're in for a storm," said the man, nodding to the dark wall of clouds approaching from the southwest.

Before Jonah could respond, the window next to him rolled back up. Removing his earbuds, he glanced over to size the guy up. He was middle-aged, hair combed straight back over a high forehead, kind of shabby looking, although he had on a bunch of gold jewelry. Under his sport coat was a brace of some kind. Jonah wondered if he had an injured arm or shoulder. After riding with some strange people in his time, Jonah liked to think he could read people well. Generally, he got along with everyone. He preferred to sit quietly and look at the scenery. This guy, however, seemed to want to talk.

"You from around here?" asked the man.

"I grew up in Lost Lake."

"Oh, sure. Beautiful spot. I stayed at Thunderhook Lodge once."

"My aunts own it."

"No kidding. So you're headed home then."

"Sort of. My parents moved to St. Louis last year."

"I don't like big cities."

"Me neither."

Rain drops began to splat against the windshield.

"Name's Otto Lindeman."

"Jonah."

"That a first or a last name?"

"First."

"I guess we don't need your last name right away."

Odd comment. Jonah's weirdo antenna cranked up.

Otto glanced over, his eyes traveling from Jonah's face to the bag at his feet.

For some reason, this brief but oddly thorough examination made Jonah feel even more uneasy. He turned away and gazed out the passenger's window, hoping to shut the conversation down.

"You got any brothers or sisters?"

"Nope."

"An only child. Same with me. I always wanted a little brother. You know, someone to look up to me."

Jonah nodded, keeping his eyes on the side of the road.

"I'm a salesman," said Otto. "Insurance. I like it because nobody checks up on me. If I don't work, I don't make any money. Simple as that."

"Huh."

"You headed to college?"

"After I graduate high school."

"You're still in high school? You look older."

The hairs on the back of Jonah's neck start to prickle.

"How old are you?"

"Old enough."

That seemed to piss the guy off. "Not much of a talker, are you."

"Nope, not much."

He began taking the bends in the road at increasingly higher speeds.

Your luck just ended, thought Jonah. This guy's a certified freak.

"I like speed," said Otto. "How about you?"

"Sure. Why not?"

"You like to live on the edge."

It wasn't a question, so Jonah didn't answer. Instead, he glanced over and saw that what'd he'd first thought was a brace was a friggin' shoulder holster.

Otto saw him looking and smiled. "Like guns?"

"Not really."

"No? This one's a nine-millimeter Smith and Wesson." He drew it out and held it up with his index finger pressed along the side. "Pretty, isn't it?"

"Beautiful."

Otto set the gun on his right thigh and kept his hand over it as he slowed the car back to the speed limit. "Wouldn't want the cops stopping us."

For the next few minutes, they drove without talking. Jonah kept stealing glances at the gun, at the slender, hairless hand covering it, yet never once looked at Otto's face. Instinctively, he knew that if he did, it would seem challenging. He'd fight him if he had to, but there might be a way out of the car without getting himself killed. Didn't his mother always say that he could talk his way out of anything?

When he couldn't stand it another minute, Jonah said, "What are you going to do with that gun?" He worked to keep the fear out of his voice. Showing weakness was always the wrong tactic with another guy.

"Don't know. Got any ideas?"

"You could stop the car and let me out."

Otto sniggered. "That's no fun. Thought you needed a ride up to Lost Lake."

"I'm not in a hurry."

Otto glanced over at him. "Neither am I."

When they reached the south end of Pokegama Lake, Otto said, "I don't like you." He was driving so slowly now that a car passed them on the long open bridge.

Just beyond an old restaurant, Otto pulled off the highway into a patch of weeds and killed the engine. With the windshield wipers stopped mid-swing, the car was instantly engulfed in pelting rain. It felt like being inside a car wash.

"Get your hand away from the door handle," ordered Otto.

Jonah pulled his hand back, repulsed by the man's rancid breath. The interior became sauna-oppressive, rank with nervous sweat, the quiet punctuated by the sounds of rain, the rumble of thunder and the distant flash of lightning.

"I'm in control," said Otto, picking up the pistol, pulling the slide back and letting it pop forward. "You do what I tell you. Got it?"

"I got it," said Jonah, sweat trickling down his back.

Otto's finger curled around the trigger. "I don't like know-it-alls, snotty kids, people who think they're better than me."

Jonah held his breath.

"Say something."

"I don't think I'm better than you. Hell, you've got a great car, nice clothes, a good job. I don't have any of that."

"You really think so?"

"Sure. Look, I didn't mean any disrespect. Honest."

"You should cut your hair. It's too long. Makes you look like a girl."

"Good advice."

"You're not a homo, are you?"

"No."

"You got a girlfriend?"

Jonah wasn't sure what the best answer was. "Yeah."

"You love her?"

"A lot."

"You're not sleeping with her, right?"

"Absolutely not."

"You keep your lousy mitts off her until you get married, you hear me?"

"Loud and clear."

Otto's face twitched. "You're lying. All you think about is sex. Sex, sex, sex."

"I—"

"Don't lie to me."

"Okay, yeah. I think about it."

"All the time. Every waking minute. You've got a filthy, dirty mind."

"Well—"

"You're just like every, other kid. You can't get enough. Your thoughts are rotting your brain and you don't even see it. You're a disgusting pervert, Jonah. I can smell it on you."

Jonah sat very still, eyes down. There was no point in arguing with a lunatic.

"You're thinking about sex right now, aren't you. Admit it."

"Actually, I'm not."

"Sex is a curse. It taints everything. God's biggest mistake. You agree?"

"One hundred percent."

Otto examined his pistol, then sat and watched the rain beat against the windshield. "A curse," he repeated, his left index finger tapping a rhythm against the steering wheel. "It kills us all in the end. Original sin. Every one of us, born in lust. Makes me sick to my stomach."

A semi roared past, hurtling a thick gush of water against the side of the car. Jonah glanced down and saw a *Penthouse* magazine stuffed halfway under the driver's seat.

"What to do," said Otto, still tapping his finger. "You're scared. I like that. You should be scared." He pointed the pistol at Jonah's stomach. "Think it's time for you to get out."

"And then what?"

"You ask too many questions."

With his eyes still on the gun, Jonah cracked the door, pushed it all the way open with his boot, and then grabbed his duffle and jumped out. The wind and rain engulfed him. Bolting for the woods, he heard the car engine catch and rev behind him. Overhead, the wind pounded the trees as lightning split the sky. When he reached the safety of a low hanging pine, he turned and screamed, "Freak! You're a friggin' freako!" Wiping the rain out of his eyes, he tried to catch the license plate, but it was no use. The car had sped off into the storm.

5

By the time Jane, Cordelia, and Jill made it to the cottage that night, the storm clouds had passed over the lake and been replaced by the dying rays of a deep violet sunset. Jane was amused at Cordelia's paranoia about the weather—or perhaps she was just an always prepared Girl Scout. Cordelia brought along a green and black golf umbrella, which she used like a cane as they strolled along the paved path that led past the tennis and shuffleboard courts. After the rain, the air was sharp with the resinous smell of pine. A few branches were down here and there, and some of the outdoor chairs were tipped over, but in general, Thunderhook had made it through with little damage.

"I need to warn you about something," said Jill, adjusting the cotton sweater she'd tied around her shoulders. "Tessa's been in a bad place since the accident. You both know she's never been a particularly sunny personality, but this seems different to me. I assume it's because she hates her invalid status. Neither of us are getting any younger. She must see it as a taste of the future."

"We didn't come to bathe in her sunshine and light," said

Cordelia. "We came because we love you two, and we wanted to help."

"How did she happen to fall?" asked Jane.

Staring into the distance, Jill said, "She came home from rehearsals last Thursday night and proceeded to get drunk."

"Tessa?" said Jane.

"I don't get it either. Something must have triggered it. When I asked her about it, she just brushed it off by saying it was stress over the show, that I was making something out of nothing."

"Were the rehearsals going badly?" asked Cordelia.

"Nothing out of the ordinary."

"Well, no worries," said Cordelia. "I'll take over starting tomorrow night."

"And I thought I could make some of the meals," said Jane. "Take a little pressure off you."

"You two are the best."

"We are indeed," said Cordelia, never one to willingly choose humility in the face of a compliment.

Jane smelled the roast in the oven even before they walked in the side door. Tessa was seated like a dowager queen on the center of a large leather sofa, pillows stuffed around her, her leg propped up on a footstool.

"Welcome to the land of the broken and the needy," she called, holding up her hand and wiggling her fingers.

While Jill stayed in the kitchen to check on dinner, Jane and Cordelia gave Tessa a hug and a kiss and then sat down across from her. Cordelia let out a tired groan as she leaned back against the chair cushion.

"Did you *walk* from the Cities?" asked Tessa, raising an amused eyebrow.

"Funny," said Cordelia, stretching her arms. She'd changed out of her leopardskin dress into a pair of black jeans and a red cotton sweater.

Jane had almost forgotten how beautiful the cottage was.

In nineteen ninety-four, perhaps feeling the same architectural urge as her great-grandfather, though on a much smaller scale, Jill had designed and headed up the contracting. Jutting out like the prow of a ship, the house was built in the shape of a T. At the end of each arm were bedrooms, one of which Tessa had made into a study. Across from the bedrooms were the two bathrooms. The floor plan was compact, a little more than a thousand square feet, although the addition of a wraparound deck nearly doubled the usable space. With the living room at the front, a two-story wall of windows facing the lake, a dining room in the center, the kitchen running along the back wall, and a vaulted ceiling open to a second floor loft, the cottage seemed cozy and yet spacious—the stuff of a city dweller's dreams.

"So, how's the ankle?" asked Jane, motioning to the foot swaddled in ice packs.

"The whole thing is completely ridiculous. I lost my balance on the deck stairs."

"Is it painful?" asked Cordelia.

"Like twelve root canals. And it's swollen like a watermelon, although it's gone down a little. Tomorrow I get the air splint and a walking boot. I'm supposed to let the pain guide me in how much and how fast I get back to walking."

Which means, thought Jane, that she'd be up and around by next Christmas.

"This is absolutely wretched timing."

"Because of the stage piece you're directing," said Jane.

Tessa's gaze drifted out the front windows. "Right."

"A true bummer," said Cordelia. "Although, I suppose there's never a really great time to tear ligaments in your ankle."

Jane thought Tessa looked restless, even a little jittery. Her hair was shorter than it had been the last time Jane had seen her, a spiky platinum instead of the dark blond pageboy she'd worn for so many years. She was an attractive woman, with beautiful aqua eyes, long lashes, and a smile that could melt ice—when she chose to bestow it, which wasn't often.

"How's everything at your restaurants, Jane?" called Jill from the kitchen.

"The economy has taken a toll, but we're holding our own."

"Same with the lodge," said Tessa. "Things have looked up a little since spring arrived, although not as much as we'd hoped."

"And your love life?" called Jill.

Jane hated the inevitability of that wretched question. The fact was, when it came to her professional life and her family she felt lucky, and yet after her partner of ten years, Christine Kane, had died, her luck with women seemed to have tapped out. "Nonexistent at the moment."

"What about that woman you were dating? Kenzie? Was that her name?"

"We broke up. It was mostly my fault."

"Don't be so hard on yourself," said Cordelia. "You simply haven't met the right woman yet. There's a goddess out there waiting just for you."

"I'm not sure I'm up to a goddess."

"Piffle."

"Let's change the subject," said Jane, leaning forward to grab a few nuts from a bowl on the coffee table.

"Cordelia, how's your little niece?" asked Tessa.

"Hattie is brilliant, as always. She'll be starting kindergarten

36

this fall. She's in South America at the moment with Radley Cunningham, her surrogate father."

Sailing past them with several terry cloth towels in hand, Jill opened the screen door and stepped out onto the deck. "Thought we'd eat outside. It's turned into a beautiful evening. I'll get the table and chairs all cleaned up, light some candles, and then we can move out here."

Cordelia rubbed her hands together. "I'm starving. With the right sauce, I could probably manage to eat one of your Navajo rugs."

"Can I help?" asked Jane.

"This will just take a sec." Jill tilted the cast aluminum table and chairs sideways to drain off the standing water. Once she seemed satisfied, she set about drying the furniture with the towels.

"Where are your crutches?" asked Cordelia, looking around.

"Leaning against the bookshelf next to the fireplace," said Tessa.

"They should be closer to you."

"I don't need a lecture."

With a huff, Cordelia got up and collected them, and then tried to help Tessa to her feet, but Tessa was having none of it.

"I'm not some helpless old woman," she said testily.

"You're hardly old," said Jane.

"What would you know about aging? What are you? Fifteen?" Brushing off Cordelia's hand, she said, "I can get up by myself."

Jane wasn't used to being compared to a teenager. She would be forty-five in the fall. Not exactly the flower of youth.

When Tessa almost fell, Cordelia righted her. "Don't be so pigheaded."

"I hate being like this."

"Well, suck it up because the age of miracles is past."

Dinner that night was a bumpy affair. No matter how light-hearted the conversation, Tessa's mood continued to sour. At odd moments she would stare into space, completely checking out of the conversation.

Shortly after ten, Tessa announced that she was cold and wanted to go inside.

Instantly, everyone stood.

"Oh, this is just fabulous. Are you planning to carry me? Maybe we should call the piano movers."

"Come on," said Jill. "Lighten up. We're just concerned."

This time, Tessa managed to get up without losing her balance. She made her way slowly through the screened door and sat down heavily once again on the living room couch. "There," she said, adding more loudly, "You can cancel the hoist and derrick."

"I'll bring you a fresh ice pack," said Jill, piling the dirty plates together.

As they were cleaning up and loading the dishwasher in the kitchen, a knock came at the back door.

"Don't answer it," called Tessa, with an unusual urgency in her voice.

"Don't be silly," said Jill, wiping her hands on a towel. She hooted when she opened the door. "Jonah?"

A tall, bushy-haired youth with a lopsided grin stood outside, soaked to the skin. "I . . . ah, I got caught in the storm."

"How did you get here?" she asked, motioning him inside.

"Hitchhiked."

"From St. Louis?" called Tessa. She sat up straight, attempting to see over the kitchen island.

"Umm . . . yeah?" He was wearing bell-bottomed jeans and

an old army field jacket and had a folded red bandana tied around his forehead. Jane was surprised by how much he'd shot up since the last time she'd seen him.

"You've got to get those clothes off," said Jill. "Are you cold?"

"A little." He dropped a two-strap duffle next to the island. "I don't have any clean clothes."

"I'll start a fire," said Jill. "You need to take a hot shower. And then you can borrow something of mine. You know where I keep my sweats?"

He smiled shyly at Jane and Cordelia. "Hey. You may not remember me—"

"Of course we remember you," said Jane. "You're Jill and Tessa's nephew."

"Looking a little the worse for wear," said Cordelia, hand rising to her hip.

"Get in here and give your other auntie a hug," called Tessa. It was the first time all evening that she looked happy.

His dark eyebrows shot up when he saw her foot propped on a pillow. "What happened?"

"Fell down the deck stairs, tore some ligaments in my ankle."

"But she doesn't want any sympathy," said Jill.

"I adore sympathy," Tessa shot back. "Just don't like hovering."

Jonah removed his wet Nikes before padding over to her to give her a kiss.

"Your parents never called and said you were coming," said Jill, following him into the living room with his mug of coffee.

"That's because they don't know."

"They don't *know*?" said Tessa.

"Nope."

"You just left?"

"They were in the middle of one of their thermonuclear

shouting matches. I wrote a note, said I was going to stay with a friend for a few days. I doubt they even realize I'm gone."

"Lord," said Tessa, scooting herself farther back against the pillows. "Jill, we better call your brother."

"Not before I talk to you," said Jonah, standing his ground. "Look," he said, shoving his hands into his back pockets, "I *hate* St. Louis. I refuse to spend my senior year there. The school is totally lame. All those kids talk about is computer games and sports. I want to stay here, with you two. I want to be able to graduate with my class at Lost Lake High. Is that so much to ask? I can help out, like I always do. I can even do more now that I've got my driver's license."

"*You've* got your driver's license?" said Tessa, clutching her hands to her throat. "Oh, my God, no. No one will ever be safe again."

"Cut it out," said Jonah, clearly annoyed by her attempt at humor. "I promise. I'll be as quiet as a mouse. I'll do *everything* you ask."

Tessa snorted. "That'll be a day."

"No, I mean it," he said. "I just—" He turned to plead with Jill. "I need you both to be on my side, to talk to Mom and Dad and get them to agree. I could stay in the basement room next to the garage. I've stayed there before. The couch is plenty comfortable."

Jill gestured to his clothes. "Go take that shower. I'll build a fire."

"But—"

"You need to give Tessa and me some time to think about it. Are you hungry?"

"I'm always hungry."

"When you're cleaned up, I'll fix you a plate of food."

He took a quick sip from the coffee mug. Handing it back to Jill, he said, "Think fast, okay?"

After he'd retreated to the bedroom, Cordelia sauntered out from behind the counter and draped herself over one of the living room chairs. "Kinda stinks that he had to move away. Senior year is a big deal."

"I don't blame him for wanting to stay," said Tessa. "I think we should let him."

"Thank you!" shouted Jonah, as he zipped, shirtless, from the bedroom to the bathroom.

"We're still considering," called Jill. "Get in that shower." When the water came on, she said, more quietly this time, "My brother and his wife have had marital problems for years. Sometimes Jonah gets lost in the shuffle."

"He's like our own kid," said Tessa, grimacing as she changed her position. "I vote yes."

"But would it be fair to my brother and his wife?"

"Was leaving Lost Lake last summer fair to Jonah?"

Jill crouched down next to the fireplace and busied herself with the newspaper and kindling. "I need more time to think about it."

"Oh, hell," said Tessa. "Fine. Think away. Cordelia, let's talk about tomorrow night. There are some papers in my study that I'll need if we're going to have a substantive conversation."

Jane was still in the kitchen, so she offered to run get them.

"Should be on my desk," called Tessa. "In a manila folder marked *Relatively Speaking*. Or it could be in the right bottom drawer. Just look around."

Jane closed up the dishwasher and switched it on before heading back to the study. The only light in the room came from a green-glass banker's lamp perched on a bookshelf above the desk. To the right of the desk were two good-sized double-hung windows partially covered by gauzy white curtains fluttering in the evening breeze.

As she bent over to examine the papers on the desk, she noticed that water had rained in on the hardwood floor. Crossing quickly into the bathroom, she came back with a roll of paper towels. She crouched down and sopped up the water, wiping the floor until it was completely dry. She didn't want the wood to warp. As she straightened up, she came face to face with the dark visage of a man standing outside one of the windows.

"Who the hell are you?" she demanded.

The man backed away and jumped over the deck railing, disappearing into the darkness.

She stood for a few seconds, eyeing the French doors, her curiosity and her better judgment fighting over whether or not she should chase after him. The longer she considered it, the less the the idea of chasing him appealed. Forgetting about the file she'd been sent to find, she returned to the living room.

"The folder?" asked Cordelia, giving her a quizzical look.

"What?"

"The F-O-L-D-E-R?"

"Oh."

"Something wrong?"

She eased down on the edge of a chair. "There was man standing on the deck outside one of the study windows. He was looking inside."

Jill turned away from the small kindling fire she'd managed to get going.

"He took off when he saw me."

"It's probably nothing," said Jill with a shrug. "Sometimes a guest at the lodge wanders down here. Even though we posted a sign that says this is private property, they either don't see it or they don't care."

Jane was relieved to hear it.

"Describe him," said Tessa, a forced composure on her round face.

"All I remember is his cap. It was black or dark blue, had white letters on the front."

"Did it say *Sox*?" asked Tessa.

"Yes, I think it did."

"Do you know him?" asked Cordelia.

"I might," said Tessa, her lips barely moving.

"A friend?" asked Jill, twisting all the way around.

"Not exactly."

"You're not going to tell us anything about him, are you," said Cordelia, adopting a bored tone to hide her impatience.

"I don't know much, except that I don't want him anywhere near this cottage."

"Should we call the police?" asked Jane.

Tessa gave her head a stiff shake. "No. Here's what we do. I want all the doors and windows locked and every shade pulled." She clapped her hands. "Come on, folks. I can't do it, so you have to."

"Is that really necessary?" asked Jill.

"And someone go get my Mossberg twenty gauge. It's in the closet in my study."

"Aren't we being a wee bit melodramatic?" asked Cordelia.

"*We* may be," said Tessa, pulling her shawl more closely around her shoulders. "But just in case *we* happen to be right, why don't you all pitch in and humor me."

6

Standing on the front porch and peering in through the open blinds hanging over the living room windows, Emily Jensen could see her mother and Wendell Hammond sitting on the faux suede couch, holding hands and watching TV. Even though Emily didn't much like Wendell, he had a sad quality that appealed to people like her mother, a woman who never met an underdog she didn't want to champion. Wendell also had a reputation in town for being an honest businessman, a churchgoer, and, once upon a time before his wife had died, a good husband. And yet Emily didn't like him. She berated herself for introducing him to her mom.

A question kept swirling through in her mind. What if her mom decided to marry Wendell? They were spending so much time together that Emily couldn't help but wonder. She was a born catastrophizer. In her opinion, a person might as well get the most dreadful idea out there on the table because, more often than not, it would have to be considered sooner or later. Catastrophizing was as necessary to Emily as air and water because it gave her an emotional head start.

Sitting down on the steps, she gazed silently up at the stars and made a wish. At nineteen, she wanted nothing more than to see Lost Lake in the rearview mirror as she sped out of town. The fact that she didn't have enough money to buy a decent car, one that wouldn't break down before she hit the highway, was hardly an unexamined issue. The rusty piece of junk Kenny had given her as a birthday present last year had bald tires, a bad starter, and smelled like a turkey had died in the trunk. It had been his car for a couple of years. Since he was buying a new—used—Dodge Avenger, he gave it to her, saying that it had a few thousand good miles left on it, and that when—not if—it broke down, he'd repair it free of charge, as long as she paid for the parts. It did break down all the time, and yet it would have been impossible for her to turn down an offer of free wheels, even when it kept her tied to him in a way she didn't like. Money was the solution to her problems, so that's where she was putting every ounce of her effort.

Emily's mother had worked at the local Piggly Wiggly for sixteen years. She'd begun as a checkout clerk the year Emily started kindergarten. Emily's dad was diagnosed with ALS a year later, none of which Emily remembered firsthand, although she did recall how quiet the apartment became—and stayed—after her father returned home from his first visit to the hospital in Duluth.

Eventually, they moved into Grandma Birgitta's house. It was a time of scrimping and scraping for everyone because her father was no longer able to work. He died when Emily was eleven. She'd been catastrophizing about his death for so long that when it happened, the tears she'd been crying for him for years had all but dried up.

Her grandmother, a dour woman who spoke with a Swedish accent, medicated her general grimness by baking cookies and pastries for the family and always seemed to be working on some craft project on the dining room table. She died the year Emily turned fourteen, leaving Emily wondering who would go next. She catastrophized constantly about losing her mother, her best friend, Karin, and her dog, a little Yorkshire terrier named Pastrami. Her world seemed to forever be growing smaller and lonelier.

For a while after her grandmother died, it looked as if she and her mom might have to leave the house and move back to an apartment. Although her mother had inherited the place, she still had to come up with the mortgage money each month. There simply wasn't enough money to go around. Emily would lie in bed at night and picture the two of them moving into a rat-infested tenement like the ones she saw on reruns of the TV show *Homicide: Life on the Street*. Weird as it might sound, what had saved them in the end was her mother's obsessive knitting.

Every evening for years, her mom would sit in the living room in front of the TV and knit late into the night, mostly mittens—because she loved the shape—but also sweaters, baby clothes, hats, purses, and scarves. She said it helped to keep her centered and to ease her stress. She enjoyed being productive. Mostly, Emily figured she knitted because she didn't like to admit that she was addicted to so many late night TV shows. She had trunks full of her finished projects, gave her wares away to friends, relatives, neighbors, the mailman, the refrigerator repair man, anyone and everyone who looked like they could use one of her creations. She eventually started selling her knitting at several gift shops in town. The extra cash began to add up and after a while her mom stopped talking about moving. Even so, Emily continued to imagine herself in one of those bleak Baltimore tenements.

"I might end up there yet," she said, trotting down the front steps and crossing around to the side door. She'd just removed a can of Pepsi from the refrigerator when the overhead light snapped on.

"I was getting worried," said her mom, coming into the kitchen carrying two empty wine glasses.

Emily gave her a quick hug. "I was out with Kenny."

"You see a lot of that boy."

She shrugged. "He's leaving for boot camp next month."

"What's that?" asked her mom, nodding to a black and blue mark on Emily's left wrist.

"It's nothing."

"Honey, that looks nasty. How did it happen?" She set the wine glasses down on the kitchen counter, took Emily's hand and gently touched the bruise.

"I don't remember how it happened."

"Did Kenny do that to you?"

"Of course not."

"He's got a temper, everyone in town knows it." She looked Emily square in the eyes. "Tell me the truth. Are you getting serious about that boy?"

"Kenny?" She laughed. "No way."

Taking both of Emily's hands in hers, she said, "Everything's okay, right?"

"Sure."

"That new job's working out?"

"It's fine."

"Because you could still go back to your old job."

How could Emily explain that working as a checkout clerk at the Piggly Wiggly was utterly and totally demoralizing. Her mom had done it for years without complaint. Did that mean Emily thought she was better than her mom, that she was too good to do that sort of work?

Emily's mother was the best person Emily had ever known, and yet her mom's life had been made up of nothing but getting by and going with the flow. She rolled with the punches, as she liked to say, and always ended up on her feet. A haphazard life wasn't what Emily wanted. She'd been given one significant gift—her beauty. The problem was, professional models and actors were hardly in demand in Lost Lake. That's why she had to get out. The kind of life she craved couldn't be found in a small town. Maybe she was selfish. If so, she'd live with it. All she knew for sure was that her future would never include a fishing- and sports-crazed husband, a crummy part-time job at the local grocery store, and a bunch of squalling kids sucking up all her free time, not to mention the pregnancies that would ruin her figure. She had to run before she got stuck.

Changing the subject, Emily said, "I saw you having coffee with Fontaine this morning."

"Don't get me started on that," said her mom.

"Something wrong?"

"Not with Fontaine. With other people in this town."

"Such as?"

"Lyndie LaVasser, for one. I'm so angry with her I could spit nails."

"Want to talk about it?"

"Not now, honey." Lowering her voice, she added, "Wendell's here."

"I know. Look, I'm kind of tired. Think I'll head up to bed."

"We'll turn down the TV so we don't bother you."

"Oh, Mom," said Emily, wrapping her arms around her mother and holding on tight. "I love you so much."

"Where did that come from?" she asked, backing up a step.

"Just . . . like . . . wanted you to know."

7

As the first rays of the morning sun burst over the lake, Jane showered and dressed in jeans and a heavy flannel shirt. She spent some time writing in her journal, and then went downstairs and grabbed herself a cup of coffee from an urn in the lobby. She carried the paper cup down the broad concrete steps in front of the lodge, breathing in the fresh morning air and drifting out to the beach. She was glad now that she'd let Cordelia talk her into coming along.

Finding a wood bench a dozen feet from the water, she sat down and stretched her legs. Her English mother would have called the moment "agreeable." Jane had always liked the word. It carried such a wealth of meaning for her, a taste of her past, her first nine years growing up in England. After yesterday's late afternoon storm, the weather had turned deliciously cool. The sky was cloudless, a beautiful azure blue, and the sunlight turned the chop on the water into glittering jewels.

Cordelia hated mornings. She was back in her room, buried under a feather quilt, fast asleep. Jane had learned her lesson long ago and didn't even try to wake her. And anyway, spending time alone was what she'd been hoping for. She'd been wrestling with a decision for over a year, one she'd made and then unmade, an idea she'd toyed with and discarded, teetered on the brink of, then pulled back from, only to wonder if she'd made a mistake. She usually wasn't this ambivalent. This decision, however, was a big one.

Jane's father was a criminal defense attorney in St. Paul. As a child, she remembered listening to him discuss his cases at the dinner table—never in any great detail and yet enough so that she would become intrigued. Later in the evenings, after she was in bed and was supposed to be asleep, she would tiptoe to the top of the stairs, where she would listen to her father and mother down in the living room discussing the case in greater detail.

As Jane grew older, she followed her father's trials in the newspaper, always fascinated, trying to work out in her own mind what had really happened. Her first love had been food, which was why, ever since she'd spent a summer working at her uncle's restaurant as a teenager, she'd wanted her own. She'd made good on that wish with a career as a restaurateur, but in her late thirties, she'd come to see that she'd left a significant part of her interests unaddressed.

For many years, Jane had engaged in what others might term risky behavior. She'd helped friends, friends of friends, and even a few strangers with various criminal problems. She already knew she enjoyed the intellectual part of crime solving—connecting the dots, thinking about motives and means—and yet now, as an adult, she also discovered that she liked getting her hands dirty, liked the chase. She might not admit it out loud, but that frisson of danger made her feel more alive. There wasn't much physical danger involved in owning a couple of restaurants. Financial danger, yes. Danger to her health because of the stress, for sure, but not the kind of danger for which she had a growing itch. And then she met A. J. Nolan.

Jane remembered a time, not all that long ago, when she'd been absurdly pleased by his comment that she was a natural at criminal investigation. Shortly after he made the statement, he began to push. He wanted her to come work with him. He promised that he'd teach her everything he knew. He told her it was what she wanted, too, and, although the comment touched a chord inside her, she'd never liked it when people tried to tell her what she wanted.

Then came the ultimate incentive. Last spring, Nolan had offered to make her his partner. He'd even made up some business cards with both their names on it, cards she still carried in her wallet. She could work under his license until she'd put in enough hours to earn her own. Nolan was getting older and couldn't continue doing some of the more labor-intensive aspects of the job forever. If she signed on, he sweetened the deal even more by saying that he would leave the business, which included his name, his reputation, his files, his connections, and his client list, to her. Nolan & Lawless Investigations. It was a heady idea.

Jane *almost* jumped. But just as she was about to say yes, the economy tanked. She saw immediately that she needed to turn her entire focus on her restaurants. Nolan didn't understand. When he took a bullet a couple months ago while saving her life, the discussion was tabled. True to form, he'd brought it up again last week when he'd come to Blackberry Lake to stay with her at her family's lodge. Her inclination this time was to give him a firm no, and yet when the moment came, she hedged again.

This time, however, she did offer a promise. She would decide by the end of August. She set the deadline more for herself than for him. Her ambivalence was driving her nuts. In many ways, spending the week in Lost Lake was a godsend. Nolan could recover in the tranquil setting of her family's cabin and she could continue to think, while at the same time feeling no immediate pressure from him. And yet the pressure was on.

Last night, she and Cordelia had stayed at the cottage until just after eleven. Tessa finally consented to take a pain pill after Jonah offered to sleep in the loft above the living room instead of his usual spot in a room off the garage. He was apparently a light sleeper and would know instantly if someone tried to break in.

Jane had hoped to stay and talk to Jill about the possible identity of the Peeping Tom, but Jill said she was tired. Jane figured she wanted to talk to Tessa alone. What bothered her about the evening were the undercurrents she couldn't identify. Something was bothering Tessa that had nothing to do with her ankle. Her reaction to the Peeping Tom had made that clear.

Glancing at her watch, Jane recalled the she'd made a promise to come down to the cottage by nine to fix everyone breakfast—everyone, that is, except Cordelia, who would undoubtedly sleep until noon unless a tornado intervened. Since it was just after eight, that meant she had time for a walk.

Strolling along the shoreline, she watched a family of ducks paddle past the tip of the main dock. If the weather had been a little warmer, she would have removed her sandals, rolled up her jeans and waded in, but there would be plenty time for that later in the day.

As she passed the cottage, a group of gulls soared overhead, gliding into the water just a few feet from where Jill had moored their pontoon. Jane couldn't wait to get onboard and take a tour of the lake. It was amazing what enough sleep and a little rest and relaxation did for a person's general sense of well-being.

Half a mile down the beach, Jane saw an elderly woman in a light blue sundress come trudging through the sand toward her. The woman waved as if she knew who Jane was.

Jane waved back, then realized it was Helen Merland. "Hi," she called.

"I thought I might find you out here," Helen called back.

Jane wasn't sure why she thought that, though she was happy to see her.

Helen was a dear friend of Jill and Tessa's. Jill and Helen were related in some distant way that Jane could never remember. Nobody had to explain how complicated small town relationships could be. Pretty much everybody in town was linked to six major families—the Merlands, the Ivorsens, the Benoits, the Houtalas, the Dimitch clan, and the Welches. It was a microcosm of some of the ethnicities in northern Minnesota: Norwegian, Swedish, French Canadian, Finnish, Serbian, and Irish.

Back in the late nineties, Helen had come to stay at Jane's house during a spring graduation weekend. One of her many great-grandchildren was graduating with honors from the University of Minnesota. Over the years, Jane and Cordelia had been invited to dinner at Helen's home on at least half a dozen occasions, the most recent of which had taken place during their last visit to Thunderhook three years ago. In the intervening years, Helen had aged dramatically. Her white hair, usually done up in a loose bun, was worn wild and uncombed, and her erect posture had grown stooped.

Once upon a time, Helen Merland and her husband, Conrad,

had been local royalty. Helen had been a whirlwind of activity, tall and hardy, full of ideas and high spirits. She ran a philanthropic foundation and in her spare time tended a flower garden in the back of her house that was a showpiece for the entire community.

"Nice to see you again," called Jane.

Helen walked straight up to her and threw her arms around Jane's neck. "Come back to the house with me. I've got breakfast waiting. Fresh fruit. Yogurt. Tea and toast. Everything you like."

"Waiting for *me*?"

"What? I can't make breakfast for my daughter?" She laughed, pressed her hands around Jane's face.

"But . . . I'm not your daughter."

Helen adjusted her bifocals, her expression turning uncertain. "Of course you are."

"No, I'm Jane."

The elderly woman seemed to falter. She backed up, extended her hand, then retracted it. "Not Sarah?"

"I'm Jane. Jane Lawless. Remember?"

The old woman looked suddenly drained. "I—" She held a hand to her forehead. "I'm sorry. I . . . I get mixed up."

"We all do."

"But you must have seen her." Her gaze drifted over Jane's shoulder. "I'm sure she came this way."

Helen had two children, a son and a daughter. Jane remembered seeing pictures of them on the mantel in the living room. If she recalled correctly, the son had died in Vietnam, leaving behind a wife and two children. The daughter had died several years later in a car crash, leaving behind a husband and several more children. "I came from Thunderhook," she said. "I didn't see her."

"Oh, dear. What if she got lost?"

"I think she knows the area pretty well, don't you?"

Helen bit her lower lip. "Of course, you're right."

"Why don't I walk you home?"

She hesitated. "No, I'd rather stay here. Just in case she comes this way."

Jane looked around the beach. There was nowhere to sit, and Helen wasn't exactly a candidate for lounging on the sand. More to the point, Jane couldn't just leave a clearly confused woman to wander the beach. "Do you have on sunscreen?"

"What?" The elderly woman ran her hands along the paper thin skin of her arms. "I never thought to put any on."

"You shouldn't be out here on such a sunny day without it."

"Oh . . . beans," she said, making a face. "I don't suppose you have any with you."

"Back in my room at Thunderhook."

"We'll go there."

"It's much farther away than your house."

She raised a hand to shade her eyes. "I guess I am tired." Scrutinizing Jane's face, she added, "You know, I do remember you now."

"The last time I was at your house you made cassoulet."

"Yes, one of my husband's favorites. And we had an old-fashioned floating island for dessert."

Jane slipped her arm through Helen's, surprised at how thin and twiglike it felt. "Come on, I'll walk you home."

On the way back down the beach, they talked companionably about the weather, always a conversational staple in Minnesota.

When they reached a pine tree downed by yesterday's storm, Helen pointed to her house atop a steep sandy ridge. From this vantage point, it looked like a mini-mansion. The back faced the lake, while the front looked out on Conrad Merland Drive, one of Lost Lake's main drags.

Jane was about to help Helen up the narrow concrete steps that led from the beach to the back lawn when she saw a man rushing toward them from the direction of the lodge.

"Mrs. Merland?" he called, skidding to a stop in the sand on the other side of the downed pine.

She turned to face him.

"I need to ask you a couple of questions."

"You are?"

"Steve Feigenbaumer. I'm a journalist."

Still holding on to Helen's arm, Jane could feel the elderly woman's startled response.

"Your family used to own the Merland Brewery, isn't that right?"

"Yes?"

The man pulled a black Chicago White Sox cap out of the back pocket of his khaki slacks and slapped it over his thinning dark hair. "You also have a foundation."

Jane figured there weren't that many men running around Lost Lake wearing a White Sox cap. He had to be last night's Peeping Tom.

"I no longer run it, but yes, we take on progressive causes," said Helen.

"By progressive, I assume you mean liberal."

Jane wondered how the guy could conduct an interview without taking any notes.

"Liberal, progressive. Either is fine with me. For your edifi-

58

cation, in the early part of the last century, you could find progressives in both major parties. Teddy Roosevelt was a Republican and a progressive. Woodrow Wilson a progressive and a Democrat. We've forgotten our history. We do that at our peril."

He didn't seem the least bit interested in a history lesson. Removing a photo from his shirt pocket, he handed it to her. "Do you recognize the woman in that snapshot?"

Helen adjusted her bifocals. "Should I?"

"Her name is Judy Clark."

"Doesn't ring a bell."

"You've lived here all your life?"

"What are you after, Mr. Baumgartner?"

"*Feigenbaumer*," he said, clearly annoyed that she'd mispronounced his name.

Jane sensed that Helen had done it on purpose. Glancing over the old woman's shoulder, she took a look at the photo.

"I'm afraid I can't help you."

"Can't or won't? The woman in that picture may not look like it, but she's a cold-blooded killer. If you know anything about—"

"I've already told you that I don't. Now if you'll excuse me—"

Helen handed back the snapshot and was about to head up the stairway when a voice shouted, "There you are. You had me worried sick." A pudgy-faced blond man in a short-sleeved dress shirt and a brown tie stared down at her. "I thought we were having breakfast together."

Helen whispered to Jane, "The Amazing Mr. Hammond. My house guest." She winked. "Hold your horses," she called back. "I'll be right up."

"I'm not leaving," said Feigenbaumer, his voice carrying a distinct threat.

Helen responded with a smile. "I hope you don't. Lost Lake is a lovely place to spend a few idyllic summer days."

A sudden gust of wind off the lake revealed a bulge near Feigenbaumer's ankle. An ankle holster, thought Jane. If she hadn't been convinced of the seriousness of this man's appearance by Tessa's reaction last night, the sight of the holster surely flipped an alarm switch this morning. Whatever Tessa was mixed up in, it was dangerous.

With a kind of thuggish swagger, Feigenbaumer headed back down the beach.

Returning her attention to Helen, Jane found the elderly woman halfway up the steps.

"Will you be in Lost Lake long?" Helen called down.

"I'm here for the week."

"My keepers don't allow me to drive anymore. Do you have a car?"

"I have access to one."

"Wonderful. I'll take you to breakfast in town tomorrow. Mr. Hammond," she added, and here she winked, "will have to get along without me for a few hours."

8

Jonah tiptoed down the stairs from the loft to the living room, tucking his tie-dyed T-shirt into his bell bottoms as he went. He'd washed and dried his clothes last night before going to bed. The book he'd taken with him on the road, Kingsley Amis's *The Green Man*, was a little worse for wear because of the storm, but still readable. He always read until the wee hours. This particular story was hilarious. He loved the ghost scenes and the cynical narrator's voice and laughed to himself when he thought about the sex-phobic freak in the Toyota. Maybe he should have left the book as a parting gift. The guy could have gnashed his teeth over the sex scenes.

If it hadn't been for the growling in his stomach, which woke him from a vivid dream, Jonah would've still been asleep. He'd been dreaming about his girlfriend, Emily. While he'd been gone they'd texted each other a few times a day, though for Jonah, it was never enough. He'd made a snap decision to leave St. Louis, but hadn't called to tell her because he couldn't wait for the moment when she first saw him standing right in front of her. It was all he'd thought about on the road.

Jane had promised last night to come by and make everyone

breakfast. Probably some form of eggs. Jonah didn't eat anything in the morning that wasn't submerged in milk, so waiting wasn't an issue. Digging through the pantry, he found an unopened box of Cheerios. It wasn't his first choice. He would need to hit the grocery store in town later and buy himself some Cinnamon Toast Crunch, his current fave.

His aunts had refused to make a decision last night about letting him stay, mostly because Jane had caught some stupid guy outside Tessa's office window, which set everyone spinning, locking doors and windows. Jonah had no idea his aunt Tessa owned a shotgun, and it both surprised and amused him to see her packing. He didn't want to let his amusement show because his aunt was in a wretched mood. Even so, he felt confident that the answer to his request, when it came, would be yes. He'd always fit in better with his aunts than he had with his mom and dad. His parents were so incredibly boring, fighting all the time about anything and everything. Tessa and Jill were cool—especially Tessa. If he could pick a mother instead of being issued one, she would be his first choice.

Carrying his cereal bowl into the study, Jonah shoveled spoonfuls into his mouth as he stood in front of a wall of books. This had been his playground as a child. While other kids were out fishing or swimming or inside watching TV or playing video games, Jonah was reading. Tessa had been clever about the way she'd suckered him in. As a little kid, his main interest had been superheros. From age five on, he couldn't get enough of them. For a time he was convinced he really was one. He still wanted to be a superhero, although it was a personal goal he usually kept to himself.

Tessa read him *The Count of Monte Cristo* when he was ten. As silly as it sounded, that first introduction to world of Dumas had rocked his world. Next came *The Three Musketeers* and *The Man in the Iron Mask.* From there, he began reading the books himself. Tessa suggested Jules Verne and H. G. Wells. Later, he began to pick his way through her library. Fiction first. He read *To Kill a Mockingbird* and *Lord of the Flies,* all of Vonnegut, all of Marge Piercy. His favorites were the books by Mary Renault, historical novels sent in ancient Greece. As he got older, he moved on to *Their Eyes Were Watching God, Narcissis and Goldmund, One Flew Over the Cuckoo's Nest, One Hundred Years of Solitude, The Bell Jar,* and *Pale Fire.* He also dug deeply into nonfiction, reading histories of Woodstock, of the culture and music in the sixties and early seventies. Tessa had so many books written about or during that period that he eventually fell into reading more difficult subjects such as the civil rights movement, the cultural revolution in China, Vietnam, the counterculture, antiwar and socialist movements in America and Europe, and books on feminism. He also read dozens and dozens of plays. As Jonah ran his hand along the volumes on the bookshelves, they were all still there—his friends, his mentors.

He had to admit to a particularly embarrassing period in his life, his freshman and sophomore years in high school, when he was never without a book in his hand, not because he was actually reading it, but because he liked the way it looked. His friends thought of him as an intellectual, and he didn't want to disappoint. He actually carted around a copy of Plato's *Five Dialogues* for a while waiting for people to ask him what he was reading.

On the bottom shelf were all of Tessa's record albums, again, most from the sixties and early seventies. She insisted that he handle them with care. As often as possible when he stayed at the cottage, he would lock himself away in the study and play those songs until, over the years, they became more familiar to him than the current bands. He was powerfully drawn to the the sixties and sad, in a strange way, that he'd missed all the excitement.

As he sat down at the desk to finish his cereal, he heard voices. His Aunt Jill had left around seven, and Tessa never got up willingly before nine. She said it was one of the perks of her profession.

The voices were soft, muffled. Returning to the kitchen, he positioned himself as close to his aunts' bedroom door as possible. Peaking around the corner, he saw Tessa propped up against her pillows. She was faced away from him. The double doors that led to the deck were open and Lyndie LaVasser was pacing in front of the bed. Jonah's best friend was Kenny Moon. Mrs. LaVasser was his grandmother. Jonah liked her well enough, although he could never quite figure her out. One minute she seemed totally religious, and the next she'd be cussing a blue streak. People often confused him, which was another reason he liked fiction. At least in a book you got a chance to get inside a person's head and see why they acted the way they did.

Eavesdropping wasn't cool, and yet he had no intention of moving. Taking one more quick peek, he withdrew his head and stood as quiet and rigid as a stick. He hoped that they were talking about him coming to live in Lost Lake for his senior year. Tessa and Mrs. LaVasser weren't exactly best buddies, although they did have coffee together every now and then. Nobody had "coffee" in St. Louis the way they did in Lost

Lake—crowded around the kitchen table shooting the breeze and eating coffee cake. Sure, people drank coffee in St. Louis. Mostly, as far as he could tell, they did it in coffee shops while texting, talking on their cell, and working on their laptop.

Mrs. LaVasser was speaking, keeping her voice low:

"If he came here last night, he's got to know. He's watching us—that's why he visited the emporium first."

"If he's watching, he's not acting."

"We've got to *do* something."

"You keep saying that. What are you suggesting?"

"Sometimes," said Mrs. LaVasser, her voice sounding more and more depressed, "I think I should just turn myself in. End it."

"*That's* your solution? Tell me, how would you do it and not implicate me? You make that choice and you take me down with you. No way is that going to happen. This has to be a joint decision."

"Keep your voice down." She was silent for a few seconds. "You're willing to wait it out? See if he comes after us?"

"What's the alternative?"

She didn't answer. "We're sitting ducks."

Jonah didn't have a clue what they were talking about. He wondered if it had something to do with last night's unwanted visitor.

"How could we have been so stupid?" asked Mrs. LaVasser, an ache in her voice.

"We were young."

"That hardly covers it. Most young people never did what we did."

"We were angry. Hurt. We wanted to hurt back."

"You've come to terms with it. I never have."

"You think it's easy for me?"

"You've gone on with your life, made a success of it."

"Is that the way it looks? People see what they want to see, I guess." Tessa paused. "We have two choices. We can wait it out, or we can go after him."

"I knew you'd get there sooner or later."

"Me? Isn't that what you were suggesting?"

"I don't know. Maybe."

"We couldn't do it ourselves. We'd have to find someone."

"Just like that?" Mrs. LaVasser snapped her fingers.

"Why did you come here, Judy? What do you want from me?"

Judy, thought Jonah. Why was his aunt calling Mrs. LaVasser Judy?

"Honestly?" said Mrs. LaVasser. "I don't know."

"If you push me to make the decision, does that make you any less a part of it? We always have choices, even if none of them are good."

"Just like in sixty-eight."

"Hardly. Back then we mistook passion for insight. This would be simple survival."

"I can't, Tessa. I just can't."

"Fine. Then we wait to see what happens."

"I can't do that either. I . . . I need to pray about it."

"Go ahead. Pray. Nobody's stopping you."

"You're such a heathen."

"Don't start."

"I feel like I'm *drowning*."

"So do I."

"I have to talk to George. He'll know what to do."

"No way," said Tessa. The bed creaked with her weight. "The

more people who know about what happened, the more danger we're in."

"But I feel so *alone,*" she cried. "Look, I'm going to kneel down right here. You can pray with me if you want. I wish you would. Or you can just sit there and listen."

Jonah peeked again, saw Mrs. LaVasser get down on her knees. She closed her eyes and rested her elbows on the bed. Pressing her hands together, she said, "Please, *please*, Lord. I'm sorry. Look into my heart and see for yourself. I made a mistake, and yet that's why your son died for my sins, right? If people didn't make mistakes, we wouldn't have needed a sacrifice. And remember . . . I'm just bringing this to your attention in case you forgot . . . I didn't have anything to do with the bomb. Tessa's friend built it. Sure, I went along, so I guess I'm almost as guilty as they are. Please remember that I've gone on to live a good life. Doesn't that count for something? I may have been divorced a couple of times——"

"Four times," said Tessa.

"But Tessa's gay, so that should make us even. Also, please dear God, if there's any way you can make Steve Feigenbaumer forgive us, will you try? Either that, or make him go away. I'll devote myself to you and your will for the rest of my life if you'll only help me."

"I don't think bargaining works," said Tessa.

"Shut up," hissed Mrs. LaVasser. "This is *my* prayer." She straightened up and began again. "Lord, forgive my trespasses as I forgive those who trespass against me. Lead me not into temptation. And deliver me from evil. That means Feigenbaumer, Lord." Bowing her head, she said, "In Jesus's name, amen."

Jonah withdrew his head. Stepping over to the counter, he

stuffed two more spoonfuls of cereal into his mouth. The business about a bomb had really grabbed his interest.

Back in position again, he heard Mrs. LaVasser ask, "You still have a handgun?"

"I do," said Tessa.

"I want it. I'm not saying I'd use it, but if it comes down to that, I need some way to protect myself. I can't stand to think he's out there lurking, that he's going to put it all together any moment and come after us. I still look a lot like I did when I was young. You—you've changed, dyed your hair, exchanged your glasses for contacts, packed on a bunch of weight."

"Thanks."

"Well it's true. If he gets his hands on a better picture of Judy Clark, I'm toast. If he has one of you, he might not be able to make the connection quite so easily."

Tessa said nothing.

"I feel like I'm glowing in the dark!"

"Okay, okay," said Tessa, shooshing her. "You can have it. It's in my study."

Busted, thought Jonah. Sensing the need for a bold move, he called, "Hey, Aunt Tessa, are you up?"

Both women looked stricken as he sauntered into the bedroom.

"Hi," he said, trying to look both sleepy and innocent. He stretched his arms, gave a yawn. "How're you doing, Mrs. La-Vasser?"

She poked her thumb at him and said to Tessa, "What's he doing here?"

Tessa motioned him over to the bed, put her arm around his waist. "He's staying with us for a while."

"For a long while," corrected Jonah.

She glanced up at him with a sly look in her eye, rubbed his back. "That remains to be seen, mister. Listen, will you do me a favor?"

"Anything. Want me to put the coffee on?"

"Go into my study. In the top drawer of my desk you'll find a small gold key attached to a maroon, gold, and black Loyola University keyring. You know that wooden cedar chest next to the printer?"

"Yeah?"

"Open it. There's a box inside, sort of a rusty blue metal. Bring it to me."

"Sure," he said. Racing back through the kitchen to the other side of the cottage, he found the keyring next to a box of black Sharpies. He crouched down in front of the chest and pressed the key into the lock. Raising the cover, he found the metal box on top of what looked like a treasure trove of personal journals. Each volume had a date on the spine. Removing a large black one that said "1968," he quickly paged through it, finding his aunt's familiar small, neat handwriting. On a whim, he shoved the volume under his arm. Lifting out the box, he closed the chest and heard the lock click. After returning the key to the desk drawer, he looked around for a someplace to hide the journal.

Taking the stairs up to the loft two at a time, he shoved it under the couch and then rushed back down. Seconds later, he was handing the box to his aunt.

"Now," said Tessa, smiling up at him, "if you don't mind, this would be a perfect time to make coffee."

"Happy to." What he really wanted was to stay and get a first-hand look at the gun.

"When you're done, maybe you'd stick around the living room. Jane's supposed to be by in a little while. She'll need someone to let her in the front door."

He wasn't stupid. He knew she was not only attempting to get rid of him but also trying to prevent his immediate return.

Instead of making coffee, he ran back to the kitchen and took up his post, watching as his aunt opened the cover and lifted out a snub-nosed revolver.

"Is it loaded?" asked Mrs. LaVasser.

"Of course not." She rummaged around inside the metal box and withdrew another box, this one small and red. "These are the shells." She handed everything over. "My advice is to take it out somewhere in the woods and shoot it until it feels comfortable in your hand. It's a thirty-eight, so it has a fairly big kick. Have you ever shot a pistol?"

Mrs. LaVasser shook her head.

"It's been cleaned and well oiled. You shouldn't have any problems with it."

Jonah couldn't help himself. He was riveted.

Mrs. LaVasser opened her purse and dropped the shells inside. She continued to hold the pistol, examining it, touching the hammer, pulling back a tiny latch that allowed the empty cylinder to fall out. "It's so heavy."

"Make sure you hide it from George."

She held out her arm, pointed the gun at the wall.

"Careful. Always keep your index finger pressed along the side, never on the trigger, even if you think it's not loaded."

"Unless I want to use it." She kept her arm outstretched for a couple more seconds, then stuffed the gun into her purse and snapped the clasp. "Call me if you see Feigenbaumer again."

"You do the same."

70

She was about to turn around when she stopped herself. "I couldn't live with myself if people in this town found out what we'd done." Gazing down at the purse, she mumbled a quick thank-you and then turned and disappeared out the French doors.

9

Jane returned to Thunderhook Lodge a little before noon, stopping by the reception desk because she wanted to have a word with Jill. She found her all but sprinting towards the back hallway.

"A problem?" asked Jane, falling in beside her.

"Plumbing," said Jill. "We had a leak in one of the second-floor rooms. We thought we had it fixed. Now I'm told the ceiling in one of the first-floor rooms is showing signs of water damage. It's always something."

Jane's first reaction was to say she was sorry to hear it. Her second was more selfish. She was glad someone else had to field the problem, not her. Not being the one in charge had its advantages.

Slowing her pace, Jill asked, "How was breakfast?"

"Tessa seemed to enjoy it. Listen, I know you're busy. Just answer one question. Do you know a guy named Feigenbaumer?"

Jill stopped. "No. Should I?"

"I think he was the man standing outside Tessa's study last night. Did she say any more to you about it?"

She dug her hands into the pockets of her sweater, looking bewildered. "She took that pain pill, so by the time I had Jonah settled in the loft and got myself ready for bed, she was asleep. And then I was up early, so we never had a chance to talk. Honestly, in all the years we've been together, I've never seen her behave like that before."

"Look, I know you need to go," said Jane. "I'll catch you later."

Climbing the main stairs up to the second floor, Jane headed for Cordelia's room. If she wasn't up by now, she should be.

Dressed in a white terry cloth bathrobe, compliments of the lodge, Cordelia answered the door with her hair wrapped in a towel and a mud mask covering her face. The only part of her visage left uncovered were her eyes and lips. She looked like she belonged in a minstrel show.

"Oh. Drat. I was hoping you were room service." She tapped several keys on her iPhone as she shambled back into the sitting room.

Jane closed the door behind her. The room was a mess. Every chair was covered with clothes. Instead of sitting down, she stepped over to the windows, noting that clouds were moving back in. "Did you sleep well?"

"Except for the pea, yes."

"Oh, no, not another pea."

"I'm beset by them whenever I'm away from my own bed. It's why I don't travel well."

"Couldn't your Princess-ness find it and get rid of it?"

"Not unless I wanted to rip open the mattress in the middle of the night."

"We can change rooms if you like."

"I might be up for that." Slipping the phone into the pocket of her robe, she sailed into the bathroom, snapped on the light and gingerly touched the mud mask.

"Want to look your best for the northern Minnesota moose population?"

"One would think *you* have a thing about moose."

"Only because I know you're so fond of them."

"Well, yes, if they're discriminating, then of course I want to *dazzle* the moose, the bears, the lions and tigers."

Jane coughed into her fist. When it came to the natural world, Cordelia was less than encyclopedic in her general knowledge. Knowing it was impossible to disabuse her of her notion that the northern woods were lousy with elephant and zebra—after all, one forest was much like the next—Jane removed a red cape from a rustic log chair and sat down. The cushions were comfortable enough, although they weren't exactly like sinking into whipped cream. By the looks of the papers laid out on the coffee table, Cordelia had been busy with the script.

"All ready for tonight?"

"Boo-ya," she shouted, giving a fist pump.

"In northern Minnesota, boo-ya is a stew."

"I'm using it in the street sense of the term." Removing a pair of Frye boots from the couch, Cordelia flopped down, stretched out and placed cucumber slices over her eyes. "You're coming to the theater tonight, of course."

"If I won't be in the way."

"I called the four people in the cast, reminded them that it's tech week. Initially, they weren't asked to come tonight, but I need to do a quick run-through with them—just a couple of scenes to get a sense for where they're at. And then we can start the dry tech."

"Speak English. What's a dry tech?"

75

"You've been my intimate lo these many years and you don't know basic theater lingo?"

"Must have slipped my mind."

"It's a rehearsal without the cast. All the tech people show up—the lighting designer, sound, set designer, stage manager, the entire crew—and we go through everything, from beginning to end, checking each cue in order. There are a few moving set pieces that we'll have to time and get right, thankfully not many. It takes a couple hours, depending."

Jane decided to bring along a book.

"I assume you prepared breakfast for Tessa, et al. Was she in better humor this morning?"

"Hard to tell." While Jane had been working in the kitchen, Tessa said she needed to make a grocery list. She sat on her throne in the living room with a pad and pen and stared at the blank page with a concentration too intense to be real. "Jill is taking her to see the doctor this afternoon."

"Ah, yes. The air cast and walking boot. She say anything more about last night's Peeping Tom?"

"No, and I didn't bring it up. I probably should have."

"Because?"

"I ran into him this morning on the beach."

Cordelia sat bolt upright, the cucumber slices falling from her eyes. "You did? You're sure it was him?"

"How many people do you figure are walking around Lost Lake wearing a cap with the word *Sox* on the front?"

"Could be others. Did he recognize you?"

"Thankfully, no." Jane briefly detailed what had happened with Helen, ending with the guy stalking off.

"So he's looking for someone."

"A woman named Judy Clark. He said she was a cold-blooded

killer. I couldn't really tell what she looked like from the photo. It was taken a long time ago."

"Why did he think Helen would know anything about her?"

"Maybe because Helen's been living in town all her life. If this Judy moved here, she might remember a stranger coming to town with that name. He didn't get very far with his questioning because Helen's house guest showed up. Name's Wendell Hammond."

"Hammond? I think there's a guy in the cast with that name. Small world."

"Small town."

Cordelia stretched out and placed the cucumber slices back on her eyes.

"I was thinking," said Jane, not sure how Cordelia would take her next comment.

"Hmm?"

"What if Tessa is somehow connected to this Judy Clark?"

Cordelia sat up again, cucumber slices dropping to her lap. "How?"

"No idea."

"Kind of a big leap in the dark."

"Maybe. You have to admit that, while Tessa was physically present last night, most of the time she was a million miles away. And her reaction to that guy outside her window was beyond bizarre."

Before Cordelia could respond, there was a knock on the door.

"You get that while I wash the mud off my face," said Cordelia. "I charged the food to the room, so all you have to do is sign for it." She breezed into the bathroom.

Jane held the door open for the waiter. He looked around for an empty spot to put the tray. "Just set it down on the couch," said Jane.

Seeming grateful for the direction, he removed the metal cover from the plate, revealing an assortment of bagels, a crock of cream cheese, sliced red onions and tomatoes, and a generous portion of lox. Next to the plate was a carafe of coffee, several mugs and a glass of orange juice, and next to that was a tiny vase containing a fresh pink daisy. Jane signed the receipt and then held the door for him as he left.

"Ah, sustenance," said Cordelia, rubbing her hands together as she emerged from the bathroom, her face looking excessively pink. "There's plenty for both of us."

While Cordelia poured the coffee, Jane sat back down on the log chair. "I think we may have stumbled over something fairly nasty here."

"Mustn't jump to conclusions, especially about an old and dear friend."

As Cordelia piled a bagel slice with lox and cream cheese, Jane's cell phone rang. She slipped it out of her pocket and took a look at the caller ID. "It's Tessa."

"Tell her I have a question," said Cordelia.

"Hi," said Jane. "Everything okay?"

"No," came Tessa's angry voice. "Look, I don't like beating around the bush. We're friends, right? That means I can take the liberty of being blunt."

When, thought Jane, was Tessa anything but?

"Back off. Stay out of my business."

"Excuse me?"

"I'm sure you've figured out that I'm dealing with a problem right now. It's *my* problem, Jane, not yours."

It dawned on her that Jill must have called Tessa and dropped the name Feigenbaumer.

"You think you're God's gift to private investigation. Well, you're not. You're a dilettante. A dabbler. An amateur."

"Whoa," said Jane. "Let's dial this back a little."

"Butt out. Do I make myself clear?"

"Admirably."

"Good. I don't expect that we'll talk about this again. Enough said."

More than enough, thought Jane as she closed up her phone.

"What about my question?" asked Cordelia, wiping her mouth on a napkin.

"I'd suggest you call her later, when she's had a chance to cool off."

"Tessa? Hot under the collar? How unlike her."

Jane wondered if she was growing paranoid, seeing intrigues and subterfuge where none existed. The comment about being an amateur stung—more than she cared to admit. "I need a vacation," she muttered.

"Then I'd say you've come to the right place."

Paranoia aside, Jane wasn't so sure.

10

Standing in front of the bathroom mirror, Jonah rehearsed his speech, the one asking Aunt Tessa if he could please borrow her Volvo. He figured she was kidding about the world not being safe now that he could drive, although she had a weird sense of humor so he couldn't be absolutely sure.

After Jane left, Tessa had stared out the front window, not saying a word. Normally, when he was around, she always started a conversation. She wanted to know what he was up to or she'd rattle on about what she was writing or reading. They would have long talks about politics, movies, philosophy, girls, sex, love. She was one of the few people in his life who treated him as an equal, not like some dumb kid. Jonah looked forward to those talks. Today, however, Tessa seemed distracted—so distracted that when he asked to use the car the question barely registered.

"We'll eat dinner around six, if you're interested. Otherwise, be back by midnight," was all she'd said, waving him off.

He wanted to get a better look at that journal she'd written, wanted to see if it talked about her setting off a bomb some-where, though he'd concluded that reading it was probably something better left until late at night when nobody was around. He didn't think his aunt would notice that it was gone. She maintained that she didn't have the mental focus to work, which he assumed meant that she wouldn't be using her study anytime soon. Before he left, he made sure that the table next to her was stocked with her favorites: a wedge of triple-cream brie and crackers, an assortment of olives, several cans of sparkling water, a pitcher of OJ, and a plate of Jill's homemade chocolate chip cookies.

Jonah's first order of business was to drive over to Emily's house and surprise her. Emily had mentioned in a recent text that she might be starting a new job cleaning cabins at one of the small fishing resorts over on Harris Lake. Sure enough, as he passed her house, Kenny's old rust heap of a car was nowhere to be found. Kenny and Emily had been friends in high school, had graduated together last spring. It irked Jonah to no end that Kenny had given her a far bigger gift than anything Jonah could ever have afforded. He'd sent her a book and a pair of earrings. How pathetic was that?

Thinking that he'd see Emily later, Jonah headed east out of town. The road meandered through woods and open fields. He loved it out here. In the fall, these same woods were full of hunters and the sound of rifles, but spring and summer were peaceful—except for the mosquitos. He'd brought along a spray can of bug repellant for that. Mosquitos didn't like smoke, and if the texts Kenny had been sending him were accurate, he intended to make some mighty smoke in the next few hours.

The paved road eventually ended and a dirt road began. Half a mile farther on, two muddy tire lanes in the weeds continued the trail, this time deep into the woods. Jonah stopped the car next to a huge dead oak, which was one of the markers they used. Making sure the windows were up and the doors were locked, Jonah set off toward the hideout.

As he made his way though the underbrush, mosquitos dive-bombed him from every direction. Near the lake, there was always a breeze to cool a person off, but here, with the sky grown overcast, the humidity rising, and the air still, his T-shirt was soaked with sweat. Bugs loved human sweat. He pulled the can of repellant out of the pocket of his cargo shorts and took a moment to spray himself down. He liked the smell. It made him think of summer, of good times swimming off the point, make-out sessions with Emily, beer, and smoking pot at the hideout.

Sure enough, as he came into the clearing, he saw a motor-cycle parked next to the ancient shed. Instead of Kenny's used Honda Motard, which Jonah thought was one of the ugliest bikes ever made, he beheld a used Harley touring cycle, all black and menacing, with chrome as shiny as a mirror and heavy leather saddlebags emblazoned with the Harley-Davidson insignia. Jonah couldn't imagine where Kenny got the money to buy it.

"Hey, how's it goin'," called Jonah, seeing his friend's head poke out the door. More changes had taken place around the hideout. Some of the rotted wood had been replaced, as had part of the roof, and yet it still looked old and rundown. "You do that?" asked Jonah.

"Yup," said Kenny with a grin.

They hugged, slapped each other on the back.

Kenny looked the same. Big and tough and musclebound. Reddish-brown mullet. T-shirt with the sleeves cut off to show his badass tattoos.

"Found some old barn wood to do the repair," said Kenny.

"Can't let the place fall apart, now can we. We also don't want to advertise that it's being used." He glanced at a buzzing two-way radio clipped to his belt. "Just a sec." He picked it up to read the text message.

"How come you've got one of those?"

"You know what cell phone reception is like up here. Even in town it's spotty. This is more reliable." He turned it off and slipped it into his pocket.

"That's a cool bike. Your finances must be looking up."

"You could say that."

"You working somewhere?"

"Gran's emporium. Oh, and I'm doing carryout at the Piggly Wiggly a few afternoons a week."

"Can't pay all that much."

"Nah, but I got some other irons in the fire." He gave a conspiratorial wink. "What the hell are you doing back here?"

"Hitchhiked from St. Louis."

"No shit." He sucked in a lungful of smoke from an overstuffed joint. Kenny prided himself on rolling them as fat as Cuban cigars. They had a ton of the stuff all to themselves. They'd made a pact early on. Everything they grew they kept. No selling allowed. They could give it away, if they felt so inclined, as long as neither of them became a dealer. Kenny passed him the joint.

Taking a hit, Jonah held the smoke in and said, "Nice."

"This is some of the newer stuff."

"How's this year's crop?"

"Mega awesome. The best yet."

Jonah exhaled. "Let's go look."

"Relax, man."

They each took another hit.

"Sorry I wasn't around to help you plant," said Jonah.

Kenny shrugged. "No sweat. I like grubbing around in the dirt. Just call me farmer Kenneth."

"Kenneth?"

"Yeah. Sounds more adult than Kenny. I'm ready for some adult respect."

They stood smoking, looking around, waving bugs away from their faces.

"Let's sit," said Kenny.

"Yeah, good idea. This stuff is dynamite."

They propped themselves against the side of the shed. Jonah plucked a blade of sweet grass and stuck it in his mouth, feeling for the first time like he was really home.

"How you been, man?" asked Kenny, his head lolling back against the rough wood.

"If you want the truth, not so hot. That's why I'm here. I plan to spend my senior year in Lost Lake, not St. Louis."

"Good for you. You finally grew a pair. Me, I'm done with all that kid shit."

Jonah took another toke, mainly so he wouldn't say something snarky. Kenny was a year ahead of him in school, which meant he'd graduated last spring. Actually, they were only eight months apart. Big freakin' deal. Sometimes, particularly when he was high, Kenny would cop this moronic attitude about the difference in their ages, as if eight months had any meaning at all.

"Still headed for the army?"

"Damn straight," said Kenny.

"You talked to a recruiter?"

"Didn't I text you about that?"

"Nope."

"Thought I did. Yeah, saw the recruiter right after school was out. He came to the house after I passed the ASVAB."

"The what?"

"The Armed Services Vocational Aptitude Battery. I scored a forty-nine."

"Is that good?"

"It's fucking genius, man. I'm interested in ground combat. Heavy artillery."

"Blowing things up."

"What else is there?" he said, cracking a smile.

"Aviation. Computer technology. Special ops."

"The special ops might be okay. Ain't thought about that much."

Kenny wasn't interested in books. *At all*. Reading bored him silly. He liked sports, liked motorcycles, liked smoking dope, and liked girls. Beyond that, he was somewhat limited in his natural curiosity. He and Jonah had been best friends since they were in sixth grade. Their parents thought the friendship was beyond strange, and yet Jonah had figured it out long ago.

Kenny wasn't into philosophizing the way Jonah was. He was actually downright pitiful when it came to anything other than superficial conversation. Jonah had plenty of people in his life that he could talk to. What he didn't have was someone he could do stuff with. It was a side of his personality that people sometimes missed. He liked adventure. Kenny was the same way. He didn't just dream about stuff or talk big, like all of Jonah's other friends, he *made* things happen. Together, the two of them were like a buzz saw. They were Tom and Huck lighting out for the territory.

Jonah had been the one to suggest they grow their own

dope. For a while, it was just pie in the sky. Then, one day, Kenny found a rundown shack in the middle of an empty field that nobody seemed to own. Next thing Jonah knew, Kenny had the seeds and was digging up part of the field. Jonah busied himself finding information online about how to care for the plants, how to make sure they grew straight and strong. For a time, he got really interested in horticulture, read everything he could find. Together, he and Kenny carted out what they'd need to make the hideout their home away from home. Coolers for pop and beer. A couple of big plastic containers for the munchies. The truth was, without Kenny, Jonah's idea might never have seen the light of day—or the Bic at the end of the pipe. Jonah saw himself as the idea man. Kenny was the enforcer.

Kenny Moon was six foot five and built like a pro football defensive back. He could eat five Big Macs in one sitting and still have room for a couple chocolate triple-thick shakes. Girls loved his Irish good looks—his mother's name was Flannigan—his mischievous smile, and the glint in his eyes that suggested he was up to something, which he usually was. He could be generous, and he liked to laugh and party-hardy. That was Kenny's good side. His dark side was equally big.

Kenny was so pigheaded that, as a kid, he'd refused to let his parents show him how to tie his shoelaces, which meant that he'd been condemned to wear dorky loser loafers until he figured it out himself, somewhere around fifth grade. He wasn't exactly dumb, although he didn't understand the finer points of . . . well, just about anything. He also didn't like to spend the time or effort it took to think things out logically, so he tended to overreact for all the wrong reasons. He was ridiculously sensitive to criticism, hotheaded in general, and tended to throw a punch rather than try a less physical route to solve a problem. He made for an exciting friend, but Jonah doubted he'd make a great husband, lover, employee . . . or army recruit. Then again, that was the army's problem.

"So," said Jonah, holding in another lungful of smoke, starting to feel pleasantly drifty. "I'm gonna need a key for that new padlock you put on the shed door."

"Check."

"Did you take the army physical yet?"

"Last week."

"Man, with all the dope you smoke, how'd you pass it?"

"Not to worry."

"Have you seen the results yet?"

"Should have them this week."

Jonah thought he was living in dreamland. "So what's next?"

"Boot camp. No pussies allowed." He elbowed Jonah in the ribs. "You're too soft, man. You gotta harden up."

This was one of their biggest differences—their values. They were polar opposites when it came to virtually everything that mattered. The last thing Jonah would ever do was join the military so that he could be sent off to fight some foreign war for the political bullshitters in Washington or the fat cats on Wall Street. His body wasn't going to be used as fodder to fuel anybody's pocketbook or political empire. It was all black and white to him. No shades of gray in an equation like that.

"You're one of those softie liberals, Jonie."

"Don't call me Jonie, *Kenny*."

Kenny slapped the back of Jonah's head.

"Hey," he said. "That hurt."

"Remember, it's Kenneth."

"What*ever*."

"What's it called when you're a psychic and you hear dead people's voices?"

"Huh?"

"You know? You see these people on TV sometimes. They talk to the dead. What's that called?"

"Channeling?"

"Yeah, that's it. It's like you're channeling some douche-bag hippie from the sixties. 'Course, you know what they say about the sixties."

"What's that?"

"If you remember them, man, you weren't really there." He began to giggle and couldn't stop—another stranger-than-fiction thing about him. He didn't have a hearty, deep male laugh. He giggled.

Because Jonah didn't want to get hit again, he decided not to point that out. "I'll take your assessment as a compliment."

"Not meant that way."

"Peace."

Kenny rested his head against the shed wall and gazed disinterestedly up at the dark clouds scudding across the sky. "Wonder if it's going to storm again?"

Jonah's thoughts happened to be on the freak in the Toyota. His love of hitchhiking had been severely shaken. On the other hand, what was a guy to do who didn't have much money and had no other way to get around? "Listen," said Jonah, feeling a raindrop hit his forehead.

"If it's about Emily—"

"What about Emily?"

"Nothing."

"No, what about her? I drove past her house. The car was gone."

"She's working at a resort."

"You know the name of it?"

He pulled out a roach clip and attached it to the end of the joint. "Can't remember."

"I need to see her."

"Doesn't get off work until five."

"But she's okay, right?"

He examined the tip of the roach to make sure it was still lit. "She's fine."

"You see her much?"

"Now and then."

"God, but I've missed her."

"She'd be easy to miss."

"You got another joint on you?"

Kenny produced one from his shirt pocket. Holding the clip in one hand, he stuck the joint in his mouth and lit it with the Bic in his other hand. "Here," he said, handing it to Jonah. "This stuff is older. Still primo."

While Kenny sucked in the last of the first doobie, Jonah started in on the second. Even if it rained, he doubted he'd get up.

"Okay," said Jonah, blowing smoke slowly out of his nostrils. "You gotta focus for a minute, man, because this next bit is important. Are you focusing?"

The question might have elicited another punch if Kenny hadn't been so high. "Just spill it."

"Something's going on with your grandmother and Aunt Tessa."

"Going on? You mean sexually?"

"Huh?"

"They sleeping together?"

"Hell no. Where did you get that idea?"

Kenny shrugged.

Jonah decided to leave out the part about the gun exchange. For the moment. "Last night, a friend of my aunt's caught some weird dude in a White Sox cap looking in Tessa's study window. Jane Lawless. You remember her?"

"Sure. The dyke restaurant owner."

"You used to call her that 'foxy' restaurant owner."

"That was before I found out she was a dyke."

"Tolerance in action."

"Never claimed to be tolerant. Get back to the subject."

"Far as I can make out, your grandmother and my aunt set off a bomb someplace."

Warming to the topic, Kenny said, "Like where?"

"Not sure. Your grandmother's first name isn't Lyndie. It's Judy."

"Well, shit." He digested that for a few seconds. "Judy. Yeah, I can see her as a Judy. What else?"

"They think the guy looking in the window last night is after them. I mean, really out to hurt them."

"There was a dude in the emporium the other day. Gran acted really weird after he left. And then she took off, put me in charge. Ain't never done that before."

"So you know what he looks like."

"Kind of." He closed his eyes. "Narrow face. Dark eyebrows. Dark scruff."

"Your grandmother said she and my aunt were sitting ducks. They even talked about . . . well, about taking care of him."

"You mean as in really . . . taking *care* of him?"

"I got the impression they thought it was either him or them."

"Hell," said Kenny, shoving the roach clip into the dirt.

"Nobody's gonna threaten my gran. I don't care what she did."
Glancing at Jonah, he said, "Did you tell me what that was?"

"A bombing."

"Well, hell. If shit happens, they had a reason."

Jonah hated to admit it, but he felt the same way. That's why he'd hightailed it to the hideout. He pretty much anticipated what Kenny's reaction would be. "So what do we do?"

"Find the guy and send him back to where he came from."

"And if he won't go?"

Kenny smiled. "He'll go. Or I'll break every bone in his freakin' body. You think I'm kidding?"

"No."

"Damn straight."

They touched fists and went back to smoking their dope.

11

Once upon a time, Tessa had fed off risk. It had been her drug of choice. She understood intimately the kind of pleasure—and pain—that came from knowing you were risking something important. And yet, during her time in the wilderness of northern Minnesota, she seemed to have lost her taste for it.

It had bothered her at first, this lack of courage. It took her years to understand such a fundamental change in her nature. What she saw now, a truth that she'd been blind to as a younger woman, was that risk, the kind she relished, was bound to certainty; they were halves of the same coin.

If you were, for example, engaged in fighting for a righteous cause, the cosmos, by its very nature, had to be on your side. Thus, while risk might exist, it was mitigated. In the end, if you failed, if you were caught, beat up, fired from a job, evicted from your apartment, jailed, if you lost your lover or even your family, you could still hold your head high because what you'd been working for was the cause of the Greater Good.

What Tessa had lost wasn't simply her love of risk, but her absolute belief that she had the keys to the kingdom of the

Greater Good. Once lost, she doubted those keys could ever be recovered.

Strange as it would have seemed to to her twenty-five-year-old self, her sixty-five-year-old self thought that lack of certainty was not only good but a huge step forward morally.

A quiet life, a settled routine, a room of her own to work on her craft, the love of a good woman—those were what Tessa craved now. Perhaps it meant that she'd buried her head in the proverbial sand. What she also knew was that all human beings shoved their heads as far into the dark as they could just so they could continue to live and not go quietly insane. Everyone turned their backs on the horrors in the world, otherwise no one, with the exception of sociopaths and fanatics, would be able to sleep at night.

From the very first, Tessa understood that Judy was the biggest threat to her continuing freedom. If it wasn't for their shared goal of staying under the radar, they would have parted company long ago. They had nothing in common except for a single violent act, one they both regretted. Still, Tessa continued to keep her finger on Judy's emotional pulse because she needed to know they were still on the same page. The problem at the moment was, she was no longer sure they were.

Two years ago, when Judy met George Sunderland and found the Lord, a new element had been tossed into the mix. Tessa had never been religious herself, although she respected the spiritual instinct as universal. And yet, instead of adding an authentic sense of ethical and moral underpinnings to Judy's internal life, Tessa felt a new slipperiness take hold. Now more than ever, Judy's ideas and actions seemed inscrutable. After years of being philosophically to the left of the average anarchist, Judy's values, such as they were, had turned murky. Tessa had no way to predict where she'd come down on any given issue, which provided her with another good reason to keep Judy close.

Hearing footsteps on the deck, Tessa hoisted herself to a standing position, pulled her crutches under her arms, and went to unlock the front door. Right after Jane and Jonah had left, she'd called Fontaine, asked him to stop by. He was the one man in the world she could go to with the kind of favor she needed to ask.

"Afternoon," he said, removing his snap-brim cap, bunching it together in his large, rough hands. These days, his once thick black hair was shot through with gray. "How's the ankle?" he asked.

"Awful."

"You been taking your pain meds? Always important to keep up with that."

"Come in," she said, making her way back to the couch.

Fontaine closed the door and stood for a moment taking in the large, open room. "Smells good in here."

"A friend came by to make me breakfast. A frittata. There's some in the fridge if you're hungry."

"No thanks."

She motioned him to a chair.

Still glancing around, he adjusted his small, round, wire-rimmed glasses, then lowered his muscular frame down on the leather La-Z-Boy. He was dressed in his usual gray work shirt, jeans, and heavy work boots.

Fontaine Littlewolf, a full-blooded Ojibwe, was a Gulf War vet, a man who'd served his country with honor. On the out-skirts of Lost Lake there was a sign that said WE SUPPORT OUR TROOPS. In Fontaine's case, it was only minimally true.

While society was changing, many folks in town still looked down on Native Americans. Fontaine had come home from Kuwait with headaches, odd skin rashes, and chronic fevers, what doctors eventually began to call Gulf War Syndrome. Because he was Ojibwe and couldn't exactly hide his heritage, he had a harder time than most finding a job when he returned. His fatigue made it difficult for him to hold on to one once he'd found it.

Tessa had been elected president of the board of the Lost Lake Community Center the same fall she'd first met Fontaine. In a conversation over coffee, he mentioned that he'd been evicted from his apartment because his sporadic attempts to pay the rent had created problems with his landlord. For the time being, he was living in a tent in the woods. He said it was no big deal. It might have been alright then, but winter was coming on.

It took a few weeks for her to finally get the go-ahead to offer Fontaine the job of janitor at the center. With a BA in history from the University of Minnesota and seven years of high school history teaching under his belt, he was overqualified, although nobody seemed to notice. She figured that if he was in charge and had to take time off, he could find someone to cover for him. She arranged for him to report directly to her, which gave him the option to take as much leeway with his hours as he needed.

Within a year, he was doing far more than simple janitorial work. He'd become the community center's part-time handyman, periodic set designer and stage manager, and was beginning to take over the ordering for the gift shop. Tessa had no doubt that he'd be running the place sooner rather than later.

Wincing at a stab of pain in her ankle, she jerked her head up to see the clock above the mantel. She had to get this over with before Jill came home to take her to her doctor's appointment. She was actually looking forward to the walking boot. Mobility was crucial. If she didn't start walking, and fast, she would be an easy mark for anything Feigenbaumer wanted to pull. She had to push through the pain, no matter how much it cost her.

"I need to ask a favor," she began.

"Anything."

"There's a man in town. Arrived a few days ago. His name is Steve Feigenbaumer. I need to know where he's staying. All I can tell you is that he's middle-aged, medium build, dark hair, and has been seen wearing a White Sox cap—black with white letters."

"Okay."

"If you can locate him, I'd like you to follow him, see what he's up to, and then report back to me if you learn anything."

"That's all?"

"For now."

"He some kind of threat to you?"

"Possibly."

"I'm sure I could find a way to convince him to leave."

If it was only that simple. "I wish you could."

"Just say the word."

"He won't go. And if you could convince him, he'd come back with the police in tow."

Fontaine frowned.

"This is serious. I can't really say any more."

Standing, he nodded. "No need. I'll find the information you want."

She reached for his hand. "You're saving my life."

"Just returning the favor."

Tessa was practicing with her crutches on the steps down to the garage when Jill strolled up the paved driveway holding a pie. "What are you doing out here?" she demanded. "You're supposed to rest, keep your leg up."

"Not every minute," said Tessa, thumping down the last step. "You're early. We don't need to leave for another half hour."

"This is crazy. You could fall and hurt yourself."

Tessa was winded, but pleased to see that Jill had remembered the pie. "What is it? Blueberry?"

"Strawberry rhubarb."

"Awesome, as Jonah would say. Have I told you lately that I love you?"

Jill rolled her eyes.

"No, really," said Tessa, turning all the way around to face her. "You . . . make my life worth living." The sentiment was way too Hallmark card. Probably residual effects from last night's pain killers. Tears filled her eyes.

"Are you crying?"

"At my horrific use of clichés."

Jill leaned forward and cupped her hand under Tessa's chin. "Earth to Tessa. I don't want anything bad to happen to you."

It was amazing that the touch of Jill's hand could still cause her heart to speed up. "I'm so sorry."

"Good." Clearly thinking there might be more to the apology, she said, "For what?"

"The way I've been behaving. I've been taking all my frustration out on you."

"I wasn't sure you'd noticed."

"Am I that thick?"

"Sometimes. You took some of your *frustration*, as you call it, out on Jane and Cordelia last night, too."

Tessa caught the amused gleam in Jill's eye. "I know. I'll apologize. Do you forgive me?"

"I'll consider it."

When they kissed, Tessa lost her balance and ended up sitting down somewhat askew on the steps.

"See," said Jill. "You shouldn't be outside alone."

"I'm not. You're here."

"I'm going to throw the pie at you."

Waiting a beat, Tessa asked, "What do we do with Jonah?"

Jill's shoulders drooped "I called my brother this morning."

"And?"

"We had a long talk. Apparently Jonah was suspended from school a couple of times last year. Once for smoking pot. Once for getting in a fight. It sounded like it was a bad one. Jonah completely lost his temper. Gavin says he's been doing it a lot lately. He thinks he's acting out because of all the problems at home, which is why he agreed to let him spend his senior year here with us."

"Score," said Tessa, thrusting her fist in the air. "He's a good kid with a great heart. He just needs to get away from all that strife."

"My brother wasn't happy that Jonah left the way he did or that he lied and then hitchhiked all the way up here. It sounds like things have gotten pretty rocky between him and Shannon. They're seeing a marriage counselor."

"A good idea."

"I don't know. Gavin said that marriage counseling made him feel like they were one step closer to divorce."

"Is there anything we can do?"

"Keeping Jonah away from the worst of their problems is a good start. I think he should move into the downstairs room. We should probably take out the couch and buy a bed."

"I'd like him to stay up in the loft, just for a few more days."

Twisting the gold band on her finger, Jill said, "Look, I know you don't like it when I push, but you have to tell me what's going on. Who is this Feigenbaumer? Was he the man outside your study window last night?"

"I can't say for sure. I've never met him."

"But you're afraid of him."

Tessa covered Jill's hand with hers. "Give me some time to work this out."

"Are you in physical danger? I mean, do you think he'd hurt you in some way?"

"It's nothing like that. I overreacted last night. I feel so vulnerable because of this ankle." More lies. She hated herself because they flowed so easily.

"I wish you'd let me help. All this secrecy makes me feel like you don't trust me."

Tessa's eyes softened. "I trust you with my life."

"But not with whatever this is."

"Please, honey, let me work this out in my own time and in my own way."

In a halting voice, Jill said, "I guess I don't have a choice."

"You do have a choice. You can give me the space I need or you can be angry or hurt, which will make everything ten times worse for me."

"Oh, all right. We'll leave it at that. For now."

Tessa eyed the pie. "Do we have any vanilla ice cream?"

"Vanilla and cinnamon."

"Let's have dessert first tonight."

"I knew there was a reason I married you." Jill kissed Tessa tenderly, then leaned back and ordered her up the stairs to change her clothes before the doctor's appointment.

"I love it when you get all militaristic."

"I know."

12

Wendell Hammond had never been in a stage play before, although he believed he had a natural talent for acting. As a professional portrait photographer, he had to be a good actor to get people in the right mood for a photo shoot. This was especially true of children, his primary focus. One minute he would do his Barney impersonation, the next he would get the kid laughing with jokes or make balloon animals, a speciality of his. If all else failed, he'd bring out his dog, Boomer, a Jack Russell terrier. Boomer usually put a gleam in a kid's eyes. That was before the fire, of course. Before his life changed forever.

Wendell thought of himself as a wizard with kids. It was funny, too, because he didn't much like them. His wife had wanted at least two, but they had never been able to conceive. She had to make do with animals—six cats and eight dogs over the course of a twenty-two-year marriage. Mary Jo was gone now, as was Boomer. Both had died before the fire, thank God. Wendell had to admit that until he'd met Ruth Jensen, he'd been a lonely man. In a short time, he'd grown to care about Ruth a great deal, and yet nothing would ever fill the place in his life that his wife—and their collection of the sweetest animals on earth—once had.

During Mary Jo's final illness, he'd done everything in his power to make her happy. The fact remained, however, that what she wanted most—a trip to Italy, to the spot where they'd first met—had never happened. It all came down to money. Even with medical insurance, the bills the company refused to pay had plunged them deep into debt. One thing led to another. When Mary Jo couldn't continue working, they fell behind on their mortgage. The bank foreclosed on them the year before she died. They'd bought the house shortly before she was diagnosed—bad timing, of course, though their finances at the time had been solid. Their final lifeline—two credit cards—had been maxed out when he paid the last of the funeral expenses. That was two years ago. He'd felt like a failure then and he felt like one now.

As far as Wendell was concerned, the American Dream was nothing but a sophisticated scam. He'd done everything right and yet he could never get ahead. After years of fading into the woodwork, of being the kind of guy who had a hard time catching a waitress's eye because he was so forgettable, so dreary and colorless and boring, he'd made a decision to turn the page. He'd stood at his wife's gravesite on a windy March afternoon and promised her that he would start over, that he'd become the man he'd always wanted to be. Life *had* changed for Wendell, although his dream of becoming a new man was turning out to be much harder than anything he'd attempted before. He wasn't sure he had the steam, the grit, or the stamina to stick with the program. Perhaps he'd set his sights too high. After all, it was hard to imagine Pee Wee Herman turning into Clint Eastwood overnight, especially when it was so much easier to simply stay home and watch TV.

The only part of his life that was going well at the moment, other than Ruth, was the play he was in at the community playhouse. His first glimpse of the dressing room at the theater, however, had been a disappointment. Because he'd watched too many movies about great actors in private dressing rooms being attended to by a staff of hairdressers, makeup artists, and other assorted minions, he hadn't expected something quite so grungy. The long narrow room was meant for both the men and women in the cast, and contained one long Pepto Bismol–colored Formica table facing mirrors surrounded by bright lights.

Making himself comfortable on one of the beat-up chairs, Wendell leaned toward the mirror and studied his face. He decided that the thin mustache he'd grown for the part was a good touch. It made him look raffish. Cosmopolitan. At forty-five, his hair remained thick and blond, although his hairline was beginning to recede. When he thought about being directed tonight by the legendary Cordelia Thorn, his palms grew clammy. He wanted desperately to do a good job acting the part of the wolfish Philip. He needed to succeed at *something*.

Feeling the cell phone in his pocket vibrate, he fished it out and checked the caller ID. "Hi, Frank," he said. "Anything new on the insurance front?"

"I should have some good news for you soon," came Frank's friendly voice.

"Great. Appreciate your returning my call." Emily came in though the door on the other side of the room. He nodded to her. "Talk to you soon then?"

"In a day or two."

Returning the phone to his pocket, Wendell rose and walked over to where Emily had taken a seat. Resting his hands on her shoulders, he said, "Are you ready to be touched by greatness?"

"Excuse me?"

"Cordelia Thorn."

"Oh, yeah. Ready as I'll ever be."

"This could be a big break for you. You're the one who wants to become a professional actor."

"All I can do is my best, Wendell."

"True. Still, a lucky break for you, her turning up here."

She began to apply her stage makeup.

"You should be more excited."

"You can be excited for both of us."

"You're jaded. Nineteen years old and you're jaded."

Her jaw set.

"I'm seeing your mom tonight after rehearsal. I'm taking her over to Thunderhook for dinner."

"Kind of pricy."

"I'm not completely broke. Besides, she's worth it."

Emily glanced up at him. "You really mean that?"

"I do. I think she's wonderful. Not as beautiful as her daughter, of course."

"You're a sleaze, Wendell."

"Why? I'm merely stating the obvious. I'm not coming on to you, if that's what you think."

"Right."

"I'm not." He was hurt that she would jump to such a ridiculous conclusion.

"Look," said Emily, running a comb through her hair. "My mother's a grown woman. She makes her own decisions, just like I do. Now why don't you go bother someone else?"

"Am I bothering you?"

"What do you think?"

"Well, jeez, sorry for living." He pressed a hand to his stomach, sucked in his gut and walked away, feeling sulky and misunderstood. So what else was new?

"Stop! Cease! Halt!" Taking a deep breath, Cordelia hollered one last command. "Desist, dear ladies and gentlemen." Under her breath, she whispered, "I can't take another second."

Jane had been sitting next to Cordelia, five rows up from the stage, all through the early part of the second act. Every so often, Cordelia would start to quiver, cover her mouth and clear her throat. Jane had no idea why she was behaving so oddly—that is, until she burst out laughing right before erupting out of her chair and calling for an end to the proceedings.

"Did Tessa provide you with a dialect coach to help you with your English accents?" she asked, having trouble keeping a straight face.

"No," said Wendell. Jane recognized him as Helen Merland's house guest.

"Do we need help?" asked Camilla Strom, Wendell's wife in the play, the confused and slightly ditzy Sheila.

"Seth and Emily," called Cordelia. "Front and center."

The other two actors emerged from one of the voms. These were Ginny and Greg in the production, the young lovers. Seth was sensitive looking, with dark brown hair worn long and shaggy for the play. Emily was thin and lovely, with long blond slightly frizzy hair and a grace and presence on stage that she lacked entirely when she stepped off.

Vom was a theater term Jane was familiar with. Short for vomitory, it was a word with a theatrical history dating back to ancient Rome. Jane had first come across it when Cordelia had done work at the Blackburn Playhouse in Shoreview many years ago. A vom was an exit or entrance through the banked seating of any theater-in-the-round. The Lost Lake Community Theater had four voms, one that led to the dressing room, two that allowed the audience to enter and exit, and one that led to the prop room and stage door.

Barreling down the steps from the audience, Cordelia smiled like a cobra about to strike. "Comrades," she said, hopping up on stage. "Your English accents are . . . how shall I put it?"

"Substandard?" offered Wendell.

"Yes, that's a good word. Better than atrocious, miserable, or criminally inadequate."

The actors all stared at the floor.

"Here's what we're going to do. Instead of London, we're going to set the first part of the play in Boston. The Willows' country garden will take place in a small town outside of the city. The programs haven't been printed yet, so the change won't be a problem."

"Lower Pendon, Bucks?" chirped Camilla. "Sounds rather English to me."

"The audience will just have to work harder to suspend their disbelief. Now. Please drop all pretense of an English accent and resume your normal mode of speech. Think you can do that?"

The actors shuffled and grumbled, and all said they could.

"Dandy. I believe that to be our only major problem. We want people laughing at the play, not at us. Are any of you free during the afternoons this week?"

"Camilla and I are," blurted Wendell, backing up a step and looking sheepish as he once again dropped his gaze to his loafers.

He wasn't the best pick to play the assured, lecherous Philip. Tessa had explained that everyone in town felt sorry for him because of his string of bad luck, and that's why she'd given him the part.

"Depends on the day," said Seth, his arm draped across Emily's shoulder.

Emily agreed. "I work most afternoons."

"I'll have the stage manager, the amazing Mr. Littlewolf, contact you. I would like to work with each of you briefly, one on one. Tonight, as you all know, is the dry tech. We won't need you to stick around for that, although if you want to, feel free. Tomorrow will be our first dress rehearsal. I'd like all of you here by six. Any problems with that?"

"No, Miss Thorn," said Wendell, clearly in awe.

"Marvelous." Motioning to Fontaine Littlewolf, who had been standing up by the control booth door watching the action, Cordelia called, "Bring your play book down here and let's get going on the cues."

Jane had met Littlewolf on several occasions. Tonight, as a way to welcome Cordelia to the playhouse, he'd given them a mini-tour. Cordelia was most interested in the costume department, such as it was. She examined each piece of clothing to determine the size. Jane could see her lusting after some of the more outrageous specimens—male or female, it didn't matter.

Wriggling her hefty form into the seat next to Jane, Cordelia leaned close and whispered, "I may take you up on changing rooms at the lodge tonight."

"Because of the pea?"

"I am not cut out to live in Sparta."

When Jane broke into a laugh, Cordelia puffed herself up like a great bird. "You think my discomfort is amusing?"

Before Jane could answer, she heard a shout and then a crash.

"What the——" said Cordelia, rising.

Littlewolf, who had been on his way down from the control booth, shook his head and started for the vom that lead to the dressing rooms.

"Is it a fight?" called Cordelia.

"Wendell and Seth. Wendell doesn't like the way Seth leers at Emily. I know this may seem out of character for him, but he decked Seth a couple of weeks ago."

"Lord," said Cordelia, sitting down with a thump. "I absolutely love it when there's brawling in the ranks. Makes for such a collegial atmosphere. This play is supposed to be light comedy. If the actors all hate each other, guess how it's going to come off?"

"I wonder if Littlewolf will need some help," said Jane, still looking in the direction of the shout.

"Breaking up scuffles among the thespians must be in the stage manager's job description. It's certainly not in mine. I think we should stay here and hope that makeup can handle any potential black-and-blue issues. If a gurney becomes necessary, we cancel the production." She pulled a Snickers bar out of her purse. At Jane's questioning look, she said, "What? It's a health food. It has peanuts."

Monday nights were the pits, even in high summer. Lyndie sat on the stool behind the counter at the emporium and gazed forlornly at the empty display aisles. She didn't even need to hide her cigarette. It was probably silly to be open, although it gave her time to clean and dust—and sometimes, when she was in the right mood, to think.

Lyndie wasn't as dumb as some people assumed, especially Tessa, who never had anything good to say about her mental abilities. True, she wasn't an intellectual. Philosophical discussions bored her. She would rather talk about people, celebrities, or concrete things like recipes or vacation spots or children. Tonight, however, Lyndie was feeling reflective.

The one quality all her husbands had in common was confidence. In George's case, he had God on his side. His relationship with the Almighty was one of the things she loved most about him. She could sink into his convictions and warm herself by them. And yet tonight, when she needed them most, she was forced to the conclusion that borrowed convictions were useless.

Her cell phone rang. Removing it from her purse, she glanced at the caller ID before pressing it to her ear. "Hello?"

"Hi, Lyndie. It's Wendell."

"Ah, hi," she said, wishing now that she hadn't answered. Lyndie had dated Wendell's father once upon a time. She'd always felt sorry for the boy because he had so little natural spunk.

"Have you thought any more about my idea?" he asked.

"Honey, you know I would love to be able to help you out, but right now I've got so many other things to deal with. And money is tight. I don't think I'd be able to swing it. I'm beginning to wonder if I should sell the emporium."

"Really? That's so sad."

He sounded depressed. "You're still at Helen Merland's place, right?"

"Thanks for putting in a good word."

"And you're helping her out?"

"Every chance I get."

"That's a good boy."

"I am *not* a *boy,*" he erupted.

She was momentarily stunned into silence. He'd never raised his voice to her before. "Are you all right?"

"Gotta go. Thanks for nothing."

"Wendell? Are you there? Wendell?" It was no use. He'd hung up. She wondered what had gotten in into to him, and yet with so many other pressing issues on her mind, she soon forgot about it.

A few minutes before nine, as she was reaching to remove the OPEN sign from the window, Feigenbaumer startled her by pushing through the front door. She stepped back. "We're closed. You can't be in here."

"I need to show you something."

"Not interested." She inched her way back toward the counter, to her purse and the loaded revolver that was tucked inside. She was glad now that she'd listened to Tessa's advice and taken the gun out in the woods to do some target practice.

"I want you to look at a couple of photos."

"No more photos," she said, nearly knocking over one of the displays in her eagerness to get back to her purse.

"I think you may recognize this woman."

"Why can't you just leave me alone?"

"Am I ruining your evening? Such a shame."

The threat in his voice was unmistakable.

"Here," he said, stepping up to the counter.

She edged onto the stool. "I'm not interested."

"You will be in this one." He dropped it in front of her, pressed it to the Formica with his finger. "You recognize her?"

She only had to glance at it to realize he'd found her senior photograph, the one that had appeared in her high school annual. "I've never seen that person before."

He let out a laugh. "That's good. You don't think she looks an awful lot like you?"

"No, I don't."

"Really, Judy?"

"I'm not her. I've lived my entire life in Lost Lake."

He made a buzzer sound. "Ennhh. Wrong. Ten points off for lying. I did a little research in the last couple of days. You arrived in town in February of nineteen-seventy. Your first place of employment was Sibley's clothing store on Elm and Walnut. You had a Minnesota driver's license in the name of Lyndie Reynolds. Since your arrival, you've been Lyndie Becker, Lyndie Taggert, Lyndie Niemi, and Lyndie LaVasser. I'd say that makes you the town's official gold digger."

"My personal life is none of your business." She lowered her right hand to her lap.

"You killed him, Judy. Admit it."

"I want you to leave."

"What I need to know is, where's Sabra Briere?"

"I'm telling you, I don't know what you're talking about."

He came at her, fist clenched. "Stop with the bullshit. You think this is all I have? What I've found will send you to jail for the rest of your life. I want a straight answer to my question and I want it now. "

Her hand curled around the handle of the revolver.

"Where's Sabra?" he demanded, shoving his face close to hers. "Did you hear me?"

"I heard you," she replied softly.

"Well?" he said. "I'm waiting."

13

Jonah relaxed in his aunt's car two doors away from the Jensen house, listening to a CD Kenny had given him and waiting for Emily to get home. The Hold Steady was Kenny's current favorite band. Normally, Jonah and Kenny didn't like the same music. This time, however, Jonah had to admit that the band was hot. He liked the convoluted lyrics. He wasn't sure he understood them, though that was probably the point.

After spending the afternoon smoking dope at the hideout, he and Kenny had met up at a pizza joint in town and in record time they'd downed an order of Italian cheese bread; two extra meat, extra cheese pizzas; a side of spaghetti; and, when Jonah left, Kenny was chowing down on a piece of apple pie à la mode. Jonah had to admit that Kenny had done most of the eating. He'd put on a bunch of weight in the year Jonah had been gone. From certain angles, he almost looked fat. Basic training would beat that out of him soon enough.

By the time Emily got home, the clouds had parted revealing a perfect crescent moon. Jonah slipped out of the front seat, but then remembered the rose he'd bought at a convenience store. He ducked back inside and retrieved it from the dash. By the time he reached the Jensens' front lawn, Emily was on her way inside.

"Hey," he called, unable to stop himself from grinning. He felt like an idiot. Pretty soon he'd start drooling, with no more ability to stop the drool than his stupid-ass grin. He'd been thinking that he should have hid somewhere, popped out and scared her. She would have been mad at first. By the time she realized she was pissed, they would have been locked in each other's arms.

Turning and squinting into the twilight, Emily said, "Jonah?"

"It's me." He walked right up to her and handed her the flower, enjoying the shocked look on her face.

"What . . . how?"

"I wanted to surprise you." He had to admit that he was a little disappointed. He'd expected her to be all over him, which was her usual MO. Instead, she kept her distance. She almost seemed afraid. He didn't get what was happening *at all.* "Aren't you happy to see me?"

She held the rose to her nose, sniffed it, passed it back and forth in front of her mouth. "Give me a minute, for Pete's sake."

All of a sudden everything seemed all weird. He wasn't even sure if he should hug her.

"When did you get here?" she asked.

"Last night. Got caught in a storm. It was kind of a miserable trip up. I hitchhiked. Kenny and me, we hung out this afternoon. I came by first thing this morning, but you were gone."

"I was around this morning."

"Well, I mean, after I got up. I slept late."

She gave a careful nod. "Kenny say anything else?"

"Like what?"

She shrugged.

116

"Come on, Em. Are you happy to see me or not? Maybe things have changed between us. Maybe you don't feel the same way about me anymore. If that's the case, be straight about it. But please, whatever's going on inside that head of yours, stop acting so freakin' peculiar."

She continued to hold the rose under her nose. "When you left, I thought it was forever, that I'd never see you again."

"I worried about that, too. But I'm back. And this time, I'm not leaving."

Resting her arms on his shoulders, she said, "Honestly, Jonah, the rose is perfect. Nobody's ever been as sweet to me as you."

He couldn't help himself. He kissed her so long and hard that he felt as if he'd taken a dive into a deep pool. Coming up for air, he said, "I've got my aunt's car. Want to take a drive?"

"Where?"

"Does it matter? God, but you're beautiful."

"So are you."

"Do you have to tell your mom where you're going?" he asked, running his fingertips up and down her bare arms.

"It'll just take a second. I don't want her to worry. "

"I'll wait in the car." He had a bottle of Jagermeister in the trunk, compliments of Kenny, and a bunch of joints inside a small metal box taped inside one of the wheel wells.

Before he took off, Emily put a hand on his arm. "Do you still love me, Jonah? For real?"

He brushed her honey-gold hair away from her face. "Far as I'm concerned, it's you and me forever."

14

Lying on her stomach with a pillow over her head, Jane groaned when the phone on the nightstand gave a piercing ring, waking her from a sound sleep. For an instant, she thought she was back home, that someone from one of her restaurants was calling with a problem only she could fix.

"Hello?" she said, picking up the receiver and holding it to her ear, her head still partially covered by the pillow.

"Who's this?" came a worried voice.

"Jill? Is that you? It's Jane."

"I thought I was calling Cordelia's room."

"You were. She had a crisis of comfort, so we switched. Long story. What's up?"

"Lyndie LaVasser's missing. Her fiancé stopped by the cottage a few minutes ago hoping we could join the search party. I guess he didn't remember about Tessa's ankle. I'd like to help, but I don't want to leave her alone. She's pretty upset."

"What about Jonah?"

"He's not home yet. Tessa let him take her car earlier in the day. She told him to be back by midnight."

Jane checked her watch. It was going on two.

"I figured Cordelia would still be awake, which is why I called her number first."

"It's fine," said Jane, swinging her legs off the bed and sitting up. "One or both of us will be down in a few minutes."

"Thanks. Sorry I woke you."

"No worries." Jane wrapped herself in her robe and went to knock on the door that connected the two rooms. Opening it a crack, she saw that Cordelia was sitting on the couch, dressed in a black-and-white-striped hoodie, jeans, and red socks, with the script notebook propped against her knees. She was talking on the the hotel's landline.

"I'm sorry, Hatts. I can't hear you very well. Why are you up so early? It must be five in the morning there. What?" She listened. "Yes, I'm glad you're finding lots of bugs in Argentina. They have bugs pretty much everywhere. Say that again?" She waited, chewing on her lower lip. "Honey, I think a dead bug collection is macabre, even for you. Macabre? It means dreadful. Morbid. What? Morbid means, well, grotesque. Have Radley explain it to you. No, no, I'm not saying you can't have a dead bug collection. It is, one would suppose, preferable to a live bug collection. But, honey, all around you they're shooting a movie. Isn't there anything about the movie business you find interesting?" Eyes rising to the ceiling, she said, "The horses. I should have expected that." She listened a moment more. "I know we have cats and Melissa has a dog and that we all get along famously, but a horse is a big animal. No, he couldn't sleep with you. What did you say?" Her eyes nearly bugged out of her head. "A giant *termite* nest? How did we jump from a horse to a giant termite nest? No, honey, you can't bring it home. Have Radley take a picture of it so you can remember what it looks like." Cordelia held the cordless away from her ear and made a strangling sound. "What? No, Hatts, that was just me clearing my throat. Yes, I love you, too. Call me tomorrow. I miss you, baby. You're listening to Radley, right?" She waited, smiled. "Good girl. What?" She listened again, this time with apparent teeth grinding. "The giant termite nest conversation is over. I will not change my mind. Bye now, Hattie. I love you."

Seeing Jane standing in the doorway, Cordelia asked, "Are you interested in providing a good home for a giant termite nest or a horse?"

"Maybe in my next life."

"I heard your phone ring. Who called?"

"Jill. Remember Lyndie LaVasser?"

"Miss flirt and wiggle? She owns one of the gift shops on Main."

"She's missing." Jane explained that one or both of them was needed down at the cottage right away. "Jill wants to join the search party, but doesn't feel like she can leave Tessa alone."

"I'll go," said Cordelia, closing the notebook with a tired sigh. "I need to talk to her about the play anyway. Might as well do it now."

"This might not be the best time."

"Because?"

"Jill said Tessa was upset. I doubt many people go missing in a town this size."

Ten minutes later, Jane and Cordelia were inside the cottage with an obviously agitated though silent Tessa. The strain in her eyes betrayed how seriously she took the situation.

Jill busied herself in the bedroom getting dressed, shouting for Tessa to relax, that Lyndie had probably had one too many and stopped her car somewhere to sleep it off.

"Is Lyndie a drinker?" asked Jane.

"Not like that," mumbled Tessa.

"She live alone?"

"She has a house a couple blocks from the emporium. Her fiancé, George, usually comes over when she's done working. She calls him when she's home. He got worried when she didn't call, so he drove over. She wasn't there. And she wasn't at the emporium."

"You two have been friends a long time," said Cordelia, standing in the kitchen filling the coffeemaker with water. "She ever do anything like this before?"

Tessa gave her head a stiff shake.

"Maybe her car broke down," called Jill. "Depending on where she was when it happened, cell phone towers are few and far between up here."

"Maybe," said Tessa. She didn't sound convinced.

As Jill emerged from the bedroom, Jonah came through the back door.

"You're late, young man," said Jill, giving him an angry look. "I doubt your aunt will be letting you use her car again anytime soon."

Jonah examined his fingernails and said nothing.

"Where were you all day?" asked Jill, grabbing a leather jacket from off the back of a chair.

"With friends."

"It's after two," said Tessa.

"I know. I'm sorry. The time got away from me."

"We'll talk later."

"Where you going?" asked Jonah, stepping back as Jill rushed past him.

"Lyndie LaVasser is missing. I'm going to help George look for her."

"Mrs. LaVasser?" repeated Jonah.

"I'll call if I learn anything," said Jill.

"Come in here," called Tessa.

Jonah dragged himself into the living room, still mostly looking down at his nails.

"Did you find Emily?"

"Yeah."

"Is that where you were tonight?"

"Yeah."

"Bend down."

"Why?"

"I want to smell your breath."

"No."

"You've been drinking?"

"No. Well . . . maybe a little."

"You drank and drove my car?"

"I'm not drunk."

"Go to bed. You can find clean linens and blankets in the closet next to the room downstairs. I don't want to see or hear from you until tomorrow morning."

"Am I in trouble?"

"What do you think?"

Jonah's shoulders sank. He slunk out of the room.

Rubbing her eyes, Tessa let out a sigh. "You start thinking that maybe he's grown up a little and then he goes and pulls something like this. He's such a smart kid. I don't get it. He's been back one day and he's already in the dog house. *This* at a time when he wants a favor from us. He's going to be eighteen in November, old enough to be sent off to fight a war, and yet he can't even look around and discern what's in his best interests. I mean, you'd think even your standard issue narcissistic teenager would be able to do that much."

When Jonah had passed by her, Jane had smelled more than booze on his breathe. Both Jonah and his clothing smelled as if they'd been marinating in marijuana.

Tessa walked with some difficulty into the kitchen. She tried the doorknob on the back door to make sure it was locked.

"You're getting around well in that walking boot," said Cordelia, waiting for the coffeemaker to disgorge enough coffee to fill her mug.

"Better than I thought."

"It's great to see you up and around again," said Jane. She felt uneasy in Tessa's presence after the conversation they'd had earlier in the day. She wanted to say something to clear the air. Nothing came to mind.

"What do we do now?" asked Cordelia, resting her elbows on the island.

"We wait," said Tessa, getting down a box of crackers from the cupboard and a slice of her homemade chicken liver and brandy pâté from the refrigerator.

Patience had never been one of Jane's virtues. "Listen," she said, moving to the edge of her chair. "I can't sit here and do nothing. Cordelia, can I borrow your car? The more people who join the search, the quicker we'll find out what's happened to Lyndie." Jane noticed Tessa's disapproving look. Not that it mattered. Lyndie's disappearance had nothing to do with Tessa's problems. Or, thought Jane, sensing the tension behind the disapproval, did it?

"Have at it," said Cordelia, tossing Jane her car keys. "But be careful. Don't do anything I wouldn't do."

"That leaves me with a lot of latitude," said Jane on her way out the door.

Except for a white cat curled on the hood of an old Ford pickup, the early morning streets of Lost Lake were deserted. A small town was worlds away from a big city, where people were out and about at all ours of the day and night. The quiet was almost eerie.

Jane began by driving around, getting the full lay of the town. After a quick tour of the residential neighborhoods, she turned onto Main. Halfway down the block, a Balsam County sheriff's cruiser sat parked in front of the LaVasser Gift Emporium, strobe lights slicing through the darkness.

Jane pulled Cordelia's car up to the curb on the opposite side of the street and got out. She spent a few minutes leaning against the hood, arms crossed, waiting to see what was going on. When nobody came out, she approached cautiously. Noticing that the door was open, she stepped inside. Two Balsam County sheriff's deputies stood about ten feet away, examining a spot in the knotty-pine paneled wall.

"Looks like a thirty-eight slug," said the woman deputy.

Both were dressed in brown pants, tan and brown shirts, with heavy patrol belts strapped to their waists.

"Should we bag it?" asked the male deputy.

"We'll let Davey take a look first."

The woman seemed to be in charge. With her back to Jane, she moved around the store, examining the floor, the free-standing shelves, the walls.

"Look at this," said the man. He was behind the main counter now, just a few feet from the cash register. "I'd say this is LaVasser's purse. Why would she leave it behind?"

The female deputy turned to face him. When she did, she caught sight of Jane standing in the doorway. "Back out, ma'am. You can't come in here."

Jane held up her hands. "I've been driving around, helping look for Lyndie."

"You a friend of the family?"

"Friend of a friend."

The deputy was maybe five-six, trim, not bad looking. Her short sandy hair was partially covered by a brown cap with the word *Sheriff* written in large gold block letters. Jane was savvy enough to know that just because the woman looked like a dyke didn't mean she was one.

"You from around here?" asked the deputy.

"I live in Minneapolis. I'm up here staying at Thunderhook Lodge. Jill and Tessa are old friends."

The deputy digested that while giving Jane a more thorough examination. "I'm the undersheriff of Balsam County." She hooked her thumb at the man standing behind the counter. "That's Patrolman Dahl."

"Nice to meet you both," said Jane. "Have you found Mrs. LaVasser?"

"Not yet, but we will." She stepped a little closer.

Jane couldn't help but notice that the undersheriff swaggered. Not an appealing characteristic.

"You're Jane, right? I'm Kelli Christopher." She stuck out her hand.

"Sorry. Have we met?"

"Jill told me about you." Lowering her voice, she said, "I thought you'd be younger. I don't much like blind dates, that's why I said no."

"What blind date?"

"The one we were supposed to go on."

"Nobody ever told me about a blind date."

"Wouldn't have worked anyway." She looked at Jane the way a person might look at a piece of gum stuck to her shoe. When she smiled, she revealed upper teeth that were straight and white, and lower teeth that could have used a few thousand dollars worth of orthodontia. "How's Tessa taking Lyndie's disappearance?"

"Not well."

"Have you seen her tonight?"

"I came from the cottage."

"Well," she said, turning Jane around and walking her out the door, "it's best if you leave this to the professionals."

Not only did she swagger, but she was patronizing.

"Go back and stay with Tessa. If I learn anything, I'll be sure to let you know."

"Gee, thanks."

Kelli cocked her head. "I say something wrong?"

All the way across the street, Jane could feel Kelli's eyes boring a disapproving hole into her back. This was the second time today that someone had called her an amateur. She didn't like it.

15

Waking to the cries of gulls, Jane looked up through the skylight to see a gray day dawning. She and Cordelia had spent what was left of the night at the cottage, Cordelia on the couch in the living room, and Jane on the couch up in the loft.

Negotiating the spiral staircase down to the main floor as quietly as possible, Jane began the search for her wallet and Cordelia's car keys. She'd promised Helen Merland that they would go out to breakfast today and didn't want to disappoint her.

As she sat down on a dining room chair to pull on her boots, Cordelia stirred on the couch.

"What are you doing?"

"Sleepwalking?"

"Why?"

"Helen Merland's taking me to breakfast."

Sitting up a bit straighter, Cordelia whispered "Where?"

"The Jacaranda Café, I would imagine."

"Think Helen would mind if I tagged along?"

"I'm sure she'd love to see you, but isn't it a bit early for you to be up?"

"I think I can dig deep and find the wherewithal within me

to cope." Pulling the blanket off her midsection, Cordelia gazed down at her black-and-white striped hoodie. "I suppose the natives will find this a bit jarring."

"Unless the café caters to fugitives from chain gangs, I think you'll be okay." Jane brushed her teeth and combed her hair while Cordelia wrote a note for Jill and Tessa and then waited impatiently for Cordelia to finish with her makeup.

The convertible was parked in the drive.

"You take the wheel," said Cordelia, sliding into the passenger's seat. "I'm in the mood to be chauffeured."

"Before we go," said Jane by way of warning. "I don't think we should mention to Helen that Lyndie's missing. Tessa told me last night that they were close friends. Since we don't know what happened, I don't think there's any reason to upset her."

"My luscious lips are zipped," said Cordelia.

Wendell sweated as he pushed an old lawnmower across the grass outside the Merland home. It usually took a good hour to get it all done. His plan was to finish early, then shower and spend the rest of the morning working on his lines. He'd just stopped to wipe the sweat off his forehead when a man he'd never seen before walked up and pointed to the roof.

"You got a couple issues up there," said the man, adjusting his sunglasses. "First off, some shingles are missing. Also, part of the chimney flashing is gone. Bet you've got a leak inside. You're going to need to replace that or you'll run into some serious problems."

"I'm not the owner," said Wendell. "I'm just living in the walk-out basement temporarily."

"Sure is a beautiful place. Probably the grandest home in town. Guess there are fat cats everywhere."

"I'm not opposed to fat cats," said Wendell, returning his handkerchief to the pocket of his tan slacks. "I'd just like to be one of them."

The stranger smiled. "I hear you. Still, some people seem to be luckier than others. Can't help but get a guy down. Takes money to make money in this world. How did these people make theirs?"

"Ever heard of the Merland Brewery?"

"Good stuff. I'm sure I've helped add to their fortune."

"Haven't we all."

"You friends with these folks?"

"Mr. Merland's dead. It's just Mrs. Merland now. One of the reasons I moved in was to help her out. She's old, forgetful. I do what I can."

"You're a nice guy."

"Yes, I am. I get her groceries, make her some light meals, do a little cleanup, a little property maintenance. She pays me."

"But not much, right?"

"I didn't ask for much."

"She should give you a decent wage. It wouldn't be any sweat off her back."

"No, I suppose not." As the weeks had worn on with no photography jobs and no word from the insurance company about the fire, Wendell was becoming more and more concerned with his financial future.

"You gotta stand up for yourself, man, otherwise people walk all over you. Especially rich people." Folding his arms over his chest, the stranger continued, "I'm looking to hire someone. It's easy money—if you can find the information I'm looking for."

"Information?"

"About the owner of this house."

"You know her?"

"Not exactly."

"Then I don't get—"

"A thousand bucks," said the stranger. "Cash money."

Wendell glanced up at the living room windows. Sometimes Helen liked to watch him work in the yard. This morning he was glad to see she wasn't there.

"Mrs. Merland used to run a foundation. You familiar with that?"

"Somewhat."

"I assume she's known around town as a philanthropist, a good and decent person. What I'm about to tell you might clash with that opinion. You can believe me or not, doesn't really matter." He hesitated.

"Go on," said Wendell, curious about what he had to say.

"In nineteen seventy, a woman moved to town. You might know her as Lyndie LaVasser."

"Lyndie? She dated my dad for a few years."

"You two close?"

"Not . . . anymore."

"Well, you may not want to hear this, but she was involved in a homicide in Chicago in nineteen sixty-eight. Her real name is Judy Clark. When it looked like she might get caught, she took off and ended up here. Helen Merland helped her financially during the two years she was in hiding. Another woman was also involved in the homicide. She might also be in town. Her name back then was Sabra Briere. I believe that Mrs. Merland helped them both acquire new identities and then brought them to Lost Lake. I'm looking for proof."

Wendell scratched the back of his head. It was a lot to absorb. "Why would Helen do that?"

"I have a theory, but I need more proof. One thousand dollars in small bills. You interested?"

It might help him pay off some of his debt. He'd been considering filing for bankruptcy. Everything in his life seemed so confusing. "What would constitute proof?"

"Does Mrs. Merland store any business files in the house?"

"She has a study crammed with filing cabinets, not that I've ever seen her go in there."

A car drawing up to the curb attracted Wendell's attention. When Cordelia and her friend got out, Wendell waved, embarrassed that they'd caught him looking so unkempt. He was supposed to meet with Cordelia at one. He hoped he hadn't gotten the time wrong.

"Find anything with the name Judy Clark or Sabra Briere on it," whispered the stranger. "You're looking at a two-year period. Shouldn't be that hard. What's your name?"

"Wendell Hammond."

The man pulled out a business card and handed it over. "My cell phone number is at the bottom. You find anything, you call me."

Wendell glanced at the name.

"Call me Steve," said the man, keeping his back to the street.

"One *thousand* dollars, right?"

"In cash."

Shaking the man's hand, Wendell said, "I'll see what I can do."

For a Tuesday morning, the Jacaranda Café was bustling. The red oilcloth-covered tables looked festive, as did the red gingham curtains The smell of fresh baked bread made Jane's mouth water. The waitress who greeted them appeared to know Helen and made sure they were seated at the first available table.

"I know what I'm having," said Cordelia, flipping open the menu and then closing it back up.

"A dozen caramel rolls," said Helen.

"Think twelve is enough?" asked Jane.

Helen hadn't remembered about breakfast. They found her in her bathrobe sitting at a table on the patio, reading the morning paper and enjoying a cup of tea. Helen recognized Cordelia instantly, though once again seemed confused about Jane's identity. She called her by her daughter's name twice before the fog of confusion lifted and she remembered who Jane was. She had no memory of their conversation on the beach yesterday morning. Thankfully, she was eager to go out to breakfast.

"My appetite isn't what it used to be," said Helen, reading through the daily specials.

"How's everything with the brewery?" asked Jane.

"I guess you haven't heard," said Helen. "We had to close it last year. Put a lot of people in this town out of work. Believe me when I say that I'm not as well-loved as I used to be. The job base was already hit hard by the economy. Lots of home foreclosures, stores going out of business. Shutting down the brewery made it even worse." She took a sip of water. "The natural spring, which was our water supply, became contaminated. I don't recall all the details, but it left us with little choice. The purity and taste of the spring was our claim to fame. It's all gone now."

"Bummer," said Cordelia, adding, "I know that hardly qualifies as an elegant statement of concern and compassion."

"Works for me," said Helen. "I might as well tell you the other bad news. I'm not keeping it a secret from my friends. I was diagnosed with Alzheimer's. So far, I think I'm doing pretty well.

I get confused sometimes. I'm on a drug that's supposed to slow the progress of the disease."

Jane assumed it might be something like that.

"I had no idea," said Cordelia.

"None of us gets through life without some pain. I will say that some days are better than others."

The waitress arrived and they all placed their orders.

"Is that why Wendell Hammond is living with you?" asked Jane, watching the waitress move behind the counter and hook the order to a check wheel.

"Not entirely. He's had a string of bad luck, poor boy. First his wife died of cancer, and then a couple of months ago his business burned down. He was living in the apartment above the photography studio, so when it happened, he lost everything. He had nowhere else to go, and very little money. He's a proud man. He insists he's not a charity case."

"Did he own the building that burned?" asked Jane.

"I assume so."

"What caused the fire?"

"No idea. He's trying to rebuild his life and his business. It's been slow going. I let him take over one of the bedrooms on the first floor to use as a studio. He's been so helpful, I'm not sure what I'd do without him."

"What sort of photographer?" asked Cordelia, leaning back as the waitress set filled coffee cups in front of them.

"He does the portraits for the schools in the area, for the yearbooks. He also does weddings, family portraits—the usual. When he finds his own place and moves out, I'll have to hire someone to help me. The truth is, I can't live alone anymore." She pulled her coffee cup directly in front of her. "Enough doom and gloom. Let's talk about you two. It's a funny coincidence, actually. I was talking to my daughter about you both just yesterday when we were out for a walk along the beach."

"Your daughter?" said Cordelia. "But she's—"

Jane kicked her under the table.

"Hey. I thought we'd call a moratorium on sneak attacks."

"So, you're up to see how Sabra's doing?" said Helen.

"Sabra?" repeated Cordelia. "Who's that?"

Touching a hand to her forehead, Helen seemed to falter. "No, no. See how I get confused? I meant to say Tessa. Didn't she break something? An arm? Am I getting that all mixed up, too?"

"She has a bad ankle sprain," said Jane.

"That's why we're here," said Cordelia, mesmerized by the sight of a plate of caramel rolls being served to the next table. "I'm taking over the play she was directing at the playhouse."

"How I'd love to see it," said Helen. "When does it open?"

"End of the week. I'll make sure you get comps."

"In fact," said Jane, "you could be my date for the opening."

"Oh," said Helen, looking down at her wrinkled cotton blouse. "I'm not sure I have anything to wear. I've lost so much weight."

"I'll take you shopping," said Jane. "We'll make an afternoon of it."

"Today?"

"Why not?"

As they were being served their plates of bacon and eggs, hotcakes, maple syrup, and caramel rolls, Jane noticed the front door open. Kelli Christopher sauntered in and grabbed a seat at the counter. She had on the same brown pants and tan shirt that she'd been wearing in the wee morning hours, except that now she'd exchanged her cap for a brown campaign hat. It was a silly look, reminding Jane of Smokey the Bear or the Canadian

Mounted Police—way too big a statement for a tiny county sheriff's department.

Aftr removing the hat and setting it next to her, Kelli's half-squinting gaze roamed the interior of the restaurant. Her scrutiny stopped when she saw Jane. In an instant she was up and heading over to the table.

"Morning, Mrs. Merland," she said, nodding to Helen. "Nice to see you out and about."

"Undersheriff," said Helen with an amused smile.

"Cordelia, this is Undersheriff Kelli Christopher," said Jane.

Between bites of caramel roll, Cordelia said a mumbled hi. She also spent a couple of significant seconds looking the sheriff up and down.

"I'm afraid I've got some bad news," said Kelli, hooking her thumbs into her belt. "I was just over at the cottage, so Tessa and Jill already know. You're going to hear this soon enough. You might as well hear it from me."

Just get on with it, thought Jane. Cut the pomposity and spit it out.

"We found Lyndie LaVasser this morning."

"Found?" said Helen. "Was she lost?"

"Her car went off the road last night just south of Fifteen-Mile Lake. It careened down the side of a steep ditch. We never would have found it in the dark."

Helen gasped. "Is she all right?"

Kelli shook her head. "Sorry. She's gone. We think it might have been alcohol related. Jim Moon, Lyndie's son, gave his permission for an autopsy. We should know more in a day or two."

"What about the thirty-eight caliber slug you found in the wall of the emporium?" asked Jane.

Helen looked at her with horrified eyes.

"Can't explain that one just yet. It may have nothing to do with her death."

"Or it may have a lot to do with it," said Jane.

"Got a gut feeling that they're not related," said Kelli.

"Is your gut always right?"

A faint smile crossed her lips. "Sometimes my first reactions can be off base. Not always good to prejudge a situation, if you know what I mean. I guess we'll just have to wait and see." With that, she walked back to her spot at the counter, tossed her leg over the stool and sat down to read the menu.

16

While his aunts sat on the couch, hugging each other and crying over Mrs. LaVasser's death, Jonah took the opportunity to
sneak downstairs and slip out through the garage. If they wanted
to yell at him about last night, they could do it later.

Running up to the parking lot at the lodge, Jonah found
Kenny waiting for him on his Harley.

"Let's get out of here," called Jonah.

Kenny hit the ignition on the bike, holding in the clutch and
revving it. Looking back at Jonah, he called over the loud rumble, "Where to?"

"Where else?"

Taking the county road out of town, Kenny kept reaching up
to wipe the tears out of his eyes. He drove fast, leaning into the
curves. They eventually reached the dirt path that dead-ended at
the hideout. Kenny ordered Jonah to dig the munchies out of the
saddlebags while he opened the padlocked door. Once he'd come
back out with a fist full of joints, a bottle of Jager, and some Red
Bulls, they settled themselves against the side of the shack.

"I'm sorry about your grandmother," said Jonah.

Kenny unscrewed the bottle cap and took a slug, then downed half a Red Bull. "Want some?"

"Nah. You okay?"

"Better now that I'm here," he said.

Jonah lit up one of the joints. "You think it was that guy? The one who came to town to find your gran and my aunt?"

"Probably."

"Me, too."

Kenny pulled his legs up to his chest, scraped his wrist over his eyes. "My dad said something about suicide. I don't buy it."

Kenny's dad was Lyndie's only son. He was also the president of one of the two banks in town.

"Does he know anything about her past?" asked Jonah.

"Hell no."

When Kenny's tears turned to sobs, Jonah looked away, trying to give his friend some space. He figured Kenny had to be embarrassed to come apart like that. He'd always been close to his grandmother—when he wasn't bitching about her, which was the majority of the time. Still.

"We gotta find that creep," said Kenny, taking another slug of the Jager.

"At the very least, we gotta ask him some questions. It had to be him. Who else had it in for your gran?"

Kenny finished the Red Bull and opened another. Heaving himself up, he held the Jager in one hand and the Red Bull in the other, kicking at weeds as he paced in front of the shack.

"I'm worried about Aunt Tessa," continued Jonah. "If that guy came after your grandmother, maybe she's next."

"Could be."

"What do we do?"

Kenny kept kicking at the weeds, obviously mulling it over.

"When we're done here, we split up. You take the north end of town, I take the south. Whoever spots him first calls the other. We jump him together. Cut him off so he can't get away."

"Sounds like a plan."

"We could use a gun," said Kenny, emptying another Red Bull and tossing the empty can over his shoulder.

"They're expensive."

Pulling a wallet out of his back pocket, he tossed it to Jonah.

"Where'd you get all this?" asked Jonah, opening the back flap and finding four one hundred dollar bills.

"Odd jobs."

"Illegal?"

"Borderline. But lucrative. Hey," said Kenny, taking a folded envelope out of his cargo shorts. "Forgot about this. It came in the morning mail."

"What is it?"

"From the United States Army. Man, I can't wait to get out of this backwater." He downed another couple of slugs of Jager.

At this rate, Jonah figured Kenny would be both wired and smashed in record time. "What's it say? Open it."

"You open it," he said, half grinning. He dropped it in Jonah's lap. "Probably tells me when and where I'm supposed to show up for basic."

Ripping open the top, Jonah unfolded the letter and read silently.

"Just give me the date," said Kenny.

"I, ah . . . I think you better look at this yourself."

Kenny grabbed the letter out of Jonah's hand. He gave it a cursory read. "What the—" he said, reading through it again, this time with more concentration. "This is bullshit. Did you see what they said?"

Jonah took a toke, looked away.

"I don't fit within 'the U.S. Army's weight parameters.' What the hell does that mean?"

If Kenny couldn't figure it out, Jonah sure could. The army had just rejected Kenny because he was too fat. "They want you to begin a fitness program."

"Fitness? I coulda broke that pip-squeak army doc in half with one hand tied behind my back." He dropped the bottle and ripped up the paper, tossing it in the grass. "All I've ever wanted to do was serve my country in the fucking military."

"Take a toke," said Jonah, holding out his joint. "Chill out. This isn't the end of the world."

"It's the end of *my* world." Kenny slammed his foot into the hideout wall.

"You're going to break the boards. I don't feel like spending the afternoon repairing them." Maybe he shouldn't have said that, although now that he had, something else came to mind. "Did you make me a key for that new padlock?"

"You want a key?"

"Yeah. The stuff's half mine."

Leaning over and whispering into Jonah's ear, Kenny said, "You think so?"

"Cut it out," said Jonah, pushing him away. "I'm sorry about the army thing, okay? Jesus."

That was all it took. Kenny reared back and kicked him, and kept kicking him—in the side, in the back, in the stomach, in the head.

Jonah rolled into a ball. "Stop it," he cried. "You're crazy."

"Crazy, huh? I'll show you crazy." Kenny kicked him a bunch more times. Punching the wall with his fist, he screamed, "Shit shit shit," shaking his fingers in pain.

Jonah struggled to his feet. "What the hell is wrong with you?"

"You're a pansy. The world is full of pansies just like you. I don't know why I even bother."

"Calm down."

"You're a weak-ass pussy. A douche. I don't need losers like you in my life."

"What did I do?"

"You *exist*," screamed Kenny, stomping over to his bike.

Jonah stood and watched him drive off in a cloud of dust and gravel. Only after he was out of sight and the sound of the motor had grown faint did Jonah collapse to the ground and wonder what the hell had just happened.

17

A floppy sun hat drooped over Tessa's eyes as she reclined on a chaise lounge on the deck overlooking the lake, a book of James Fenton's early poetry open on her lap. She found it difficult to concentrate, which meant that prose was out of the question, as was any thought of writing. She was too jittery. Her feelings were a confusing jumble of sadness, anger, fear for her safety, and foreboding. Feigenbaumer had played his first card. Lyndie was dead.

The cordless phone on the table next to her gave a sudden shrill ring. She glanced at the caller ID. In the direct sunlight, it was almost impossible to read.

Clicking it on, she said, "Hello?"

"Hello, Sabra," came a male voice.

Her entire body jerked to attention.

"I know it's you because Judy told me."

She cut the line and tossed the phone on the table as if it were a hot coal. He'd just told her everything she wanted to know. Not only had he killed Lyndie, but she was next.

The phone rang again. This time it didn't sound so much shrill as taunting. *Pick me up,* it said—*if you've got the guts.* She stared at

145

it for a few seconds, trying to assemble her thoughts. One more ring and she clicked it on, held it to her ear.

"That's better. You can't run. I assume you know that. I've spent a great part of my life looking for you and Judy. Don't you want to know who I am?"

"Who?" she whispered.

"Take a guess."

"His son?"

"His only son."

Tessa closed her eyes.

"Wanted to hear your voice. And tell you I was coming."

"A life for a life."

"For someone like you, that would be too easy."

Tessa found his mild, almost soothing tone far more menacing than if he'd been screaming at her.

"You come forward and admit to the police what you did, or I handle it my way."

"How did you find us?"

"Yeah, I suppose you would be interested in that. I was just a little kid when you murdered my dad, so you had a big head start. Not exactly fair. It all came down to Judy. She subscribed to the daily paper in Newfield, South Dakota. *The Newfield Herald*. When she read that her sister was dying of cancer, she wrote to her. There were a couple of phone calls. I've had people watching your two families for years hoping to get a lead on where you'd gone."

"Everyone in my family is dead."

"I know. Your last remaining relative, your mother, died in ninety-eight. I went all the way to Nebraska, to the funeral in McCook hoping that you'd turn up. You did, didn't you."

"Why would you think that?"

"I saw you, I know I did—standing at the edge of the grave-yard. You were placing flowers on another grave, but you kept looking over at those of us who were there for your mom. When I started for you, you ran to your car and took off."

"Look, I can give you money. I'm not rich, but—"

"You think I want *money*?"

"I'll give you anything I have."

"I want you behind bars, Sabra. I want you to suffer the way you made me suffer. I need you to grieve for the life you had be-fore it was ripped away. I want you to miss someone so bad that it claws your heart to shreds. I want you to *think* long and hard about what you did. My dad was a decent man. A loving husband and father. An honorable cop."

"There's more to the story."

He gave a bitter laugh. "I've heard enough lies from people like you. Hell, I'm giving you more than you gave my dad—a chance to control how and when it goes down. I'll be in touch."

Emily closed the front door of the small, wood-frame fisher-man's cabin, making sure that the rusted latch locked securely. She carried a backpack and a caddy of cleaning supplies over to the edge of the deck, where she set everything down to re-adjust the strap at the back of her halter dress.

Kenny had called around one and offered to take her over to the resort and then pick her up when she was done. She was a little surprised that he would offer today of all days. By sunup, everyone in Lost Lake knew that his grandmother was dead. She assumed he would be involved with family stuff most of the day. When he arrived at her house, he was in a foul mood, his breath reeking of alcohol. He shut down every attempt she made at sympathy.

Brushing a ladybug off the front of her dress, she crossed from the edge of the cabin steps to a dirt path that would take her back to the cleaning shed. As she made it to the group of cabins closest to the water, she spied a man sitting on a log. He was closing his cell phone and putting it away in the pocket of a blue jacket. She'd seen him a couple of times before, but had never said anything to him. He looked rough and unfriendly.

"Hey," he called, standing and motioning her over.

"Me?"

"You been working here long?"

"No."

"What are there? Ten, twelve cabins at this resort?"

"Fourteen. Two are set back in the woods, away from the lake."

"Fourteen," he repeated. His eyes slowly shifted from her to a rowboat, where a fisherman was tying a rope to a fixed metal pole at the end of the dock. "Just a word to the wise. You might want to find another job."

"I can take care of myself," she said, continuing on to the shed.

Kenny roared down into the gravel parking lot on his motorcycle and stopped just south of the main beach.

"You take care," called the stranger. "Hear me?"

All she wanted to do was get away from him.

"What'd that guy say to you?" said Kenny, his eyes trained on the stranger.

"I don't like him. I think he's been watching me."

Kenny's eyes narrowed. "I'll take care of it. Hop on."

"Let me change back into my jeans first."

He grabbed her wrist before she could walk away. "You seen Jonah since he's been back?"

"We talked for a while last night."

"Just talked? You told me you two were over."

"That was when I thought he was gone for good."

"You still got a thing for him then?"

He held her hand so tightly that it frightened her. "That hurts, Kenny."

"Kenneth," he corrected her.

"Come on, let go."

"He's a wimp."

"I'm not having this conversation."

"He ain't good enough for you. You deserve better."

"I think that's my decision to make, not yours."

"I thought I meant something to you."

She was startled by the hurt in his face. "You were the one who said it didn't mean anything. Just fun and games." She'd needed someone after Jonah had left. She told herself it wasn't a mistake. She'd been so alone. "We're friends. I care about you. But you can't make our relationship something it isn't."

"So I'm an asshole?" He released her hand. "Nothing new in that. Make it quick."

He revved the motor as she changed into her jeans and T-shirt. She didn't like the dank, moldy smell in the shed, so she never spent any time in it, unlike some of the other employees, who would drink their Cokes and play poker at the rickety card table. Tucking her work clothes into her locker, she attached the combination lock and gave it a spin, then ducked into the office and handed off her backpack. She told the owner that she was done for the day.

He glanced up from his newspaper and smiled at her with yellow, nicotine-stained teeth. "Thanks, honey. Have a nice evening."

When she got outside, she heard the distinct sound of wheels grinding on gravel. Rushing back to the parking lot, she saw that Kenny was driving away up the hill, leaving her stranded. "Hey, stop," she yelled. "Kenny? Stop!"

"Need a ride?"

Turning, she came face to face with the stranger in the blue jacket. He was standing just a few feet away, smiling.

18

Jonah approached Helen Merland cautiously, not wanting to wake her. She was asleep on a chaise lounge, lying in the shade of a huge elm tree on the patio in her backyard. He'd been wanting to come by ever since he got back to town. This was the first chance he had. It tugged at his heart to see how old and worn she looked.

Jonah remembered a far different Helen, a hearty woman who laughed uproariously at his antics, chased him through her house as they played hide-and-seek on wintery afternoons. She would make hot cocoa and bacon and egg sandwiches for lunch, and they'd pile their food on a tray and take it out to the living room, where they'd sit on the window seat and watch it snow. As he moved into his teens, he could always count on her for a few extra bucks to supplement his allowance.

Jonah had met Helen for the first time when he was eight. It wasn't as if he didn't already know who she was. Everyone did. He'd seen her riding her horse through the fields near her home, watched her stride into town carrying a big leather briefcase. She was glamorous the way movie stars were glamorous. She stuck out in a town like Lost Lake.

Helen loved animals. The fall their lives intersected, she'd adopted an English sheepdog. A puppy. Nobody in town had ever owned anything like that before. Jonah was mesmerized. He'd walk by her house every day on his way home from school, hoping to see the puppy out playing in the grass.

One afternoon, he heard Helen calling for the dog. Her yard wasn't fenced back then, so, as puppies often do, Maisey had gotten out. Jonah was too tongue-tied to say anything to Helen, but he decided he'd help her look. He found the dog drinking from a kid's plastic swimming pool five blocks away. Maisey was so friendly that she came to him when he called, hopped right into his arms and licked his chin. He could still remember the look on Helen's face when she answered her front door.

She said, "Oh my goodness, you found her. I was out for hours looking. I thought I'd lost her."

She invited Jonah in, offered him cookies and milk. She let him play with Maisey that afternoon until it was time for her to have dinner with her husband, then showed him out, telling him to come back anytime. Before he left, she hugged him, told him that they were going to be great friends. And they had been, ever since.

Moving up next to her, he saw her eyes flutter and then open. A soft smile spread across her face. "Tommy. I'm so glad you're here."

Tom Merland was her son. Jonah had never met him because he'd died in Vietnam.

"I'm not Tom," said Jonah.

"No?"

"I'm Jonah."

He figured it wasn't so much the Alzheimer's as it was the fact that she'd been asleep and was momentarily disoriented.

"I'm back from St. Louis, staying with Aunt Jill and Aunt Tessa."

"I hadn't heard," she said, touching his sleeve. "Help me sit up."

He repositioned the back of the chaise until it was more or less upright. After reorganizing the light cotton blanket around her shoulders, he asked if she was warm enough.

"I'm just fine," she said, gazing up at him, then switching her attention to the elm. "That one's coming down next month. It has Dutch Elm. That tree was old when we bought the place. Conrad wanted to take it down, but I said no. I liked the shade. Can you imagine a ninety-foot-high, one-hundred-year-old tree felled by something as tiny as a beetle?" Turning back to Jonah, she said, "Life is fragile. Remember that. Even when people look tough, they aren't."

He drew a chair up next to her. He wanted to sit close so he could hold her hand. "How are you feeling?"

"I'm still here."

"Of course you are."

"I went shopping this afternoon for a new dress. That's why I'm so all in."

"Can I get you anything? Water? Coffee? Something to eat?"

"Just let me look at you." Her rheumy eyes took him in. It almost felt as if she were trying to memorize him. "What do they call that?" She twirled her finger and pointed to the red bandana he'd tied around his head.

"It's kind of like a sweatband. I like the way it looks."

"Me, too. I think you've grown another foot."

"Not quite."

"And you're filling out, becoming a man. I wish you could have known my son. You two would have hit it off just the way we did."

Jonah had heard so much about Tom Merland that he felt as if he knew him.

"You know, honey, my mouth is parched. Maybe you could get me a glass of water."

He hopped up. "Be right back."

He entered the house through the French doors. As he crossed the dining room into the kitchen, he heard a noise coming from the rear of the house. Pulling a detour into the hallway, he followed the sound until he came to Helen's study. The door was partially shut. Pushing it open, he saw a man in khaki slacks and a yellow polo shirt on his knees in front of one of the metal filing cabinets, pawing through the files in the bottom drawer.

"Mr. Hammond?" said Jonah, not sure what was going on.

The man turned around. "Jonah," he said with a high squeak, his blond eyebrows shooting straight up.

"What are you doing here?"

"I, ah . . . I live here. I mean, for the moment. It's not permanent. You probably didn't hear that my business burned."

"No. Wow, that's awful."

"Helen was kind enough to let me move into the basement until I can get back on my feet."

"That makes total sense. What are you doing in here?" He nodded to the filing cabinet.

Standing up, Wendell said, "She asked me to help organize some of her files."

"Really? Why?"

"She can't stay here forever, you know."

"She's moving?"

"Well, not immediately. I've been helping her as much as I can. She's got that—" He pointed to his head. "You know."

"Alzheimer's."

"Sometimes she gets confused. She's walked off a couple of times. I was frantic the other morning when I couldn't find her. And then, since she can't drive anymore, I get her groceries for her, take her to doctor's appointments. She gives me a little money. But one of these days I'll be moving on."

If lightbulbs could actually burst on over someone's head when they were seized by a great idea, one had just burst on over Jonah's. "Well, nice to see you, Mr. Hammond."

"You too, Jonah."

Racing back to the kitchen, Jonah opened the refrigerator and found the cold water bottle. He poured a generous glass and then hightailed it back outside.

"Thanks, honey," said Helen, taking a couple of thirsty sips. "That really hits the spot."

"Listen. I just had an idea." He sat back down next to her.

"What would that be?"

"I ran into Mr. Hammond inside. He said he's living here, but won't be around much longer." Jonah explained his reasons for returning to Lost Lake. "One way or the other, I'm spending my senior year here. I asked Tessa and Jill if I could stay with them. They're thinking it over. But here's the problem. If they're not okay with it, maybe I could move in here with you. I could help you out, the way Mr. Hammond does. I could get your groceries, take you wherever you need to go. Do whatever needs to be done. I'd only be in school for part of each day. And my weekends would be free. What do you think? It sounds like a win-win situation for both of us."

She seemed hesitant.

"You don't need to give me an answer right now. But think about it, okay?"

"I'd have to talk to your parents first."

"Sure, that's fine." He was positive he could sell it to them if his aunts said no. In fact, the more he thought about the idea, the more he liked it. He had to find Emily ASAP and give her the good news.

19

"Ten minutes," called Cordelia from her usual perch, five rows back from the stage.

The actors drifted, grumbling, into the vom that led to the dressing room.

Cordelia stood and headed down the stairs. "Where do you think Fontaine is?"

"No idea," said Jane, following her to the main floor.

"Without my stage manager, this dress rehearsal is dead in the water."

"He came by to see Tessa this afternoon," said Jane. "After I took Helen shopping for that new dress, I stopped by the cottage to make Tessa and Jill a summer stew for dinner."

"Did he say anything about being sick unto death?"

"How biblical. No."

"Why was he there?"

"I'm not sure. He helped Tessa out to the deck, I imagine so they could talk without an audience. When I looked up a while later, he was gone."

"Well," said Cordelia, hands rising to her ample hips, "he better get here in the next five minutes or he's fired."

"You can't fire a guy who's donating his time for free."

With one frustrated glance up at the control booth, Cordelia swept off in a huff, leaving Jane to watch the art director put the finishing touches on a flamboyantly pink bedroom— the first scene of the play. Since Cordelia was deep into directorial mode, Jane wondered if this wouldn't be a good time to leave. Jill had suggested taking the pontoon out for an evening cruise, something Jane didn't want to miss. With the mood Cordelia was in, she figured that if she left now, she wouldn't be missed.

Turning to go, she noticed Jonah sitting way up in the semidarkness at the back of the theater. She hadn't seen him come in, which meant he must have already been sitting there when she and Cordelia arrived. His head was tipped back and his eyes were closed, so instead of calling to him, she simply walked out.

On her way past the box office, she ran smack into Cordelia again.

Pressing a finger to her lips, Cordelia yanked on Jane's arm.

"What?" Jane felt herself being pulled back through the curtain that led to the stage doors. "What's going on?"

Cordelia formed a gun with her hand, pointed it at her head and pulled the imaginary trigger, all the while making a strangling sound in her throat. She seemed unable to speak.

The room behind the curtain was full of wood crates, packing boxes, and a long wooden table and chairs that was occasionally used for meetings when the other, more formal meeting rooms were occupied. The stage door was actually two oversized wooden doors that opened into the alley behind the theater.

"There," whispered Cordelia, pointing to a pair of jeans-clad legs sticking out from behind one of crates.

Jane circled around and bent down next to the body. "It's Feigenbaumer," she said, a sick feeling spreading across her chest. The back of his head had been blown off. The sight of his blood and brains spewed across the gray brick walls forced the sick feeling to her stomach. "He's dead. We better call nine-one-one." Backing away, she held a fist to her mouth, hoping her dinner would stay put.

"You do it," said Cordelia. "I'm having a nervous breakdown."

When their eyes met, Jane felt sure they were thinking the same thing. The two people who had once shared Tessa's secret, whatever it was, were now dead.

"Who do you suppose did it?" whispered Cordelia as Jane took out her phone.

"No idea."

"Tessa?"

"That's an awful thought." Noticing something sticking out from under one of Feigenbaumer's shoes, Jane bent down to take a look. "What's that?"

"Looks like one of those cheap metal key rings."

Jane wasn't so sure. She took a couple pictures of it with her cell phone.

"What if Tessa's done something dreadful?" asked Cordelia, a quaver in her voice.

Jane punched in 9-1-1. "Let's take it one step at a time."

It felt like hours, though it was only minutes before two squad cars arrived, sirens blaring. Undersheriff Kelli Christopher entered the theater with the force of a storm, two male deputies in tow. She immediately cordoned off the back room and asked everyone to gather in the auditorium and wait until they could be questioned individually.

Since Cordelia and Jane had discovered the body, she separated them from the rest and asked them to wait in the costume shop. Half an hour later, they were still waiting. Jane assumed the undersheriff was taking her time with the crime scene, maybe calling for a tech to examine the room for evidence and a coroner—or if they were lucky, an actual doctor—to take a look at the body and give them some idea about the time of death. She doubted that Lost Lake had many homicides, and thus, Kelli was most likely in over her head.

"I know this may sound callous," said Cordelia, staring down at the can of Sprite in her hand, "but I have no idea how I'm supposed to get this production in shape for a preview on Thursday night."

"You're right. It sounds callous. But I understand your concern."

The door opened and a solemn Kelli Christopher entered. Removing her cap and wiping her arm over her forehead, she said, "A few questions," as she lowered herself down on the edge of the cutting table.

Jane and Cordelia pulled stools up and sat across from her.

"When did you find him?"

"Right around seven-thirty," said Cordelia. "I was waiting for my stage manager to show up."

"That would be?"

"Fontaine Littlewolf."

"Did he ever show?"

Cordelia shook her head.

"Any idea where he is?"

"None."

"You have any thoughts on when the guy died?" asked Jane.

"I've got a man working on that. There's no rigor, but his

skin is cool. I'd say a few hours." Returning her attention to Cordelia, she asked, "Are any of the doors to the theater kept open during the day?"

"You'd have to ask Fontaine."

It would have been fairly easy, thought Jane, for someone to come and go through the stage door without being seen. A generally deserted alley separated the theater from a two-story brick building next door. That building was empty, with a FOR RENT sign in the front window. In fact, as she thought about it, since the gift shop closed at three, the killer could have come in the front way without being seen.

"Did either of you touch anything?" asked Kelli.

"Not me," said Cordelia.

"I bent down to get a pulse," said Jane. "That was it. I did notice something under the dead man's right foot."

"The O-ring. Yeah, we bagged it. Not sure what it means."

"Did you find the gun?"

She scratched a few notes on a pad she'd removed from her vest pocket. "Not yet."

"His name was Steve Feigenbaumer," said Jane. "He was a journalist."

Kelli looked up. "Where'd you hear that?"

"I was out on the beach walking with Helen Merland yesterday morning. He came up, introduced himself and told her that's what he did for a living." For the time being, she left out his connection to Tessa, whatever it was.

Poking her cap back with one finger, Kelli said, "He wasn't a journalist. He was a police officer."

Jane's eyes widened.

"He lived in Chicago. I'd like to know what he was doing up here. What did he want from Helen?"

"He said he was looking for someone he thought lived in town. I guess he figured she might be able to help."

"He mention a name?"

"Judy Clark."

Kelli turned to Cordelia.

"Don't look at me. I wasn't there."

"You'd never met him?"

"Never."

"Take a look at this." She pulled a couple of snapshots out of her pocket and pushed them across the table. "You recognize any of those people?"

Jane had seen one of the pictures before. It was the snapshot Feigenbaumer had shown Helen yesterday morning—a young man and woman standing next to an old Chevy. The season was winter and they were dressed in heavy jackets and scarves.

"No idea who they are," said Jane.

Cordelia put her finger on the second photo. "That looks like a young Lyndie LaVasser."

"That's what I think, too," said Kelli. "And if that's the case, why did Feigenbaumer have a picture in his pocket of a woman who'd just died?"

"Maybe *she* was Judy Clark," said Cordelia.

"Was her death ruled accidental?" asked Jane.

Kelli hesitated. Wiping a hand over her mouth, she said, "It was a homicide. The coroner found evidence of a partially crushed trachea and severe blunt-force trauma to the back of her head. She was buckled in and her airbag deployed when the car went off the road, so it's unlikely it happened when she hit the ditch. Other signs suggest she was already dead, that the accident was staged. We haven't had a murder in this community in forty years. Now we've got two."

162

"Which means they're probably related," said Jane.

Kelli's lips parted, but she didn't reply.

Jane pushed the pictures back across the table.

"I understand you're directing a play at the community playhouse, Ms. Thorn," said Kelli, slipping the pictures back into her vest pocket. "I'm afraid that, for now, I'm shutting the community center down. It's a crime scene. Nobody comes in or out."

When Jane saw the look of relief spread across Cordelia's face she nearly burst out laughing.

"That's not a problem," said Cordelia.

Giving Jane one last parting glance, Kelli got up and said, "You can go. I assume you aren't leaving town immediately. I may have other questions."

"Of course," said Jane.

When Kelli got to the door, she turned to look at Jane one last time.

"Did that woman just wink at you?" whispered Cordelia after the door had clicked shut.

"I think so."

"What have you been doing behind my back?"

"Nothing," said Jane, as surprised by the wink as Cordelia. "Absolutely nothing."

20

Returning to the cottage shortly after eight, Jane asked Cordelia if she minded going inside without her. She had something she needed to do, but would be in shortly. Cordelia gave her a what-the-hell-are-you-up-to look. As a lover of the dramatic moment, however, she didn't argue. She trotted eagerly up the stairs, ready to deliver the bad news all by herself.

When they drove up, Jane had noticed that the garage door wasn't shut all the way, as if someone had been in a hurry. Curious what she might find, she hoisted the door and stepped into the semi-darkness. Jill's Jeep was gone. Tessa's Volvo sat in its usual place. On a whim, Jane pressed her hand to the hood. To her surprise, she found that the engine was still warm. She wasn't sure what to make of it, nor was she inclined to ask Tessa, especially after her "back off" message earlier, and yet clearly Tessa had gone somewhere.

As she was closing the garage door, Jill's Jeep drove in behind her.

"I'm so sorry," said Jill, hopping out. She was wearing white slacks, a navy-blue-and-white striped top, and canvas deck shoes.

She looked ready for a night on the water. "I know we planned to be out on the lake by seven-thirty, but I got waylaid up at the lodge." Opening the back door, she removed an old woven wood picnic basket. "I come bearing provisions. That should make up for the my late arrival."

"I just got here myself," said Jane.

"Tessa's probably chomping at the bit," said Jill as they made their way up the stairs to the front door. "Thankfully, she's easily placated with pie."

When they entered the living room, Cordelia and Tessa were sitting close together on the couch. It took Jane a few moments to decipher the look on Tessa's face. When she did, she realized it was elation.

"What's going on?" asked Jill, setting the picnic basket on the stone hearth in front of the fireplace.

"You're not going to believe this," said Cordelia, pressing a limp hand dramatically to her chest. "A man was murdered at the theater this evening. The undersheriff was forced to close the community center because it's a crime scene."

Jill folded herself into a chair, never taking her eyes off Tessa. "Who was he? Someone we know?"

"His name was Steve Feigenbaumer," said Jane. She'd gone into the kitchen to grab herself a beer. She figured she was owed. "He's a Chicago cop."

"He is?" said Tessa.

"Was," said Cordelia, patting Tessa's knee.

"He was your Peeping Tom, the guy looking in your window the other night," said Jane, squeezing off the bottle cap and tossing it in the garbage. "Kelli thinks his murder is related to Lyndie LaVasser's."

"But Lyndie wasn't murdered," said Jill. "It was an accident. I mean . . . wasn't it?"

Jane sat down on the La-Z-Boy. "Afraid not. Kelli said that her trachea had been partially crushed, that she was probably dead before the car left the road."

"Lord," said Jill, her hands twisting in her lap. "How did this man—"

"A gunshot to the head," said Cordelia. "Don't ask for details."

Jane's mind was spinning with questions, reservations, scenarios, suspicions, exactly the kind of thing Tessa had ordered her not to do. For her part, Tessa appeared to be trying hard to hide what she was thinking by forcing her eyes down, covering her mouth with her hand.

"Appalling," was all she said.

Turning a sharp gaze on Tessa, Jill said, "That's it. I've tried to give you the space you asked for, but this is the last straw. You know something. You've got to tell us what it is."

"I've never met the man. That's the truth. Hook me up to a lie detector if you don't believe me."

"Do you know a woman named Judy Clark?" asked Jane.

Just for a microsecond, Tessa's expression froze. "Clark?" she said, pursing her lips. "No, I don't think so. Who is she?"

Jane assumed that it was obvious to everyone in the room that Tessa was lying. "People in town knew her as Lyndie LaVasser."

Jill moved to the edge of her chair. "Tessa, come on. Talk. Tell us what's going on."

"Honestly, I don't know. Lyndie was a friend, sure, but that doesn't mean I was privy to all her secrets. If she called herself

Judy Clark once upon a time, she never mentioned it to me. Truly, honey. I'm as stunned as you are."

Tessa had recovered and was acting now, Jane was sure of it. The problem was, she was a good actor, with a willing audience in Jill.

"Feigenbaumer said that Judy Clark was a murderer," continued Jane.

Tessa's eyes collided with hers. "That's a terrible thing to say. Remember, she was a friend of mine. I stick by my friends."

The comment was a shot across the bow. A challenge. Are you with me or against me?

"Who had she 'theoretically' murdered?" asked Tessa.

"He didn't say."

"Then I think you better be careful with an accusation like that."

"It doesn't sound like the Lyndie I knew," agreed Jill.

It was a naive comment, one Jane didn't feel like debating.

"I think we should all calm down," said Tessa, leaning back and fixing her eyes on Jane. "Let Kelli do her job. She's the one with the experience."

"Not in multiple homicides," said Jane. "This one's way over her pay grade." As soon as the words came out, she realized that *that's* exactly what Tessa was counting on.

Back at Thunderhook lodge later that night, Jane was lying on her bed reading when she heard a soft knock at the door. Retying her bathrobe, she found Jill standing outside in the hall.

"Is everything okay?" asked Jane. Her first thought was, My God, has someone *else* died?

"Can I come in?"

"Sure."

In the last few days, Jill looked like she'd aged ten years. Jane wondered what had been going on behind the scenes at the cottage.

Jill sat down on the couch as if every muscle in her body ached. "I don't know what to do. Tessa's lying to me. That's not the kind of relationship we have, or . . . I thought we had."

Jane sat down next to her.

"I'm not crazy, am I? She's been lying to all of us for days, ever since that man appeared at her study window the other night. Who knows? Maybe it began before that." She searched Jane's face for an answer.

"It may have," said Jane. "You're right. She's holding something back. She's not telling us the truth."

"What do I do? I've tried being sympathetic. I've accused her of not loving me. I've dropped the subject in hopes that she would open up. Nothing works. It's like I'm living with a stone."

"I can only imagine how hard it's been."

"You know what she's like. You push too hard and she cuts you off at the knees. We had a fight after you left. She's not speaking to me at the moment. I mean, I really laid down the law to her, told her I wasn't going to stand to be shut out."

"And she said?"

"That it was her business and she'd handle it. But if she won't talk to me, what do I do?" Folding her hands together in her lap, Jill continued, "What I know for sure is that she's in trouble. And she's scared to death. That's why I'm here. I need to ask you a favor."

"Anything."

"Will you look into it for me? I know you've done investigating for friends in the past. You're good at it. I need you to help me now. I need someone on my side, someone who loves Tessa, who believes in her goodness."

Jane's first response would have been to give Jill a whole-hearted yes, and yet after Tessa had ordered her to stay out of her business, she was torn. She hadn't exactly promised that she would, she'd merely stated that she understood what Tessa was asking. Yet that was splitting hairs, wasn't it? "I'd love to help in any way I can," she said. "But Tessa asked me to stay out of it."

Jill looked surprised. "When did she say that?"

"She called me yesterday afternoon. It wasn't a friendly request. It was more along the lines of an order."

Shaking her head, Jill said, "You can't listen to her. You have to help me. There's no one else who can."

"How do I choose between you?"

"Don't choose either one of us. Choose the truth. If Tessa's afraid of that, she's not the woman I thought she was."

As an argument, it had a certain force. Not that Jane needed a lot of coaxing. Would she be a complete swine if she ignored Tessa? "What if I find information that implicates her? I can't bury it."

Her voice shaking with emotion, Jill said, "She wouldn't murder someone in cold blood. No one will ever convince me of that."

Jane sympathized. If someone came to her and said that her father, a man she loved, trusted, and admired, had committed a murder, she, too, would have said it was impossible. And yet, if Jane had learned anything in her life it was that people were complex, a mixture of contradictions, that they often had multiple faces—some that they showed to the world, some that remained carefully hidden.

"Will you help?"

Finding the truth was as important to Jane as it was to Jill. And also, though she wouldn't have admitted it out loud, she was itching to prove that she wasn't a dilettante. "I'll do everything I can."

"You're saving my life, Jane. And Tessa's."

Jane wished she was as sure. The one thing she did know was that, when it came to the need to discover and understand, she was tenacious. If she had a trip wire to her soul, that was it.

21

Emily's rusted Chevy glided to a stop in the woods just off North Gower Road. When she thought of that summer, two years before, the night she and Jonah had first found this spot, she felt an almost crushing sadness roll over her. They'd been looking for a private place close to town, a location that they could walk to quickly. They were so happy back then, so in love that they couldn't bear to be in each other's company and not be touching. And now she'd gone and blown it, wrecked any chance of a future together.

Emily was startled by the eyes staring back at her in the rearview mirror. They looked just like her mother's. All along, she'd been so sure that she was making the right decisions. She wasn't going to live an accidental life, as if she were drifting through the Miller Hill Mall in Duluth, waiting for something to happen. Emily had plans, goals that she was working toward— until late this afternoon, that is, when the wheels of her life had careened off the tracks.

"You're an idiot," she said, banging on the steering wheel. "A stupid, brainless *idiot*."

She jumped when Jonah rapped on the passenger side window.

Leaning over, she pulled up the lock. He slid in next to her and they reached for each other, holding on so tight it hurt.

"Where were you all day?" he whispered into her ear. "I called and texted but you never answered."

"We're here now."

"You're shivering. How can I undress you if you're cold?"

"You'll keep me warm."

"I am so stoked," he said, pulling away to play the dashboard like a drum. "So pumped."

"About what?"

"Everything. Maybe I am a superhero after all." He wasn't smiling, just squirreling around in his seat.

"How come you were at the theater tonight?"

"I came to see you. I wanted to watch you act."

"I'm getting better. I really am." Not that it mattered anymore.

They began their lovemaking on a blanket they'd tossed under a pine near the edge of the shore, all arms and legs, soft skin and hard muscle, rushing too fast but unable to stop until, at last, they lay content in each other's arms.

"I love you so much," whispered Emily, tears springing to her eyes.

"There are no words for how I feel," Jonah whispered back. "You're everything to me."

"Why do you love me?"

"Because you're good and kind, you're fun and funny. And you're beautiful, not just outside, but inside."

His words only sunk the knife in deeper.

Propping himself up on one elbow, Jonah looked down at her in the soft evening light, tracing his fingers from her throat to her stomach. "I have super powers, you know."

"So you said. You're a goof."

"You think I'm kidding?"

"Don't joke."

"Kenny doesn't think I'm good enough for you. He says I'm weak."

"He's wrong."

"I know. Are you cold? You're shivering again."

How could she tell him that it had nothing to do with the temperature? She was frozen inside, couldn't imagine ever feeling warm again. "If I'd done something . . . really bad, would you still love me?"

"Would you love me if I'd done something bad?"

"Nothing could make me love you less."

"Then we're a perfect match."

She felt his hair fall across her face, relaxed into the warmth of his body as it stretched out against hers, and drifted as her world was reduced once again to the single sensation of his lips.

It was after two in the morning when Jonah ducked in through the garage and let himself into the cottage. Instead of going directly to his room, he crept up the steps into the living room. As usual, no matter what was going on in his life, he was hungry. He also needed to run up to the loft to retrieve Tessa's diary.

At this late hour, Jonah assumed that his aunts would be asleep. Tomorrow he'd stick around and let them holler at him. He deserved it. But Emily came first.

Tiptoeing into the kitchen, Jonah noticed that the shades were no longer pulled. Weak moonlight streamed in through the open windows. With Feigenbaumer out of the way, there was no one for his aunt to be afraid of anymore. He started for the stairs up to the loft, stopping when he heard a voice say, "The prodigal returns."

Coming to a full stop, he turned and squinted into the darkness. Tessa was sitting in one of the leather chairs. She had a wineglass in her hand and was toasting him with it.

"Hi," he said, his voice sounding guilty even to himself. "I, ah, I thought you'd be in bed."

"Did you." She motioned him to the chair opposite her.

"I'm kind of tired. Maybe you could yell at me in the morning."

"Sit."

He skirted around the couch and eased himself down. Might as well face his interrogator.

"So," she said after a long pause during which she regarded him icily, "is this how you're going to play it? You use our home as a crash pad, come and go as you like, ignore us or any responsibilities we might choose to inflict?"

"Don't freak, okay. I was just getting used to being back. I wanted to check in with Kenny and Emily—"

"And how *is* the lovely Kenny and the even lovelier Emily?"

"They're okay."

"Just okay?"

"Emily is fabulous and Kenny's a butthead."

"Sounds like nothing's changed." She set the wineglass down and pressed her fingers together to form an arch. "Let's recap, shall we? You want to spend your senior year in Lost Lake. To do so, and not be forced to sleep in the park and eat out of Dumpsters, you want to stay with us. To impress us with your gratitude and devotion, you disappear for two days. To impress us with your maturity, you get behind the wheel of my car after you'd been drinking."

"Yes, but—"

176

She held up a hand. "You also forgot to tell us that you were suspended twice from school last term—once for indulging in a little illicit weed, once for losing your temper and attacking a fellow student. Have I misstated any of this?"

"No."

"If you were me, what would you do?"

"I'd let me stay."

"Because?"

"Because I love you and Aunt Jill. You're like my moms. And because the last two days haven't been normal."

"Not normal? What, specifically, does that mean?"

"Look, I'm sorry. You're not going to like this next part either." He hesitated, not sure he was making the right move. "I heard you talking to Mrs. LaVasser on Monday morning. I was in the kitchen getting myself some cereal."

She sat up a bit straighter. "And you decided to eavesdrop."

"Yeah, kinda."

"You listened in on a private conversation. Another charming addition to your list of sins. How much did you hear?"

"Pretty much all of it. But everything's jiggy, right, because the man who was after you is dead? I'm sorry about Mrs. La-Vasser. I would have been a lot sorrier if anything had happened to you." In the darkness it was hard to see her face. When her shoulders started to shake, he could tell that she was crying. It cut him to the bone.

"Tessa, it's okay," he said, kneeling down next to her. "That man can't hurt you anymore. You're just feeling bad because of Mrs. LaVasser. I get that. But tomorrow, in the daylight, everything will look different, I promise."

She reached out and touched his hair, ruffling it, then smoothing it, then ruffling it some more. "It's not that simple."

"Yes it is."

"You're so young."

"That doesn't mean I'm stupid."

She wiped her face. "I've missed you, Jonah. So much."

"And I've missed you. I never wanted to leave."

Clearing her throat, she said, "Jane told me you were at the theater tonight."

"Yeah, for a while. Emily's in the production. That's why I went."

She stared at him for several seconds. "That's all?"

"Huh?"

She kept staring at him with a strange look on her face.

"Emily and I are back together."

"I'm happy for you."

"This next year is going to be the best year of my life."

More hesitation. "I want that for you."

"Then you'll let me stay?"

Taking a deep breath, she said, "Jill and I talked earlier this evening. For the time being, you're grounded. You don't leave the house without permission. Understood?"

"Yeah."

"It's late. We should both turn in."

He got up and started for the spiral stairway up to the loft. He wasn't sure how he could get the notebook down without her seeing it. Maybe he'd wait until she'd gone to bed.

"And no TV," said Tessa.

"I wasn't going up to watch TV."

"No more lounging in the loft. I see you up there, you're history."

"Okay, okay. I'm sorry. Really."

She let her head sink back against the chair cushion. "I know you are."

"Night," he said, grabbing an apple off the kitchen island.

"Good night."

As he got to the door that led downstairs, he said, "You okay?"

"Sweet, sweet boy," she whispered. "Go to bed."

22

Jane tugged on Cordelia's pajama sleeve. "Wake up."

"Go away," said Cordelia, brushing at Jane's hand and pulling the quilt up over her head.

"Come on. No time for malingering."

"It's the middle of the night."

"You think ten A.M. is the middle of the night."

Yanking off the quilt, Cordelia pointed to the clock next to the bed. "It's four A.M. I'm right. You're wrong. Go away." Back went the quilt.

"You have to drive me to Duluth."

"This is a bad dream. You're not really here."

Jane sat down next to her. "I've been online trying to find out information about this Feigenbaumer guy. The connection is so slow I'm losing my mind. So I made a decision."

"It's good to be decisive. Just not at four A.M. Cease talking to me, Jane, or it's gonna get nasty."

"You need to drive me to the airport in Duluth. I checked the flights. If we leave right away, I can make the early flight to Minneapolis. From there, I'll go on to Chicago. I should be able to get everything done by tonight. I'll fly back to Minneapolis, and then on to Duluth. I'll need you to pick me up."

"Cordelia Thorn—"

"Does not haul. Yes, I know."

"And I don't run a taxi service."

"This is important. More important than your beauty sleep."

"You're on thin ice there."

"It's either that or I take your car and leave it in the lot at the airport."

Poking her head out from under the quilt, Cordelia shrieked, "Oh, no you don't. Not my cherry red convertible. It could get scratched."

"Or stolen. So get up. I'll make us some coffee to take in the car."

"A cup of coffee. What every person wants in the middle of the night."

"We can buy snacks on the way."

"What am I supposed to tell Jill and Tessa in the morning?"

"Say that I've got a touch of food poisoning." Jane headed back through the door to her room. "I'll meet you downstairs in five minutes."

"I can't get ready in five minutes. Unless I wear my pajamas."

"If anyone asks, we'll just say it's a fashion statement."

The United Airbus bumped down in Chicago just after eleven A.M. Jane located a phone book in the terminal lobby and checked for the name Feigenbaumer. She found three possibilities. Carla Feigenbaumer on Temple Avenue in Highland Park; Paul S. Feigenbaumer on Cogdill Avenue in Norridge; and Steven P. Feigenbaumer, on Tripp Avenue, just east of the loop. With a last name like that, she figured there was a good chance they were all related. She wrote the phone numbers and addresses in a small black notebook.

The one significant piece of information she'd been able to glean from last night's abortive Internet search was that Feigenbaumer had recently received an award. In the article from the *Chicago Tribune*, she'd learned that he worked robbery for the CPD. She also learned that each of the five official areas in Chicago proper had its own robbery unit. She'd been able to locate a PDF of the Chicago Police Department telephone directory, which took an amazing twenty minutes to download, and from there she'd copied down the phone numbers for robbery in each of the five areas. Sitting down in a Starbucks with a double latte, she tapped in each number. The first two were dead ends. When she hit unit 3, the line connected and a man's voice answered.

"I'm looking for Steve Feigenbaumer," said Jane.

"He's not here."

"Is it possible that I could come in and talk to someone else on the unit?"

The man gave her an address on West Belmont. She thanked him and hung up, and then she headed outside to find herself a cab.

Jane had a love/hate relationship with Chicago. She loathed the freeways, the endless cityscape, the icy winds in the winter, and the deadly heat and humidity in the summer. Politics in Chicago gave her a bad case of indigestion. And yet the city itself, the bawdy history, the wealth of historic architecture, and the ease with which a person could find an excellent meal had won her heart the first time she visited. The fact that she wouldn't have time to stop by the Art Institute—and the little Russian restaurant close by that was one of her all-time favorites—caused her more than a little psychic pain. She reminded herself that she wasn't here for fun and games.

Half an hour later, sitting in an airless room with a police sergeant named Sadler, she pulled out one of the cards Nolan had given her, the one that said "Nolan & Lawless Investigations," with Nolan's address and license number at the bottom. It gave her a cachet she'd never have without it. The cop looked it over and then handed it back.

"Were you aware that Sergeant Feigenbaumer—"

"—was murdered?" replied the cop. "Yeah, we heard."

"Were you a friend?"

"What do you want?"

So it was going to be *that* kind of conversation. "Do you know why he was in Lost Lake?"

"All he said to me was that he needed a vacation."

"Nothing more?"

"Who are you working for?"

She covered a scar in the wood table with her hand. "I can't tell you that. What I can say is that I'm trying to find out what happened to him. I'm here because I need to know more about his history, his background. There's a Carla and a Paul Feigenbaumer listed in the phone book. Are either of them related?"

The cop studied her. "Carla's his ex. Paul's a relative. A cousin, maybe. Or a nephew."

"Did he ever talk about his past?"

Sadler shrugged.

"Did he have a partner? Someone in robbery that he was friends with?"

"I was his partner. He worked narcotics for ten years. Transferred in here about six months ago. Nobody knows him all that well."

Not what she wanted to hear. "Did he have a partner when he worked narcotics?"

"Maybe."

"But you don't have a name."

"Sorry."

"Is there anything you can think of that might help me? Anything he might have told you?"

"Like I said, I didn't know him well."

It was all she was going to get. Sadler didn't trust her and so wasn't inclined to give an inch. So be it. "Thanks for your time."

She rose and was about to open the door to leave when the cop said, "His dad was a cop."

She turned around.

"A patrolman. He was murdered when Steve was a kid. Don't ask me how or why because I don't know. I just know it happened. Probably has nothing to do with anything."

"Was the murderer ever caught?"

"No idea. I'm sure you could find a record if you looked."

"Thanks," said Jane.

"Steve was a good guy. Fries me, you know? He lives his entire life in a dangerous city dealing every day with thugs, lowlifes, pimps, drug addicts, and gangbangers, then goes and gets himself killed in a tiny town that probably hasn't seen a murder in a hundred years, if ever. You find out what happened to him, you call me." He stood and handed her his card.

Jane called Paul Feigenbaumer from the cab. She didn't mention Steve's death because she wasn't sure that he'd heard about it. Reaching his voice mail, she left a message asking him to call her cell. She said she worked for a private investigation firm in Minneapolis and left it at that. A thought drifted through her mind, something to the effect that she really liked being able to say those words.

Her call to Carla, the ex, was more profitable. After Jane explained who she was, Carla asked if she'd called because of Steve's death. Jane was relieved that she already knew. The cliché was true: bad news traveled fast. Carla said she'd be willing to get together, but couldn't meet with Jane until five. Jane was still hoping to make it back to Duluth by late evening. To do that, the last flight out of O'Hare which would allow for a connecting flight was eight P.M. It might be cutting it close, especially if the traffic was bad. What do you mean *if*, she thought. This was Chicago.

Jane now had a choice. She could spend the afternoon at the Cook County Clerk of Court office looking for records that might shed some light on Feigenbaumer's father's murder, although that would be a waste of time because a case that old would be archived. She would probably spend an hour trying to locate the right form so that the records could be faxed to her—or she could call Norm Tescalia, her dad's paralegal, and ask him to take care of it. He was a good friend and was always willing to make a call on her behalf. That seemed like a much better option. Instead of spending a frustrating few hours dealing with the Chicago bureaucracy, she had a lovely late lunch at her favorite Russian restaurant.

By five, she was standing in front of a small, middle-class house on a quiet street, a one-story white bungalow with green shutters and a fenced backyard. Jane rang the bell and was met by a washed-out looking fortyish woman wearing navy blue sweat pants and a gray T-shirt. Her face was mottled with red patches and she had a tissue that she kept dabbing at her eyes. They sat down in the living room to talk.

"He was a bastard," said Carla, reaching for another tissue. "I couldn't live with him, couldn't trust him, but I still loved him." Her lips quivered as she looked over at the wall, where pictures of a young woman and young man hung in a place of honor.

Jane followed her eyes. "You had children together?"

"Two. Todd and Alissa. Todd's in graduate school in California. Alissa just started at the University of Illinois at Urbana-Champaign. Steve insisted that both his kids get a college education. He didn't want either of them to join the force. That was fine with me. Except, Alissa says she's going to do it anyway, once she graduates."

"I want you to know how sorry I am about his death," said Jane.

"Yeah. It's more the kids than me. I haven't called them yet." She blew her nose. "What did you want to ask?"

"Do you know why Steve was in Lost Lake?"

"Same wild-goose chase he's been on his entire life. It was an obsession with him. Never made any sense to me. I mean, keep your eye on the road, not the rearview mirror. If you don't, you're in a ditch before you even know what happened. See, he wanted to find the other two women who murdered his dad."

"Other *two* women?"

"Three were involved. One was caught and sent to jail. Her name was Yvonne Stein. She made the bomb."

Jane tried not let her shock show.

"Steve's dad's name was Allen. Allen James Feigenbaumer. I never knew him. He'd been a police officer for seven years when he died. One morning in late fall of sixty-eight, he kissed his wife good-bye, walked out to his car, started the engine, and the car blew. Probably never knew what hit him. Steve was as at school when it happened, thank God. He idolized his dad."

"What was the motive for the murder?"

"I'm not sure anybody ever knew. All I remember was that these three women had it in for Allen. Under pressure from the DA, the one named Stein gave up one of the other names. Judy something-or-other. The other woman was never named. Stein admitted that it had something to do with this Judy's boyfriend. She wouldn't say any more than that. What was that guy's name?" She looked down at the tissue in her hand. "Briere. That's it. John . . . no . . . Jeff Briere. I'm sure you could find out more. Steve talked about it some. This may sound cold, but I stopped listening."

"That's understandable."

Carla began to shred the tissue. "Are you here because you think Steve's death is connected to his father's? Steve said he'd chase those two women down if it was the last thing he ever did."

"Actually, yes. I think there's a good possibility they're connected."

"God, this is an awful thing to say," she said, looking up at Jane with an ache in her eyes. "Maybe it *was* the last thing he ever did."

23

Jonah and Tessa sat across the dining room table from each other, finishing the last of the summer stew Jane had made. Jonah had been the picture of helpfulness all day. He'd cleaned the garage in the morning and spent the afternoon working the front desk at the lodge. He'd been polite, contrite, and quiet as a mouse. And friendly. He didn't allow himself a moment of sulking—at least, not when anyone was looking.

When Tessa wasn't in the kitchen, she planted herself in the living room, foot up on the footstool, and thus Jonah had found no opportunity to go up and grab the diary. He hoped that after everyone was in bed later on, he might be able to finally fetch it and put it back in Tessa's trunk. He wasn't worried. He'd shoved it way under the couch. At this point, he didn't care if he ever read it, he just wanted the problem gone.

All day he kept getting text messages from Emily. He didn't tell her that there was a possibility that he could stay with Helen if it didn't work out with Jill and Tessa because he didn't want to get her hopes up if it all fell through. They'd talked once while he was on his way up to the lodge and she was at her job. She sounded strange, like her voice was underwater. He wondered if she'd been crying. Her last text had said:

HAVE 2 C U. Y HAVEN'T U CALLED? WHERE R U?

He'd texted back:

BEING GOOD BOY. AUNTS ON WARPATH. C U TONIGHT.

"Want the last bit of stew?" asked Tessa, the serving spoon poised above the pot.

"I'm full up."

"I don't think I've ever heard those words come out of your mouth before."

He laughed. "I wish you and Jill would put me out of my misery and give me a thumbs up or a thumbs down."

"We will. You worked hard today. Tomorrow I think Jill wants you to spend some time helping the maintenance guy backwash the sand filters on the pool."

"I was hoping to see Emily tonight."

Tessa pushed her chair back from the table and stretched her injured leg. "Sorry, kiddo. You're still grounded."

"For how long?"

She tapped a finger against her mouth, giving it some thought. "Until this weekend."

"Are you kidding me?"

"Do I need to repeat your list of transgressions?"

His first thought was to point out that everyone made mistakes— nudge-nudge, in the words of Monty Python. Instinctively, he knew this sort of tactic wouldn't get him anywhere. Tessa already looked like she hadn't slept in days, and, even worse, she and Jill had gotten into it again after breakfast. This time he'd resisted the urge to eavesdrop, mostly because they only fought about one thing these days—Tessa and her secrets.

Taking a last sip of wine, Tessa said, "There are so many books I wish you'd read. I've missed our talks. You up for that?"

He shrugged.

"Come back to my study. I'll find you a couple."

He felt his cell phone vibrate in his back pocket. "I'll be there in a sec." He flipped back the cover and saw the words:

R u coming? I HAVE 2 c u!

He typed back quickly:

Can't. Still on house arrest. Will call. XOXOXOXOX

Jane made it to the airport with time to spare. Rushing to the gate, she found that the incoming plane hadn't arrived yet, which meant that taking off on time might not happen. She sat down in the waiting area, removing her cell phone and tapping in Norm's number in St. Paul. Even though it was late, she knew he'd still be at work—and he was.

"Will you do me a big favor?" she asked, explaining that she needed a trial transcript. She gave him the information.

"Not a problem," came his cheerful voice. "But just so you know, it could take a while. It's just the way the legal system works in Chicago."

"How long?"

"A week? A month?"

"Can you cut any corners?"

"It's Cook County. Need I say more?"

"Yeah, I hear you."

"Aren't you going to tell me I'm a peach?"

"You're a peach, Norm."

"I know. Hey, I thought you were supposed to be on vacation."

"A friend in need."

"Sounds familiar."

She thanked him, told him to go home and watch the Twins game, and then hung up. Her second call was to Nolan. He answered on the third ring.

"Hey, Jane, how's everything?"

"Not so good." She quickly gave him the down and dirty on what had happened.

"Sounds like your friend is in deep."

"Look, I'm wondering if you could do something for me."

"As long as you're still considering my offer."

"Believe me, I am."

"Shoot."

"Could you try to find information on Yvonne Stein—the woman who was sent to prison. Is she still behind bars? If not, where'd she go."

"I'll get back to you as soon as I can dig something up. I also know a few retired Chicago cops who worked homicide back then. I'll see what I can find. You keep your eyes and ears open. And be careful."

"You and Mouse doing okay?"

"Fresh fish and cold beer for dinner every night? What could be better?"

"Mouse is drinking beer?"

"He likes lake water better."

Jane missed Mouse like crazy when she was away—missed

his beautiful, honest face and the fact that she didn't have to talk to him to communicate clearly. She loved all dogs, but he was special.

"Give him a scratch behind the ears for me. How are you feeling?"

"Okay, although my body isn't healing as fast as it used to."

"Take it easy. I hope to be back by the weekend."

"Don't worry about me. I'll call if I learn anything."

For the next few minutes, Jane sat and watched planes take off and land. When her stomach began to growl, she glanced over her shoulder at a food concession. She couldn't believe she could be hungry after the lunch she'd put away. As she headed over to see what was on offer, her cell phone rang. She still had it in her hand.

"This is Jane."

"I believe you called me—I'm Paul Feigenbaumer."

"Oh, hi. Thanks so much for calling back."

"Is this about Steve? A friend of his just called and told me what happened. I'm totally stunned."

"I'm sorry for your loss. Were you two close?"

"Cousins. He lived with me for about six months when he and Carla were breaking up. You know Carla?"

"I just left her house." She explained who she was and what she was looking for.

"I know all about that. I talked to Steve the night before last. He was pretty sure he'd chased one of the women to ground. Then he called the next morning and said he might have the other one in his sights, too."

"I thought nobody knew who she was."

"They knew, they just couldn't prove anything. She was this

Jeff Briere's sister—Sabra Briere. Steve has had people watching the two women's families for years hoping one of them would make contact. The one named Judy finally did. Something about a brother or sister being diagnosed with cancer. That's how Steve tracked her to northern Minnesota."

"What did he plan to do once he found them?" The question she wanted to ask was more difficult. Had Steve Feigenbaumer murdered Judy and did he intend the same for Sabra?

"Well, that was the problem. He didn't have enough evidence to prove that they'd murdered his father. He was hoping to convince them to turn themselves in. Like he'd lie, tell them he had the proof. I'm sure he was also nosing around up there, trying to find something to nail them with. Mainly he figured that if *he* threatened to turn them in, it would scare them and force their hands."

"So he wasn't out for revenge?"

"Revenge?" repeated Paul. "As in killing them? Hell, no. He wanted them tried and jailed. For the rest of their worthless lives."

"Did he mention any names? What Judy and Sabra were calling themselves now?"

"The one named Judy owned some sort of shop. The other one owned a resort. If he said their fake names, I don't recall what they were."

It didn't matter. He'd just confirmed Jane's worst fear. Sabra Briere was Tessa Cornell. As hard as it was for Jane to believe, Tessa *was* a murderer. "This has been incredibly helpful."

"Did he find them?"

She didn't want to give away too much. "I'm not sure."

"Who shot and killed him?"

"I don't know that either."

"Well, hell, lady. For a PI, you don't know jack shit."

He didn't need to rub it in. "I'm working on it."

The books that Tessa gave Jonah all seemed interesting enough. *Blink*, by Malcolm Gladwell; *The Shock Doctrine*, by Naomi Klein; and *The Glass Castle*, by Jeannette Walls. None of them were exactly light reading. He flopped down on his bed with a gigantic Hershey bar and began with *Blink*. He was interested in the guy's thesis, and yet no matter how hard he tried to concentrate, he couldn't stop thinking about Emily. Digging the cell phone out of his pocket, he tapped her key. The phone rang and rang until her voice mail picked up.

"Where are you?" he said, keeping his voice down. "I'm sorry I can't come over tonight. My aunts are both still super pissed. I've got to play nice or they won't let me stay. Call me."

When Emily hadn't called back by ten, Jonah's worry moved into overdrive. He tried her one more time. Again, she didn't answer.

Hearing a knock on his door, he said, "Come in."

Jill stuck her head inside. "I'm back and I'm beat. Everything okay with you?"

He held up the book. "Tessa gave me an assignment."

Jill seemed amused. "If you want something to eat before bed, do it now. Tessa's planning to sleep on the living room couch tonight."

"Because of the fight?"

"Oh, who knows. We'll work it out. I'm going to turn in, too, so eat now if you're starving."

"I'm fine."

"You know, honey, we're not grounding you just to be mean."

"I know."

"See you in the morning then." She backed out and shut the door behind her.

Jonah waited another few minutes, until he was positive no one was moving around upstairs, and then let himself into the garage, where he eased Jill's road bike away from the wall rack. Because he was a good foot taller than she was, he took a few seconds to raise the seat. Once outside in the dark with the garage door closed, he hopped on and took off up the gravel path that led past the lodge to the main road. The night air was warm and thick with humidity. He started to sweat almost immediately.

He couldn't understand why Emily hadn't returned his call. A voice inside his head kept repeating the words *something's wrong*. Anxiety cramped his stomach as he rode through the quiet, deserted streets. He slowed as he turned the corner onto Comstock. Halfway down the block, he climbed off the bike and walked it the rest of the way.

As he neared her house, he heard voices—a male voice and then a woman's voice, both hushed. Coming to a stop behind the tall boxwood hedge that divided the Jensen property from the house next door, he leaned the bike against the tight foliage and then dug both hands through the leaves to part them just enough so that he could see what was going on.

Emily and Kenny had just come out of the porch door. Kenny's Harley was parked in the driveway.

"Guess I better shove off," said Kenny, draping his arm around Emily's shoulder as they moved together down the front steps. He had on a cool muscle T, and yet he managed to ruin the sexy image with his bulging gut.

"I'll pick you up tomorrow and take you over to the resort."

"I don't want to go back there."

"Now, now. There's nothing to worry about. Everything's cool." He pulled her into his arms, buried his hands in her hair and kissed her.

Jonah stiffened. Roaring out from behind the hedge, he shouted, "What the hell? Emily? Get away from him."

A smile tugged at Kenny's lips. "Hey, puke." He pulled Emily closer, lowered his head and nibbled her ear. "You're history. I'm her man now. Tell him, babe."

With eyes that were flat and cold, Emily nodded.

"I don't believe you," said Jonah, his heart hammering. "This is bullshit."

"Believe it," said Kenny.

"Emily?"

"You better go," she said.

"This is *not* happening," screamed Jonah, catching a look on her face that sent a chill through him. "That guy is a pig. He's so fat the army doesn't even want him."

"That's it," called Kenny, letting go of Emily.

"Truth hurts, huh?" said Jonah, shoving the motorcycle over as Kenny lunged for him. Luckily, Kenny's pant leg got tangled on part of the bike. He howled with fury as both he and the bike hit the pavement.

Jonah didn't wait to finish the conversation. He grabbed Jill's road bike and skidded out onto the street. Behind him, he could hear Kenny scream, "You're a dead man, Jonah. Hear me? *Dead*."

24

Thursday morning dawned gray and rainy. Wendell and Ruth sat in the front seat of Wendell's minivan, looking through the windshield wipers at the home he'd once owned. It was a modified A-frame, with a front deck facing the water. The house was everything he'd ever wanted and more. With the prominently displayed FOR SALE signs, one on the dock and one at the end of the gravel road leading to the property, he assumed it was still on the market.

"We loved living there," he said, working some fake sadness through his vocal cords, something he'd developed to hide his rage.

"It's a beautiful home. Did you own a boat?"

"A rowboat. Nothing fancy. Mary Jo and I would row out in the evenings after work and eat a picnic dinner on the water. Those were some of our best times." He turned to Ruth, pressed his hand to hers. "I didn't think I'd ever find another woman to love. How did I get so lucky?"

Wendell had stayed at Ruth's house last night. It was the first time they'd been together. He'd been his usual clumsy, tentative self, and yet for some reason, Ruth didn't seem to mind.

He'd never thought of himself as a great lover. He did, however, know how to be gentle and tried as hard as he could to pick up the cues Ruth was sending. Waking up with his arms around her had made him happier than he'd been in years. They'd talked quietly as the light crept in through the half-open blinds, discussed how overserious they'd been about their lovemaking, and agreed to take it slow and have fun. They ended up laughing at how ridiculous they both were, completely out of practice when it came to dating. Ruth made a big breakfast—eggs and pancakes and sausage. Wendell squeezed the orange juice and put on the coffee, nothing above his level of expertise.

"I love being with you," he said, stroking her hand, listening to the soft patter of rain against the car windows.

"I feel safe with you," said Ruth. "That's important to me. We always need to be honest with each other, even if it hurts."

"Absolutely," he said, nodding, while at the same time avoiding her eyes. "Honesty is the only way to go."

Back at the Merland house, Wendell led Ruth into the bedroom that currently served as his photography studio.

"So this is where you work," she said, taking it in with an impressed look on her face. The bed and all the furniture had been shoved into one corner of the room, leaving the rest of the space open and empty, except for a raised professional backdrop with a wooden stool in front of it.

Wendell assumed she was humoring him. The room wasn't much, even though it allowed him to tell people that he still had a studio. The truth was, his photography business had almost dried up since the fire. He didn't have the money to replace everything he'd lost. He had one more month before the school year started. How could he not be worried that the school board would take his contract for student photos away from him this year? If that happened, it would sink his business for good.

Ruth slipped her hands inside his. "It'll work out. You'll see."

He tried to smile. "I have something for you."

"For me?"

"For your birthday."

"How—"

"I asked Emily about it last week. I had no idea it was coming up so fast." He handed her a small, wrapped box. "I hope you like it."

She unwrapped the paper with great care and opened the lid. "Perfume?"

"It's a favorite of mine. *Evening in Paris.* I had to send away for it. You can't find it, even in Duluth."

She removed the cap and waved the tiny bottle under her nose. "It's wonderful. I love it."

"Do you really?"

"I'd love anything you gave me."

"Put some on."

As she dabbed a few drops behind her ears, Wendell's cell phone rang. "Give me a sec," he said, walking out of the room into the hallway.

"Wendell, hi, it's Frank Lind again."

"Yeah, hi. Anything more on the insurance payout?"

"I'm afraid I've got some bad news. Our investigator isn't convinced it was a faulty space heater."

Wendell flinched. "What else could it be?"

"We have to rule out arson."

"Arson? That's ridiculous. The sheriff's department investigated and said it was the space heater in our upstairs bedroom.

It was an old building, with no circuit interruptors, no sprinkler system. The volunteer fire department said the exact same thing. *Everybody* agreed."

"Our lead investigator interviewed the man who called in the fire. John McBride. You know him?"

"No."

"He said he saw two sources. One upstairs and another on the porch at the back of the house. You got two sources, you got arson."

"That is absolute garbage," said Wendell, "and you know it."

"Look, we're not saying you had anything to do with it. And we're not trying to stiff you on the money. I wrote the policy and I wouldn't have done it the way I did if I didn't think that you were an honest guy. But you also have to understand the position of my company. One in four fires today is intentionally set."

"I wasn't there. I'd been gone for hours."

"I know that. Honestly, I think this is all going to turn out in your favor. It's just going to take a little more time because we had to call in a professional consultant."

"I lost everything in that fire. I can't work if I can't buy new equipment."

"Be patient just a little while longer."

Through the windows on either side of the front door, Wendell spied a Balsam County sheriff's car pull up to the curb. He said a disgusted good-bye to his insurance man as he watched Kelli Christopher and one of her deputies dash through the rain up to the house.

Just moments after the bell rang, he answered the door. "Can I help you?"

"We need to talk," said Kelli.

"What about?"

"Can we come in?"

"Oh. Sure," he said, immediately on the defensive. What the hell did they want?

Wendell wasn't alone in his opinion that the undersheriff of Balsam County should not be a woman. He didn't hate women, or anything like that, it just wasn't right. For one thing, he was put off by her self-assurance. And he didn't like her hard-edged, down-to-business approach. The old undersheriff had been a friendly, easygoing, talkative guy. He wanted to tell her that, behind her back, people gossiped. Some thought she might be a lesbian, like Jill and Tessa. Wendell figured that was a stretch. Three lesbians in one small town? There couldn't be *that* many around.

Kelli motioned him into the living room. "Let's sit a minute."

He glanced down the hall, wondering what he should do about Ruth.

"In here," said Kelli, giving him a look that said *don't waste my time.*

"Oh. Okay," he said. "What's up?"

Kelli claimed the piano bench, while the deputy made himself comfortable on the couch. Wendell sat down on the footstool, sensing instantly that it had been a bad choice. He was a foot shorter than everyone else. It made him feel like a kid in the company of adults.

Kelli bent forward and rested her arms on her thighs. "I need to know where you were on Tuesday, before you got to the theater."

"Tuesday? You mean the night that man died? Well, I . . . I'd have to think. I guess I was here. I took a shower, got dressed, and then walked over to the community center."

"Did anyone see you?"

"I have no idea."

"Could Helen say what time you left?"

"She was upstairs in her bedroom watching TV."

"Did you talk to anyone?"

"Why all the questions?"

She shifted back a little. "You told me when I questioned you that night that you'd talked to this Feigenbaumer once. He'd stopped by while you were out cutting the grass, told you that some of the shingles on the roof were rotted."

"Right."

"And that's all? He didn't say anything else?"

"Just the usual. We talked about the weather, where he could find the best fishing."

"He mention where he was staying?"

Wendell shook his head.

"We found the murder weapon."

"You did?" His peripheral vision caught movement to his right. Turning, he found Ruth standing under the archway.

"A thirty-eight caliber revolver with two bullets left in the cylinder. You know anything about that?"

"Me? Why would I?"

"Want to know where we found the gun?"

He shrugged.

"In a locker in the dressing room at the theater. It was wrapped in a rag and stuffed on the top shelf behind a script. It was your locker, Wendell. Can you explain how the gun got there?"

"*My* locker? If you found a gun, somebody must have put it there."

"Like who?"

"Whoever killed him."

"Did you murder Steve Feigenbaumer, Wendell?"

"Absolutely not."

"But you have no way to verify where you were late Tuesday afternoon."

"I didn't do it."

"I need you to come down to the sheriff's office with us."

"Are you arresting me?"

"No."

"But you're going to."

"I never said that."

"I want a lawyer," he said.

The muscles along her jawline tightened. The fact that he'd thwarted her so easily gave him a feeling of power. For once in his life, he felt as if he'd stood up to authority and won.

"You are, of course, entitled to have a lawyer present, although it's not necessary."

"Of course it's necessary," said Ruth, speaking for the first time.

Wendell looked up at her with grateful eyes.

Kelli and the deputy stood. She handed him her card. "I'd like you and your lawyer to call and make an appointment for later this afternoon. I can hold you on a probable cause warrant if I need to, so don't mess with me on this. Take it seriously, Wendell." She nodded to Ruth and said, "Nice to see you, Mrs. Jensen," on the way out.

25

Jane and Cordelia walked through a dispiriting drizzle, umbrellas held over their heads, to the cottage for an early lunch. They were both tired from the conversation they'd had last night, one that had lasted into the wee hours of the morning. Even after hearing what Jane had learned in Chicago, Cordelia still maintained that Tessa could be innocent because they didn't have all the details.

"Did you tell Tessa and Jill that I had food poisoning?" asked Jane.

"I almost had to physically restrain Tessa. She wanted to phone you and tell you how you should treat it. You owe me big time."

Hearing how concerned Tessa had been about her, Jane started to think that she wasn't much of a friend. She didn't have any sort of inner conviction that, given what she now knew, Tessa could still be innocent. She didn't want the trail to lead to Tessa's door any more than Cordelia did, and yet she had to follow the evidence, wherever it led.

This morning, while showering, she'd remembered something Helen Merland had said at breakfast the other day. She'd asked them if they'd come to town to see how Sabra was doing. When Cordelia called her on it, she had claimed confusion and quickly switched the name to Tessa. At the time, Jane hadn't though much of it. Now she realized how significant that moment of confusion was.

When they walked in the cottage door, Jill and Tessa asked how Jane was feeling.

"Where do you think you got the food poisoning?" asked Jill.

Jane pressed a hand to her stomach, pretending that she still wasn't a hundred percent. "I'll probably never know. But I feel better."

It looked as if Jill had brought sandwiches down from the lodge. She stood behind the kitchen island, arranging them on a platter.

Tessa was already at the table, leg propped on low footstool, pouring glasses of lemonade. "This should be good for what ails you," she said. "Made it myself. A little lemon goes a long way to ease the digestion."

Jonah sat across from Tessa, looking miserable. "I'm under house arrest," he said, his eyes fixed on the gloomy day outside the front windows. "Hey," he said, pointing. "Kelli Christopher's here."

Jill skirted around the island, set the platter on the table, then dashed to open the front door. "Hi," she said, her voice betraying her nervousness. "You've come at the perfect time. We've got lots of food."

"Thanks," said Kelli, removing her cap, "but I'm afraid this is business."

"Have you learned anything more about Feigenbaumer's demise?" asked Cordelia. She taken the chair next to Tessa and was scrutinizing the platter of sandwiches.

There were six chairs at the table and only five people gathered to eat, so Kelli helped herself to the chair closest to Jane and sat down. "We found the gun that was most likely used in Feigenbaumer's murder."

"Where?" asked Jane.

"At the theater. It's a thirty-eight caliber Smith and Wesson double-action revolver. Five rounds. Blue aluminum alloy frame. Three of the rounds were spent. Two were still in the cylinder. We checked the serial number. The gun was sold to one Tessa Cornell at a gun shop in Grand Rapids in June of nineteen eighty-three."

Jill's hand flew to her mouth.

"Calm down," said Tessa. "The gun was obtained legally and registered. And I did not kill that man. How could I? I can barely walk."

Tessa had been in her walking boot for two days when Feigenbaumer had been shot, and seemed to be getting around pretty well, although she claimed great pain, and when anybody was around, rarely got off the couch. As alibis went, this one wasn't all that solid. There was also the matter of the Volvo's warm motor on Tuesday night. Jane didn't intend to keep it to herself much longer.

"Can you explain how your gun came to be used in a murder?" asked Kelli.

"I gave it to Lyndie LaVassar on Monday morning. I didn't know it was used to kill Feigenbaumer. The last I saw it, Lyndie was stuffing it into her purse."

"Why on earth would you give a gun to Lyndie?" demanded Jill.

"Because she asked me for it. She was frightened and said she needed protection."

"Did she say why?" asked Kelli.

"No, and I didn't ask. It was her business."

Kelli hooked her arm over the back of the chair. "Can you prove you gave it to her?"

Tessa seemed annoyed that her word would be challenged.

"I saw it all," said Jonah.

Everyone turned to stare at him.

"I was in the kitchen getting myself some breakfast. I heard Tessa and Mrs. LaVassar talking. It was just like Tessa told you. She called me in and asked me to go get an old metal case she keeps in this trunk. I saw her give the gun to Mrs. LaVassar. Saw her leave with it."

"So," said Kelli, thinking out loud as she scratched her cheek, "how did the gun get from Lyndie to the person who murdered Steve Feigenbaumer?"

"What about the bullet you found embedded in the wood paneling at the emporium the night Lyndie went missing?" asked Jane. She didn't mention that Kelli had thought the bullet had probably been there for years. "That was a thirty-eight caliber slug, right? Have you run the ballistics?"

Kelli flicked her eyes to Jane. "Not yet."

"Seems to me that the gun used to fire a shot into the emporium wall, if it was Tessa's gun, might have been taken away by Lyndie's murderer. That's more proof that the two murders are connected."

"It's an interesting theory," said Kelli.

Tessa could have left the cottage in her car on Tuesday afternoon and had a hand in Feigenbaumer's death. On the other hand, it seemed highly unlikely that she had anything to do with Lyndie's murder. Unless, that is, she had help.

Kelli folded her hands on the table. "Did you ever meet this Feigenbaumer, Tessa?"

"Never."

Jane caught Jill's eye, saw the guilt mixed with anxiety. Everyone around the table knew that Feigenbaumer had been looking in Tessa's office window on Sunday night. They'd all witnessed her reaction, which was clearly fear, if not outright terror, and yet nobody brought it up. For good or ill, they were all protecting her. She may never have met the cop from Chicago, so she hadn't outright lied. That, however, was a technicality. She knew who he was and what he represented.

"Jane," said Kelli, rising from her chair. "Will you walk me out to my car? I'm sorry if I spoiled your lunch," she added, nodding to everyone, "but I had to get the question of the gun cleared up."

"Not a problem," said Tessa. "If I can help with the investigation in any way, just ask. Until this ankle gets better, I'm pretty much stuck here all the time."

Cordelia's hand shot up. "Before you go, do you have any idea when we'd be able to get back into the theater? We have a production that's been put on hold."

"Maybe tomorrow," said Kelli. "Might be late in the day. When was opening night scheduled for?"

"Tomorrow."

"Oh. Well, I'd say you're looking at Saturday night at the earliest."

The rain had stopped and the clouds were starting to break up when Jane and Kelli stepped out onto the deck. Kelli led the way down the steps to her squad car. Leaning against the front fender, she said, "I have a question for you."

Jane waited.

"So I'm doing my homework last night, calling people in Chicago to try to find out just who this Steve Feigenbaumer was so I can get a handle on why he'd come to our fair town. I'm talking to his ex-wife when she mentions that a PI had come to her house yesterday to ask questions. She said the woman's name was Lawless."

Jane couldn't help but smile.

"I thought you were a restaurateur. Now I hear that you're a private investigator?"

"Not officially. I sometimes work with an ex-homicide cop. He's the one with the license."

"And you flew to Chicago to interview people?"

"Yes."

"Why?"

Jane shrugged. "I'm looking into the murders."

"Why would you do that?"

"Because Jill asked me to."

Kelli rubbed the back of her neck. "You amaze me."

"Thank you."

"It wasn't a compliment. What did you find out?"

"Probably the same information you did."

"We need to talk."

"You want to share notes?"

"I'm not sharing anything."

"Then why should I help you?"

"We both want the same thing, right? The truth? Or are you looking into this for Jill because you're trying to protect Tessa?"

"That's not my intent."

Gazing straight into Jane's eyes, Kelli said, "Who *are* you?"

"Not the bubblehead you thought I was."

"I never said that."

"No, but with your superior abilities and instincts—"

"Are you saying I'm arrogant?"

"The thought did cross my mind."

"All right," said Kelli, holding up her hand. "Truce. I've heard the criticism before. Maybe I do come across as too self-confident. I have to. Law enforcement up here is a man's job and I'm not a man."

"Makes sense," said Jane.

"Yeah?"

"Yeah. Do people know you're gay?"

"I don't go around announcing it, but sure, I figure most sentient people know. That doesn't cover everyone."

Jane laughed.

"What are you doing tonight?"

"Haven't thought about it."

"I'll pick you up at the lodge at six. I live just outside of Balsam Lake, about thirty miles away. That's where the county offices are located."

"And what would we do?"

"Eat. Talk. Commune."

"Define commune?"

For the first time, Kelli smiled. "Work on our rapport. Sound like a plan?"

Jane matched Kelli's smile with one of her own. "I guess I could do that."

"Six on the dot," said Kelli, sliding into the front seat of the cruiser.

"Should I bring my Chicago notes?"

"I kinda doubt you're the sort who needs them."

Shortly after one, Jane trotted up the steps to the community center. Yellow police tape crisscrossed the double doors that lead into the theater. Straight in front of her was the gift shop. She asked the woman behind the counter if Fontaine Littlewolf was around and was directed to an elevator. Once up on the second floor, she found Fontaine in a workshop at the end of the hall. Since the door was open and she could see him sitting at his desk writing, she didn't knock. She didn't notice Emily sitting on a folding chair a few feet behind Fontaine until she was all the way inside.

"Jane, hi," said Fontaine, looking up as he handed a check to Emily. For such a big man, he had an unusually soft voice.

"Did I come at a bad time?" she asked.

"I was just leaving," said Emily. "I'm scheduled to work at three today." She folded the check, pressing it into the back pocket of her jeans. "Thanks," she said, giving Fontaine's shoulder a squeeze.

"Call me before you make any decisions," he said. "Give your mom my love."

Once she'd left, he turned to Jane and offered her the seat Emily had just vacated.

Jane was intrigued by the number and variety of birdhouses and feeders hanging from hooks around the room, with dozens more stacked together along a wall under a chalkboard.

"I sell them," said Fontaine. The old wooden chair creaked as he leaned back.

"They're wonderful." Some were painted, some were left rustic. What they all had in common was a sense of whimsy.

214

"It adds to my bottom line," he said. "With the exception of the emporium, you can find them all over."

"Why doesn't the emporium carry them?"

"Oh, well now, that's a tricky one. Mrs. LaVassar, she told me last Saturday that they didn't sell well enough for her and she wanted them out ASAP. So I went and got them."

"Was that true?"

"Yeah, pretty much. It's a funny thing, though. They sell just fine at the other stores in the area."

Jane wasn't sure what he was suggesting.

"She didn't like Shinobs. Ojibwes. Native Americans. I heard she told customers that my stuff was badly made. Can't say I'll miss her."

"That's nasty," Jane agreed. "You still live here at the center?"

"Yes, ma'am. It's a small room, but it suits me just fine. Got my bed in there, a bookcase, a microwave, a TV, all the comforts of home—rent free."

"Sounds like a sweet deal," said Jane, standing with her hands on the back of the folding chair.

"I figured, hell, I'd live here for a while, save my money and then move into something more comfortable when I had a nest egg saved up. But I never moved. I banked most of my paychecks all these years, made investments. I was riding high, too, until the stock market fell through the floor. And then, wouldn't you know, I pulled my money out. If I'd left it in, I would have made most of it back by now. I hope Tessa stays on as board chair for a long, long time. When she goes, I'll be next."

"But she says you're indispensable around here."

"That's nice of her. It's not true. They could get a kid to take over my job, pay him half as much. I never played the game right. After I got out of the army, I let my hair grow." He pointed to his long braid. "It's the way I like it. I know it irritates people, which is partly why I do it." Fontaine didn't smile much, but he smiled at that. "Anyway, you didn't come here to listen to my tale of woe. What can I do for you?"

"I hear that the gun used to kill Steve Feigenbaumer was found in the theater."

"Yeah," he said, clasping his hands behind his neck. "Down in the dressing room. I hauled in a bunch of lockers a few years back. The high school was tossing them and I figured we could use them. No locks, of course. For every production, I assign a locker and put the name of the actor on it. The gun was found in Wendell Hammond's. I wouldn't want to be him right about now."

"Wendell?" This was the first piece of news she'd learned that gave her some hope that someone else might have had it in for Feigenbaumer. "I suppose it could have been planted."

"Always a possibility."

"I wonder where Feigenbaumer was staying?" She'd never seen him around Thunderhook.

"Fisherman's Cove over on Harris Lake. I was over there the other day and saw him coming out of one of the cabins."

"How far away is Harris Lake?"

"Oh, maybe six miles out Country Road Seven."

Jane realized she might be moving into dicey territory with her next question. "You were late to the theater the night Feigenbaumer died."

"Yeah, I was sorry about that. I was visiting my uncle over in Empire. He was making himself a will, wanted my input. When I left, I noticed one of the tires on my truck was low on air, but assumed it'd get me back to town. About three miles out of

Empire, the damn thing went flat. Didn't have a spare, so I had to hike back to my uncle's place."

"You couldn't call?"

"No cell phone service. You've probably noticed that it's spotty all over up here. Actually, the best place to get service is around Harris Lake. There's a cell phone tower just outside of town. Anyway, my uncle owns an auto repair shop. Figured he might have a tire with a rim we could switch out. It took longer than I hoped it would. I told Kelli Christopher to call him if she needed to verify where I was."

Jane didn't mean to impugn the honesty of Fontaine's uncle, and yet as alibis went, this one was even worse than Tessa's.

"You asking around because you're Tessa's friend? She had nothing to do with that guy's murder. You can take that to the bank."

"I hope you're right. If you think of anything else—" She handed him one of the Nolan & Lawless Private Investigation cards. "You can reach me at the second number."

He studied it for a few seconds. "You're a PI? I thought you owned a couple restaurants."

"Something I do on the side."

He nodded. "I'll remember that." He placed the card carefully on his desk. "Always good to know who you're talking to."

26

Tessa could feel Cordelia eyeing her from across the room. She wished that her dear old friend would go play shuffleboard or soak in the hot tub, anything that would give her some peace and quiet. Unfortunately, Cordelia was deep into her "I Am the Goddess of Healing, the Bearer of All Comfort, the Bringer of Light" mode. When her feet were firmly planted on that cloud, there was no arguing with her.

Sidling over to Tessa, Cordelia said, "I know what we should do."

"Do you."

"I think a palm reading is in order."

Tessa groaned.

"I realize you're an unbeliever, but there's no need to be churlish."

"I'm not being churlish, I'm being disinterested."

Cordelia dragged the footstool over and sat down. "It's painless."

"Says you."

"You are such a baby."

"Isn't that the pot calling the kettle black?"

"Drama mama."

"Diva."

"Prima donna."

"Megalomaniac."

Cordelia's eyes bugged out. "I am *not*."

Tessa held up a hand. "All right. I suppose it's better than being subjected to that crystal ball you carry around with you."

"If you'd rather do that—"

"No, no." At least the palm reading didn't involve a dark room, candles, and holding hands under the table. "Which palm do you want?"

"The right one."

"Is there really a difference?"

Adjusting her gold lamé turban, Cordelia said, "I am a practitioner of Chinese palmistry. In that tradition, for a woman— it's the reverse for a man—the left hand shows the cards dealt you at birth, the right shows what you made of what you were given."

"You're not going to tell me my fate? That I'll be hit by a truck or be ground up in a wood chipper?"

"You watch too many movies." Cordelia traced a couple of lines with her red fingernail. "Your love line is strong."

"See, this is what fries me about woo-woo stuff like palm reading, tarot cards, psychics. They state the obvious and people fall down and foam at the mouth because they're so impressed."

"Shut up and let me concentrate," said Cordelia.

"Now who's being churlish?"

"Hmm," said Cordelia, portentously. "Hmm," she said again. "Now give me the other hand."

If nothing else, this was light entertainment.

"Oh, my," said Cordelia, examining it.

"What?"

"Your rebellion line. Very revealing."

"Of what?"

"Your heart line is equally interesting."

"Aren't you supposed to fill me in on what you're learning?"

Still bent over, Cordelia raised her eyes. "In theory."

"So?"

"The heart line suggests a self-centered, introspective woman. FYI, my heart line is the exact opposite. I'm the kind of person who gives and gives and gives."

Tessa thought it politic to suppress a laugh.

"But the rebellion line, especially in your youth, is troubling."

She jerked her hand away. "That's enough." Grabbing Cordelia's hand, she pretended to examine the palm. "Oh, no," she said, feigning horror. "This is terrible. Your fate is dark and covered in cobwebs."

With a dignified sniff, Cordelia withdrew to the chair by the fireplace. "There's no such thing as fate. Our future is in our own hands."

"Then how can you foretell the future?"

"Palmistry, as practiced by *moi*, isn't about the future, it's about who you were and what you've become."

"I'm entirely integrated. The same yesterday, today and forever."

"I think not."

"Let's change the subject."

Tapping a finger against her lips, Cordelia hesitated and then said, "I seem to be about to tell you something I probably shouldn't."

"Oh, go ahead. We all know you're evil."

"Well, the night that Feigenbaumer was murdered, when

Jane and I came back here to tell you about it, Jane told me to run inside and give you the news while she headed into the garage."

"And why would she do that?"

"Because she's nosey. She said that the engine of your Volvo was warm. Someone had been driving it."

Tessa opened her mouth, but nothing came out.

"Let's put all our cards on the table for once, shall we? Everyone knows you're not telling the truth. Who was Feigenbaumer to you?"

"*Everyone* knows?" said Tessa.

"Don't be so stubborn. We all love you and want to help."

"There's nothing I need help *with*."

"Who drove your car that afternoon?"

Tessa heard the sound of footsteps on the basement stairs.

A second later, Jonah appeared. "I, ah," he said, holding his stomach. "I . . . I mean, did you have something you wanted me to do this afternoon?"

"Not here," said Tessa. "You should probably call up to the lodge and talk to Jill."

"Because my stomach hurts. And I have an awful headache. I think maybe I'm coming down with the same thing Jane had."

"Then take a couple of ibuprofen and go lie down."

"Yeah, I think that would be best."

"Come here first," said Tessa.

He dragged himself over to her chair.

Giving him a hug and then a kiss on his forehead, she said, "One more day and you'll be a free man. Jill and I talked about it this morning. But you're going to have a curfew from here on out."

"Like what?"

222

"Midnight."

"Even on weekends?"

Teenagers were so legalistic. "Okay, one on weekends. But twelve on weeknights."

"It's not like I'm in school."

"Don't push, buster."

"Right," he said. "Sorry."

"Now go get some rest."

He grinned at Cordelia as he walked out of the room.

Once he'd disappeared down the stairs, Cordelia stood. "I suppose I better go."

Reaching toward her, Tessa said, "No, stay. Quite honestly, I don't want to be alone. Maybe we could play Scrabble. Just . . . no more prying questions, okay?"

"FYI, I have a reputation for being lethal at board games."

"I'll chance it."

"It's your funeral."

Yes, thought Tessa. In a matter of days, it probably would be.

Before Jonah left through the garage, he hung a sign on his door that said SLEEPING. DO NOT DISTURB. He wasn't sure it would buy him any more time, and yet he had to make the effort. He'd called and texted Emily at least two dozen times since last night, and gotten no answer. He had to find out what was going on before it ate a hole clean through his stomach.

Keeping close to the side of the house, he crept up the hill into the woods and made his way around the north end of the lodge until he came out to the road that would take him into town. Running at a fast clip, he made it to Emily's house in under ten minutes. Just as he figured, her car was gone. She was at work.

Trotting back out to Main, he walked with his thumb stuck

out until a car stopped. Thankfully, he recognized the man behind the wheel. He might not have gotten in if he hadn't. It was
Mr. Dahlgren, one of the mailmen in town.

"Where you headed?"

"To the Moon place," said Jonah. The Moons lived in a small
development on the east end of town, the same area where
Jonah had once lived.

"Hop in."

A few minutes and a nonstop conversation later, Mr. Dahlgren let Jonah off at Wiggen Road.

"Have a good one," called Mr. Dahlgren as he pulled away.

Jonah sprinted down the wide open street to the largest
house in the development. Jim Moon, Kenny's dad, was the
president of Balsam County Savings & Loan. Because of his
general wealth and his standing in the community, he owned a
piece of prime property on Villniss Lake, a small but excep-
tionally beautiful piece of water. Kenny bragged so much about
what his dad had done in the Gulf War that it was like the guy
had won it single-handedly. When Mr. Moon returned home,
he was offered the job of assistant branch manager as a way to
thank him for his service. Jonah didn't know how long it took
Mr. Moon to become president, although he doubted it was
more than a few years. As long as he'd known Kenny, his dad
had held the top job.

From down the block, Jonah could see Mr. Moon standing
behind his black Cadillac Escalade. Jonah not only hated Toyotas,
he thought big cars were stupid. As he approached, he could see
Mr. Moon heft his golf clubs into the back end.

Mr. Moon broke into a grin as Jonah walked up. "Jo," he said,
clapping Jonah on the back. "What are you doing here?"

Mr. Moon shortened everybody's name. "Came to visit my aunts."

"When'd you get here?"

"Sunday night."

"Ken never said anything to me. How are your parents?"

"Good. I was sorry to hear about your mom. I always liked Mrs. LaVasser."

"Thanks. It's been a rough few days."

"You going golfing?"

"Yup." He shut the back of the vehicle, then adjusted his yellow golf hat. "Got a three o'clock tee time. Sly wants me back by six. Relatives over for dinner tonight. People coming to town because of the funeral."

Sly, known as Sylvia to everyone else in town, was his wife.

"Kenny here?" asked Jonah. He followed Mr. Moon and waited while he climbed into the front seat.

"Last I checked, he was in the basement pumping iron."

That made no sense at all. "You're not confusing Kenny with Corey, are you?"

"No, no. Cor's in Europe for the summer."

"Okay, thanks. Hope you birdie every hole."

"Oh, I will," said Mr. Moon, flashing his million-dollar smile, the one that would make him mayor one day.

Jonah stood in the center of the extrawide drive as Mr. Moon backed the monster SUV out into the street and drove away. Noticing a blue tarp pulled over Kenny's old motorbike parked at the edge of the garage, he walked over. So Kenny hadn't sold it. The tarp was covered with sticks and rotting leaves. With a Harley in the garage, he probably never used it anymore.

Jonah rang the front doorbell. Mrs. Moon appeared, looking

as cheerful and pretty as ever. She reminded Jonah of the moms in those really ancient TV shows: *The Brady Bunch, Happy Days, One Day at a Time.* Too perfect to be real, and yet too nice not to like.

"Jonah, what a surprise. Come on in."

Mrs. Moon and Aunt Jill were the only two people he knew who actually baked cookies from scratch. He thought they deserved some sort of award. The house was its usual spotless self, devoid of all clutter, unlike his aunts house, which was clean and in good repair, though never exactly neat. Floral arrangements from friends and neighbors covered every flat surface.

Mrs. Moon peppered him with all the usual questions. When had he arrived? How were his parents? How did he like St. Louis? When she was satisfied that all was well—she would have been heartbroken by anything less—she told him that Kenny had moved into the basement after he'd graduated. It wasn't really a *basement* basement, in Jonah's opinion. It was more like a furnished apartment.

"I can't believe he'll be at boot camp this time next month. My boys are growing up too fast."

"Boot camp," repeated Jonah. "Right." So Kenny hadn't gotten around to telling his parents that the army had rejected him for being a blimp. Interesting. "I'll just head on down if that's okay with you."

"Are you hungry?" she asked.

When *wasn't* he hungry? Still, he didn't want to press his luck. If Kenny decided to beat him to a bloody pulp, he hoped Mrs. Moon would intercede. "No, I'm fine."

"Well, if you boys want me to toss a frozen pizza in the oven, just holler up."

"We will."

Moving sideways down the steps just in case he had to make a quick escape, Jonah found Kenny sitting astride the bench of a huge home gym, doing leg curls, a cigarette dangling from the side of his mouth. His face was red with exertion, his body slick with sweat. With his shirt off, he looked even more flabby. It repelled Jonah to think of any girl, especially Emily, wanting to snuggle up next to that.

Kenny kept doing his reps as Jonah slunk into the room, the side of his mouth without the cigarette curling into a smile.

"You gonna hit me?" asked Jonah.

"Ain't decided. What do you want?"

Jonah wasn't really sure. He just knew he had to come. Unlike the upstairs, the basement floor and almost every piece of furniture was covered with dirty clothes, half-filled glasses, crushed pop cans, empty bags of chips, and assorted general crap. "This place is a pit."

"Suits me just fine," said Kenny, grabbing a white towel and wiping the sweat off his head, shoulders and arms.

"You trying to pump up and drop some weight?"

"Shut up about that." He tapped his cigarette above an ashtray.

"So you haven't given up?"

"Far as I'm concerned, the army had their chance and they blew it. There are other groups that would hire me in a millisecond. The pay's a lot better, too."

"Paramilitary?"

"Somebody's gotta go out there and protect dreamers like you from reality."

"Man up, right?"

"Damn straight."

"Kinda sucks when you get your philosophy of life from beer commercials."

227

"Thin ice, buddy. Thin ice." Kenny stuck the cigarette between his lips, tossed the towel and picked up a bar attached to the machine by a cable. Putting one foot in front of him and one foot behind, his elbows tucked into his sides, he began to slowly draw up on the bar.

"What's that called?" asked Jonah.

"Bicep curls. So I can intimidate pussies like you."

"Are you and Emily really together?"

"Go ask her."

"She's at work. And I haven't got any wheels."

"Boo friggin' hoo."

"Do you love her?"

"More than you do."

"So it's a contest."

"Everything's a contest, asshole. There are winners and there are losers. The entire world is divided along that one axis."

Noticing a couple of familiar keys on a keychain next to his foot, Jonah sat down cross-legged on the carpet. "If you're going to join some paramilitary organization and go fight overseas, what happens to Emily?"

"She stays home and waits for her man to come back."

"Sounds boring."

"To you maybe."

"You think that's what she wants to do with her life?"

"It's what she's gonna do."

"So you tell her to jump and she asks how high."

"It ain't like that. But yeah, if I needed to, I would, and she'd do it."

Jonah pressed his palm over the keychain and slowly drew his fingers around it. "If you think that, you don't know her very well."

Kenny dropped the bar and tossed the cigarette into the ashtray. "Really? And you do?"

"I know something doesn't add up." He sprang to his feet and began edging toward the stairs, feeling that the conversation was about to get ugly.

"Meaning what?"

"That someone like Emily doesn't change overnight."

"We've been together ever since you left."

"Bullshit."

"Ask her. I ain't lying."

That shook him. "You've found some way to manipulate her. That has to be it. What? Come on, tell me."

"It's called love, puke."

"Blackmail?" There it was, thought Jonah. The word had forced Kenny to compose his expression so he didn't give anything away. Except that the act of composure spoke more eloquently than any words. "You know, Kenny, you may have big muscles, but you don't want to mess with me."

Kenny seemed to find the comment hilarious. He let out a giggle and couldn't seem to stop.

Jonah took that as his cue to get the hell out. As he reached the top of the stairs, Mrs. Moon came out of the kitchen, wiping her hands on her apron. They both stood for a moment, listening to Kenny's giggles turn to shrieks of laughter.

"Is he okay?" asked Mrs. Moon.

"Was he ever?" asked Jonah. He headed for the front door. Once outside, he crouched down and waited by the edge of the garage, making sure that Kenny didn't come out looking for him. Breathing hard, he realized how scared he'd been down in that stinky lair. It was probably a dumb move to come by, and yet if he hadn't he might never have learned that Kenny had something on Emily. She wasn't with him because she cared about him, and that's all Jonah needed. He'd meant what he'd said the other night. He would love her no matter what.

Opening his fist, he gazed at the keys in his hand. *Score.* He needed transportation and this would fit the bill. The Moons' house was bordered by woods. Pocketing the keys, Jonah flipped the tarp off Kenny's old bike and checked it over to make sure it was in working order. The tires looked okay, although they probably needed air. Slipping it into neutral, he walked it into the woods, glad that it was light. He came out half a block away, walking it down an alley to the intersection with the county highway. Climbing on, he tried the key. The ignition coughed a couple of times and then caught. Something wasn't hitting right, and yet, when he gave it some gas, it flew, just like he remembered.

Stopping at a gas station on the way back to town, he filled the tank and put air in the tires. And then he was off. All he had to do now was find Emily.

27

Later that afternoon, Jane and Cordelia drove out to the resort on Harris Lake. Once again, Jane wasn't sure what she was looking for. Where Feigenbaumer had stayed likely played no role in his death, and yet she had to cover all the investigative bases.

"This place is a dump," said Cordelia, parking her car next to a squat wood frame building with a sign jutting off the side that said OFFICE. It was spelled out in peeling yellow and black painted letters. The building itself was painted, in Cordelia's words, "atomic tangerine."

"I wonder if this odd use of color was intentional," she asked as she opened the car door and got out, "or if the people around here are simply color challenged?"

The clump of pink plastic flamingos planted in the dirt on either side of the front door caused Jane to lean toward the latter.

The man behind the counter looked up from his magazine as they entered. "Can I help—" he said. He wasn't able to finish the question because he appeared to be struck dumb by the sight of Cordelia's gold lamé turban.

Jane pushed one of her Nolan & Lawless business cards across to him. She realized that she was getting way too attached to them.

He adjusted the glasses perched on the end of his nose and give it a quick look. "A PI, huh? That what they're wearing these days?" He nodded to Cordelia's turban.

"I like to make a strong first impression," said Cordelia. "Especially at fishing resorts."

Watching her warily, he went on. "You must be here about that Feigenbaumer guy."

"That's right," said Jane. The man's name was on a metal desktop display. Arnie L. Thompson.

"A sheriff's deputy came by yesterday. Wanted to know if he'd stayed here. I walked him over to number seven. There wasn't much to see. The deputy took his suitcase and laptop. That and a shaving kit were about all he had with him."

"Did you ever talk to Feigenbaumer, Arnie?" asked Cordelia, running her hand along a dusty corner table. "I can call you Arnie, can't I?"

"Well, you betcha," he said with a little too much enthusiasm. "The only time we spoke was when he rented the cabin. Seemed like a nice enough guy."

"You knew he was a cop then," said Jane.

The man's face blanched. "He was *what?*"

"That a problem?" asked Cordelia. Finished with her inspection of the table, she moved on to the cobwebs around the single window facing the lake.

"Well, no, a' course not."

Jane switched gears. "I understand Emily Jensen works here as a housekeeper."

"Lovely young woman," he said, opening a cigar box next to him. "As sweet as she is beautiful. You know her?"

"She's starring in a play I'm directing over at the community playhouse in Lost Lake," said Cordelia, moving over to the counter and peering into the box. "That's really generous of you to offer us cigars." She chose one, held it under her nose and sniffed.

"How can you be both a PI *and* a theater director?"

"I have multiple interests for my multiple personalities."

Jane cocked her head. She thought that was an interesting comment.

"I'm a part-time investigator, a full-time artistic director, a trained psychic, and next month I'm going to take a lateral career move and start tending drawbridges."

His eyes traveled from Cordelia to Jane. "Is she kidding?"

"When's checkout time?"

"Eleven."

"Are the people who stay here in the summer mostly fishermen?"

"Harris Lake is one of the best walleye and bass lakes around. I'm out there myself every chance I get."

"How many cleaning women do you employ?"

"Two."

"Sounds like cleaning is a real priority around here," said Cordelia.

"Oh, absolutely," agreed Arnie. He selected a cigar and flicked his lighter.

Cordelia bent toward him to catch a light.

"You're really going to smoke that?"

"Any reason I shouldn't?"

"No, no. It's a perfectly fine cigar."

"If it turns out to be the exploding variety, I'll be back."

"Cabin number seven," said Jane. "Could we see it?"

"It's rented. A couple of fishermen up from the Cities. The

deputy didn't say anything about it being a crime scene. I could show you another just like it."

"Not necessary," said Jane. "Thanks for the information."

"Ta," said Cordelia, stopping to blow a couple of smoke rings into the air before she followed Jane out the door.

Once they were back in the parking lot, Jane suggested that they take a look around.

"I wonder if Emily's here?"

"She doesn't work until three."

"How do you know that?"

Jane tapped her head. "Psychic." She led the way past a couple of the dilapidated cabins to a dirt path that ran in front of those that faced the lake.

"Not exactly thriving," said Cordelia.

Each cabin had a large brown plastic garbage can next to it. A couple were overflowing with trash.

They kept walking. The path took them through some tall grass to three cabins set deeper in the woods, with no view of the shore.

"Something's not right," said Jane coming to a stop.

"Meaning?"

"When checkout time is eleven in the morning, why would you schedule a cleaning woman to arrive at three?"

"Well," said Cordelia, examining the red polish on her fingernails. "Maybe that's when they do their deep cleaning. You know, like shampooing the rugs." She laughed at her own joke.

"So why does Emily come at three?"

"We could ask Arnie that question."

"You think we'd get a straight answer?"

"Not if he's hiding something."

"Why would he have something to hide?"

"He wouldn't. Unless it's illegal, immoral, or fattening."

"Let's think about this for a second," said Jane. "Since Feigenbaumer was staying here, maybe he saw something and put two and two together."

"Whatever two and two added up to," said Cordelia.

"If he discovered something illegal, maybe he threatened to tell."

"And they, whoever *they* are, got rid of him before he could talk. You think Emily's mixed up in this?"

"Seems like a theory with more holes than Swiss cheese."

"And Arnie doesn't look all that dangerous to me. Besides, we've already established that Lyndie LaVasser's and Feigenbaumer's deaths were connected, right? I can't see how what's going on here could have any bearing on that."

Frustrated at her lack of answers, Jane said, "You're right."

"Of course I'm right."

"Let's get out of here."

"My thoughts exactly."

Kenny's piece-of-junk motard had cost Jonah a hundred bucks and two hours of sitting in a dirty repair shop. He had some cash with him, but ended up charging the repair to the credit card his parents had given him. What he didn't have was time. He was on the road now, headed for Harris Lake. He'd called Emily's mom from the repair shop, found out that Emily was starting work at three today, which meant he might not be too late after all. His plan was to find her, talk to her alone, without Kenny there to apply his not inconsiderable intimidation skills, and then he'd nail down what was really going on. Once he understood the problem, he'd solve it. There was no way on earth that Emily loved Kenny more than she loved him.

Pulling up to the office at Fisherman's Cove shortly after four, Jonah swung his leg off the bike and set the kickstand, and then he went inside and asked the old man behind the desk where he could find Emily.

"Not sure, son. What do you need?"

"I need to talk to her."

"What about?"

"I don't think that's any of your business."

"How'd you find out about Emily?"

Jonah had no idea what he meant. "She's my girlfriend."

"Oh. I see."

"I'll just walk around until I find her. Thanks for nothing."

Coming around the back of the building, he saw a guy he knew walking to his car. "Sam," he called. "Wait up."

The guy stopped and turned around. "Jonah?"

"Have you seen Emily this afternoon? I need to talk to her."

"Emily?"

"You know. Emily Jensen. She's my girlfriend. She cleans cabins here. I don't see her car in the lot. Her mom told me she'd be here."

Sam unlocked his car. "Sorry, man. Can't help you."

"Are you working here, too?" asked Jonah.

"Nah, just visiting a friend. Hope you two hook up."

He seemed to be in such a rush that there was nothing else to do but let him go. "See you around," he called.

Shifting his focus toward the dirt path, he couldn't believe Emily would take a job in a place like this. The cabins all looked like slums. Rotting wood. Rusted screens. Concrete blocks used to prop up drooping decks.

"Emily?" he yelled, jogging slowly along the shoreline. "Emily, I gotta talk to you. Come on out. Emily, please. This is important. Life or death." He kept calling. When she didn't show, he followed the path through the weeds and found three more cabins separated from the rest. One of them had a light on above the door.

"Emily," he yelled again. "Come out. We gotta talk."

"Hey, there, young man," came Arnie's voice.

Jonah twisted around, saw Arnie steaming toward him.

"You have to stop that. You're annoying my customers. You either leave now or I call the sheriff."

Jonah glared. "She's here somewhere, right?"

"Out."

Standing his ground, Jonah screamed Emily's name.

Arnie took out his cell phone. "I'm calling the sheriff's department."

Hands clenched into fists, Jonah started for the guy.

"Now, now," Arnie said, backing up, holding up his hands. "Don't do anything we'll both regret."

As he stormed past, he bumped into Arnie's shoulder, flipping him a full one-eighty. "This is total bullshit," he muttered, spitting on the ground as he walked away.

28

Kelli Christopher picked Jane up from the Thunderhook parking lot at six. They made small talk all the way to Balsam Lake. When they reached the outskirts of town, Kelli pulled her squad car into a gravel driveway next to a barn. About thirty yards back from the highway stood an old farmhouse—white clapboard walls, two stories, screened front porch, with a big backyard, a picnic table a few feet from the entrance to a fenced garden, and a hammock tied up between two huge oaks.

"Welcome to my homestead," said Kelli, cutting the engine and then leaning back and smiling. "This is my oasis. My refuge and sanctuary. And sometimes, when it's been a particularly bad day, my asylum."

Behind the house were fields and trees that stretched as far as the eye could see.

"It's beautiful," said Jane.

"That it is. Come on. Let me introduce you to Duchess."

They made their way across an expanse of grass up to a back door. As soon as Kelli put her key in the lock, the deep barks began.

"You have a dog?"

"Not just any dog. Duchess is my soul mate."

An Airedale bounded out of the house and ran in circles through the grass.

"She always does that. Has to work off her energy before she gets around to saying hi. My neighbor comes by to let her out if I have to work late. Sometimes I take her with me. She's the most generous, decent, loyal creature I've ever known. I suppose that sounds strange."

"Not a bit. I feel the same way about my dog."

"Name? Statistics?"

"Mouse. He's a chocolate lab. Not sure how old he is. He's been with me for a few years, and, yeah, I love him pretty insanely. How old is Duchess?"

"Four. Got her when she was a pup." She crouched down and held out her hands. Duchess spread her front paws and dropped her head playfully, then came racing over and let Kelli scratch her from muzzle to tail. The dog was big, maybe sixty pounds, mostly brown, with a dark patch around her middle that extended to her tail.

"Hi, there," said Jane, extending her hand to be sniffed. She sat down in the grass and let the dog examine the rest of her.

"I think she likes you."

Jane stroked the dog's ears. "This really is a terrific place."

"The farmhouse was built in nineteen-oh-two. My dad and brother helped me rehab it after I bought it eleven years ago."

"You have a brother?"

"Jim. He's three years younger than me. My mom died when I was fourteen."

"Weird."

"Why?"

"I have a younger brother, too. And my mother died when I was thirteen."

"Maybe we're the same person," said Kelli.

Jane laughed.

The interior of the house was casually decorated, comfortable and homey. The biggest surprise came when they entered the kitchen. In many respects, it was still an old farmstead kitchen, large and open, with an oilcloth-covered table in the middle of the room and all the original painted wood cupboards. And yet the stainless refrigerator was high-end, the stove was the commercial variety with six burners and two ovens, and there was a wine refrigerator tucked under one of the counters. It definitely wasn't your grandmother's workplace.

"You like to cook?" asked Jane.

"My whole family does. We spend a lot of time here together. And when I'm alone, it's how I unwind. Cooking and my garden."

Jane liked the feel of the place and the sound of the kind of life Kelli lived. It wasn't what she'd expected.

"I made some fresh chimichurri sauce last night. Thought I could grill us a couple of steaks, slather it with the sauce, and then serve it with some bread. You could make a salad. That sound okay?"

"More than okay."

They worked companionably to make the meal happen. Jane prepared a classic vinaigrette, using fresh tarragon and adding a dollop of heavy cream to the mix before whisking it into an emulsion. After washing the leaf lettuce and cutting up a cucumber and a big Brandywine heirloom tomato, all fresh from the garden, she piled the salad, a loaf of bread, butter, and a couple of beers on a tray and carried it outside, joining Kelli by the gas grill. Duchess was chasing a ball around the yard, nosing it away from herself and then pouncing on it.

Jane squeezed off one of the beer bottle caps and handed it to Kelli. She opened another one for herself and sat down at the wood picnic table a few feet away. Kelli had already brought out some plates, silverware, napkins and salt and pepper. A bottle of old vine Zinfandel had been opened and placed between two wineglasses.

"I noticed a photo of you and another woman on the mantel in your living room," said Jane. "You look a lot alike."

"That's Laura," said Kelli. "We were together for five years. I asked her to move out last fall."

"I didn't mean to bring up something painful."

"I'm surviving. More or less. It's been a hard winter. Laura went back to Duluth after she moved out. I told her that I loved her too much to watch her kill herself." At Jane's questioning glance, she added, "Booze. I wanted her to get into a treatment program, said that if she did, we could talk about getting back together. I'm nowhere near ready to date someone new, which is why I said no to the blind date with you."

Duchess dropped her ball next to Jane's foot. "Here you go," said Jane, tossing it almost to the garden fence.

Sprinkling some garlic salt on the steaks, Kelli continued, "Because I'm the stoic sort, people get the idea that I'm tough, that nothing gets to me. The truth is, I'm . . . not immune. Laura called me a couple of weeks ago. She's been in treatment for three months. Wants to drive up and talk."

"How do you feel about that?"

"I want to believe she's getting her life together, that she can change."

"People do change," said Jane. "I've seen it."

"What about you?" said Kelli. "You're not with someone?"

"I lived with a woman for ten years, until she died of cancer. I've had a few relationships since then. The last one ended in November. It was my fault. She said I was a workaholic and I have to admit that I am."

"Oh, yeah, I've had that thrown at me, too. I happen to love my job. Not going to apologize for it. Laura's a dental hygienist. She likes it okay, but it's not part of who she is."

That was it exactly, thought Jane. If you couldn't step back, draw a clear line, it was harder to separate the two.

"So, should we talk turkey now or later?" asked Kelli, testing one of the steaks doneness by pressing on it with her finger.

"Might as well do it now."

"Tell me more about what you learned in Chicago."

Jane had concluded that there was no point in holding back. If she cooperated, maybe Kelli would be more inclined to give a little, too. "I assume you know all about Feigenbaumer's father. How he was murdered in nineteen sixty-eight. That three women were involved. One, Yvonne Stein, went to jail. The other two took off and were never seen again."

"And the other two were?"

"If we're to believe Feigenbaumer, and that photo he had, Lyndie LaVasser was one."

"Which was the reason he'd come to Lost Lake."

"Yes, but there's more. He evidently believed that both of the women he was looking for were here."

Kelli raised an eyebrow. "Who's the other one?"

"That's the big question. Whoever she was, she was the sister of the man Lyndie was dating back in sixty-eight. The brother's name was Jeff Briere. The sister's name was Sabra."

"You think it's Tessa?"

"I don't think there's absolute proof one way or the other. Feigenbaumer was planning a confrontation. Because he couldn't prove guilt beyond a reasonable doubt, he intended to lie."

"Get them to turn themselves in."

"Exactly."

"So did he murder Lyndie?"

"It's possible. Maybe she refused to bite. Wouldn't admit who she was. Who knows what happened that night at the emporium? The bullet in the wall suggests that something went wrong. If he did kill her, he needed to make it look like an accident for multiple reasons."

"But then, how did Tessa's gun go from Feigenbaumer to his murderer?"

Jane had been wondering about that. "Maybe he had it with him the night he died. Someone took it away from him and then killed him with it."

"I don't buy that for a minute. That gun would have been dropped in the middle of the nearest lake. He wouldn't walk around with it."

"So maybe he didn't kill Lyndie."

"Then who did? You think Sabra—"

"That's one theory."

"You have others?"

Jane took another sip of beer. "I gave you something. You give me something."

"Like I said, it doesn't work that way."

"Fine, then let's move on to another topic. Politics? Religion?"

Lifting the steaks onto a platter, Kelli covered them with the chimichurri sauce. "You're an infuriating woman, you know that?"

"I've been called worse."

"What do you want?"

"Well, for one, tell me about Wendell Hammond. You found the gun in his locker at the theater."

Kelli set the platter on the table and then sat down. Duchess settled next to her, chewing on a stick. "Hard to say. It's possible that the gun was planted. Although there are a couple of things that give me pause."

"Such as?" said Jane, forking one of the steaks onto her plate.

"He phoned Lyndie a few hours before she died. When I asked him about it, he said it was a simple social call."

"You believe that?"

"Yeah, I do. And I don't. It was something about his eyes. He wasn't telling me the whole truth, I know that much. And then there was the fire at his photography studio."

"Fire?"

"His business burned down a couple of months ago. The guys on the scene—it's an all-volunteer fire department in Lost Lake—said they thought a space heater in the second-floor apartment, where he was living at the time, had started it. Except, a week or so later, when the insurance people brought in their own investigator, I began hearing the word *arson*. Wendell was here in Balsam Lake having dinner that night, and then he claims he spent a few hours taking photographs of wildflowers on his way back to Lost Lake. People saw him at the restaurant. It's hard to put an exact time on when the fire started, which means his alibi doesn't entirely eliminate him." She forked the remaining steak onto her plate.

"The interesting thing is, the insurance investigator found another source for the fire on the back porch. Fires can be unpredictable. They can burn everything to the ground and yet leave a few things completely untouched. That's what happened. The investigator found a partially melted plastic gallon water jug and tested it. The lab found a gasoline residue. It looked like an athletic sock had been stuffed into the neck of the jug and used as a wick. Part of the sock was still intact, so they sent it to the BCA down in St. Paul to see if they could find any DNA. Haven't heard anything yet, but I expect to any day. We also found DNA under Feigenbaumer's fingernails. I imagine he must have scratched his attacker. If he did and the two samples match, Wendell's in deep shit."

"That's a lot of *ifs*," said Jane.

"Yeah, well, it's about all I've got at the moment."

"For him to be a double murderer, he would've needed something against both Lyndie and Feigenbaumer. What was it?"

"Probably nada."

Digging into the food, Jane said, "This steak is great. So is the sauce."

"It's nice to know I can please a restaurateur." Slicing off several pieces of bread, she continued, "So that brings us back to Tessa. What's her involvement?"

"She could barely walk the night Lyndie was murdered. And she was no match for someone like Feigenbaumer."

"Maybe she found someone to do it for her."

"Like who?"

Chewing for a few seconds, Kelli said, "I don't even want to think this."

"What?"

"Fontaine Littlewolf. They've been friends for years. He'd

do anything for her and he's no stranger to violence. He nearly killed a man in a bar fight in Coleraine after he got home from the Gulf War. The case was tossed because witnesses said the other man started it by threatening him with a knife. Not a smart move. You ever looked at Fontaine's arms? They're the size of pot roasts."

Jane had wondered herself about Fontaine. Before she could weigh in on the matter, Kelli's cell phone buzzed.

Removing it from her pocket, Kelli glanced at the caller ID. "I better take this." She rose and walked a few paces away. "What is it?" As she listened, her eyes lost focus. "Jesus. No, I'll come. Call the coroner and get him there ASAP. Make sure you keep the gawkers away. Call for backup if you need it. I'm leaving right now." She dropped back down on the bench. "Damn it."

"What happened?"

It took her a few seconds before she could respond. "This guy, his name's Otto Lindeman—he's an insurance salesman over in Empire. He just shot his wife, hauled her body into his Toyota, doused the car with gasoline, and set it ablaze. And then he put the gun in his mouth and blew his brains out. My deputy said that the garage was filled to the rafters with porno magazines. I knew this was going to happen. I warned her to get away from him. We had so many domestic calls on that house that we gave up counting."

Jane suddenly lost her appetite.

"Listen, I'm sorry, but I've got to go. I don't have time to drive you back to Lost Lake, so I'll ask one of my neighbors to do it. That okay with you?"

"Sure. I'll clean up the food, put everything away. No worries."

Kelli rose, digging in her pocket for her car keys. "The

neighbor can lock up. Duchess," she said, bending over and giving the dog's back a scratch, "you be a good girl."

"We'll be fine," said Jane.

Leaning in, Kelli kissed Jane's cheek. "I like you. We aren't meant for romantic greatness, but I can always use another friend."

"Me, too," said Jane.

"Take good care of my dog," she shouted as she crossed the lawn.

Jane waved, surprisingly sorry to see her go.

29

Wendell dropped a file folder on top of the desk. He'd finally found what he'd been looking for. If he wanted to put Tessa behind bars for the rest of her life, he had the proof. The question was, what should he do with it now that Feigenbaumer was out of the picture?

Hearing a timer go off in the kitchen, he raced to check on the hot dish. The Tater Tots looked perfectly browned and the cheese was melted. Underneath, the noodles and tuna looked positively creamy. This was his one specialty. Thankfully, Helen loved it. The tray was already set out on the counter. He dished up a plate, found a chocolate pudding in the refrigerator, filled a glass with water, and poured the coffee. And then he headed up the stairs to Helen's bedroom.

"Dinner," he said, smiling.

She was sitting in bed in her bathrobe, watching TV. "Smells wonderful."

He set the tray across her lap. "Is there anything else I can get you before I go?"

"You're leaving?"

"I told you, Ruth and I are going for a walk along the beach."

"Ruth?"

"Ruth Jensen? You know her."

"I—" She ran her fingers lightly across her forehead. "I get so mixed up."

"I know. But you're fine if you stay here in your bedroom. Promise you won't leave the house while I'm gone?"

She held up her hand. "Scout's honor."

"You've got the TV remote. Are you too warm, too cold? I could put on the air-conditioning."

"I'm absolutely wonderful. Thank you so much . . ."

"Wendell." She was having a bad evening.

"Of course. Wendell."

"I've written the name and phone number of your neighbor, Marla, by the phone. I made sure she'd be home tonight in case you need anything while I'm gone."

"I'll be just dandy. This dinner you made will hit the spot."

He couldn't believe that he'd actually grown fond of her. It occurred to him that it was even more than that. He felt protective, responsible for her. He was beginning to worry about her all the time. What if she walked off, got lost? What if she fell when he wasn't there? In the five weeks since he'd moved in, he could see a big change in her mental acuity. It saddened him.

"I'll be back in a couple of hours."

"Enjoy your evening."

"We'll have our usual bowl of ice cream before you go to bed. I bought your favorite this afternoon. Rocky Road."

"You know," she said, looking up into his eyes, "you're a fine man. Don't ever doubt that."

"I'll wait in the car," said Cordelia, stirring her double chocolate milkshake.

"Where's your inquiring mind?" asked Jane.

Cordelia lifted bored eyes to the sign above the store. Huta-maki Hardware & Supply. "Still every bit as inquiring as ever. But a hardware store? I think not."

"It won't take me long." Jane slid out of the driver's seat.

Cordelia was in the mood to be chauffeured again tonight. After being ferried back to Lost Lake by a neighbor of Kelli's, Jane was at loose ends. She wanted to borrow Cordelia's car and just drive around, but the only way that was going to happen was for Cordelia to come along. Jane threw in a milkshake to sweeten the deal.

A bell rang over her head as she entered the store. She hadn't been able to get the O-ring she'd found near Feigenbaumer's shoe out of her mind. It was time to ask an expert.

Stepping up to the cash register, she nodded to the gray-haired man behind the counter.

"Help you?" he asked.

"I hope so." She showed him the photo she'd taken with her cell phone. "I'm told it's an O-ring."

"Yes, ma'am, that's correct."

"What would something like that be used for?"

"Oh, heavens. Hundreds of things."

"Such as?"

"Well, off the top of my head, horse bridals, belts, jewelry, clothing, choke collars for dogs, various seals, gaskets, all sorts of mechanical applications—and, of course, artwork. Its uses are pretty much endless."

Not helpful. "Have you ever seen one just like this?"

"I've got dozens of them over at the end of that counter." He pointed.

"Anybody in town buy a lot of them?"

"Don't keep track of details like that."

"No, I supposed not." Unable to think of anything else to ask, she thanked him for his time. If she did take Nolan up on his offer, she assumed she'd better get used to dead-ends.

On her way out the door, she noticed a man crouched in the gardening supply section, examining the back of a box. He looked familiar, though she couldn't place the face. It finally dawned on her. It was Kenny Moon, Jonah's best friend. The ham-faced kid she'd once known had blossomed into one mega-sized adult.

A walkie-talkie on his belt gave a sudden beep.

Kenny unclipped it and said hello. "Oh, yeah, Brian. Sorry I didn't get back to you. Tomorrow is fine. Say three-thirty? Right, right. She'll be there. No, man. Cash only. Yeah. Bye."

"Kenny?" called a voice Jane recognized. Halfway down the aisle, standing with her back to Kenny, was Emily Jensen. She seemed agitated, pulling at her hair, her clothes, biting her fingernail. Her body jerked as she swiveled to face him.

Jane quickly ducked behind an endcap stocked with motor oil.

"If we don't leave soon, the store in Balsam will be closed."

"Hold your horses," mumbled Kenny, clearly annoyed that she was bothering him while he was reading. "We've got over an hour."

"I'm *nervous*. Don't you get that?"

"Go sit in the car. I'll be right out."

"Maybe I'll go get my car and drive myself."

"Hey," he said, grabbing her arm as she walked past. "Who's your man?"

"You are."

"And don't you forget it."

252

Jane found the exchange odd. For the last few days, Jonah had talked about nothing but Emily, how glad he was that they were back together. Could it be that Emily was two-timing him?

With a resigned look on her face, Emily pushed out the door, the bell jingling overhead.

Kenny continued to read the back of the box for another few seconds, then stood and carried it up to the counter.

"Hey, Kenny," said the manager. "How's that Harley runnin'?"

"Kenneth."

"Huh?"

"The name's Kenneth. Kenny's a kid's name."

"Sure. Well, anyway, your mom was in the other day. Said you'd been helping Arnie Thompson out over at his resort on Harris Lake."

"She talks too much."

"Now, now, she's just proud of you, son. She said you'd be leaving for boot camp any day. Congratulations on that."

"Yeah. Listen, I need something for spider mites."

"You doing a little gardening?"

He held up the box. "Will this work?"

"Inside or outside gardening?"

"Outside."

"What you want is a product called Avid. You mix it with water and spray the plants down. It's expensive."

"Where is it?"

The man stepped over to the wall, grabbed a quart of the product and returned to the counter. "You got a sprayer?"

"Just tell me how much."

"Let's see." He adjusted his glasses. "That will be—" He tapped the price into the register. "Four hundred and forty-seven dollars and eighty-four cents."

"You're kidding."

"Still want it?"

Kenny handed him a credit card.

"Remember, this stuff is poison."

"That's what I'm counting on."

The clerk gave him a quizzical look. "You get any on you, be sure to wash it off right away. And read all the directions. Four ounces for every hundred gallons of water."

Kenny signed the receipt.

Jane stood inside the door and watched him return to his car. Once he'd backed out of the parking space, she rushed out to Cordelia's Mercedes and hopped in. She made sure to stay far enough back so that Kenny wouldn't notice that he was being followed.

"What are we doing?" asked Cordelia, lazily spooning the last of her milkshake into her mouth.

"Following that black car."

"I figured. And why would we do that?"

Jane explained what she'd learned inside the store.

"Let me get this straight. We're tailing Kenny and Emily because Kenny bought bug killer?"

"Pretty much."

"You think he's going to use it to, oh I don't know . . . rob a convenience store?"

"I think he and Emily are mixed up in something illegal." If she had to bet, she'd put her money on marijuana. Growing and selling. If they got lucky, Kenny would lead them straight to his personal greenhouse.

Approximately four miles outside Lost Lake, Kenny slowed and then turned left into a tight opening in the woods. All Jane could see was a dirt trail big enough to accommodate a car going one way. It clearly wasn't an actual road.

She kept on driving.

Making a U-turn half a mile on, she parked a hundred yards or so from the trail, the car hidden behind the branches of a low-hanging pine.

"You scratch the paint, you pay for a new paint job," said Cordelia ominously.

"You're so fussy."

"Probably doesn't help that our car is fire-engine red," she continued, removing a fingernail file from the glove compartment.

Thankfully, thought Jane, the light was fading. "We'll wait here. Shouldn't be long."

"At least this wasn't a high-speed chase. I'm not, strictly speaking, a fan of those."

"Do you have a flashlight?"

"In the trunk."

"Good woman."

"Speaking of good, I can't believe our Emily would step out on poor Jonah. I guess the age of femmes fatales isn't over."

Twenty minutes on, they were still waiting. Jane used the time to fill Cordelia in on what she'd learned from Kelli—about Wendell Hammond, the fire, and the DNA that was found under Feigenbaumer's fingernails.

"What are Emily and Kenny *doing* in there?" demanded Cordelia, filing her nails with growing impatience.

"Spraying bug killer, I would expect. They must have a serious infestation to do it at this time of night."

"What if we've dabbled in this silly skulduggery only to find that he's growing corn? Or that he's planted an apple grove."

Before Jane could answer, she saw the nose of Kenny's car poke out of the trees. His lights were off. Swinging out onto the highway, the lights came on. As he drove past, Jane was glad to see that he wasn't looking in their direction.

"Let's leave your car here and walk in."

"Good thing I'm wearing my Adidas."

Jane retrieved the flashlight from the trunk and led the way across the highway.

Cordelia swatted mosquitos away from her face as they trotted along. "I hope this isn't a wild-goose chase."

"If it is, I'll buy you another milkshake."

"You'll buy me milkshakes for the rest of my life," she puffed. "What's it been? At least five miles?"

They'd barely gone more than a few hundred yards. Coming to a clearing, Jane pointed the flashlight at a wooden shed. "It's locked." She walked over to examine the padlock.

"It smells funny around here," said Cordelia, still swatting mosquitoes. "Let's go back."

Around the rear of the shed Jane discovered four large plastic barrels of what she guessed was rainwater. Lifting the cover off one of them, she found that it was empty. Next to it was a pump action gallon sprayer. Following a dirt track into the brush, she came out into another clearing. There, with leaves sparkling wetly in the dying light, was a small field of marijuana plants.

Stumbling up behind her, Cordelia said, "Ah, the smoking gun."

"Almost literally."

"My kingdom for a match."

"Cute."

"I'd say Kenny and Emily are prime candidates for the rack and the rope."

"They surely would not have wanted this discovered."

"A motive for murder?" asked Cordelia.

"Might be. Was it *the* motive for Lyndie LaVasser and Steve Feigenbaumer's murders? Remains to be seen."

"What kind of bugs did you say were infesting the garden?"

"Spider mites."

Slapping her neck, Cordelia said, "Do they bite?"

"How should I know?"

"Can we leave now?"

"Yes, Cordelia," said Jane, feeling that the investigation was about to crank into high gear. "Now we can go."

Jonah parked the motard in the woods behind the cottage. Once inside, he took the sign down from the door of his room. He'd placed a piece of tape at the top of door so that he'd know if anyone had been inside. The tape was just the way he'd left it. So far so good.

Trudging up the stairs to the first floor, Jonah found Tessa in the kitchen making herself a sandwich. "How's it going?" he asked, sitting down on a stool in front of the island.

"It's going," she said noncommittally. "How about you? You feeling any better?"

"Yeah. It might not be the same thing Jane had."

"You want a roast beef and cheddar sandwich?" she asked. "It would just take me a second to make you one."

"Nah."

"You *must* be sick."

He laughed. "Listen, can I ask you something without you getting mad?"

She seemed hurt by the comment. "Do I do that?"

"Not usually, but, you know, since I've been back, I've been slightly annoying."

"True."

"Except, I've been good yesterday and today. You said the dungeon doors wouldn't open until tomorrow."

"Such a lovely image of our little homestead."

"You know what I mean. I was thinking that you might open them tonight instead of tomorrow morning. I haven't seen Emily in forever."

Tessa cut her sandwich in half. "I'm sure it feels that way to someone your age."

"Wouldn't you miss Jill if you hadn't seen her in days?"

She took a bite and chewed slowly, thinking it over. "I wouldn't implode. Then again, given the right circumstances, maybe I would."

"You two are my role models."

"It's not necessary to lay it on that thick."

"No, it's true." And it was. If his aunts ever broke up, it would feel like the sun falling from the sky. Unlike his parents, who were no good at the relationship thing, Tessa and Jill gave Jonah hope that he could be happy someday, too.

Taking another bite of her sandwich, Tessa leaned on the counter. "So you want to see your girlfriend tonight. I loathe being a jailer. So does Jill."

"Does that mean I can go?"

Drumming her fingers on the counter, she said, "Oh, hell. Sure. Take off. As long as you promise to be home by eleven."

"Word of honor."

"I'm holding you to that, mister," she said, limping out of the kitchen with her plate.

Jill called from the lodge a while later. "Everything okay?"

It was the exact wrong question. "Great," said Tessa.

"I'm going to be a little late."

"No problem."

For the last hour, Tessa had been thinking about making her way out to the shore to sit in the sand and let the waves lap against her one good ankle. It was such a peaceful evening. If only she could draw some of that peace inside her. And yet, with Feigenbaumer's murder shining a light on everyone around him, the authorities would need to be totally incompetent not to figure out who she was. It was only a matter of time before the sheriff, the FBI, or a US Marshal came knocking at her door.

"Just so you know," said Tessa, "I told Jonah he could go see Emily."

"Probably a good idea."

"I figured there was no point in torturing the lad. Young love and all that."

"Don't go to bed before I get there."

"Why? Hey, you want me to dig out our Victoria's Secret duds?"

"If we had any, it would be okay by me."

"Maybe we should get ourselves a catalogue."

"I think not. But I'm not kidding. I'm sick of all this tension between us."

"You're saying we need to spend some *quality* time together?"

"Don't make jokes."

"Honey, I'm not." Tessa's voice turned tender. "I'll see you when you get here."

The only thing that sounded good to Tessa right about now was a glass of wine. She crossed into the kitchen, but stopped when she heard a noise come from the basement. Moving cautiously to the top of the stairs, she called down, "Jonah, is that you?"

The question was met with silence.

She called again, "Jonah? Are you back?"

This time, the sound was more subtle. A kind of scraping. Faint, but unmistakable.

She backed away from the stairs.

Flipping off the overhead light and plunging the room into darkness, she grabbed a flashlight from the island and clicked it on. Shining it down the stairs, she could see now that the door to Jonah's room was open.

"Who's there?" she called, surprised by the trembling in her voice.

The silence was oppressive. Seconds ticked by. Where was her shotgun? If she couldn't find it, she was sure there was a baseball bat in the coat closet. All of a sudden, she heard a crash, a door creak, and a screech as something zipped past her in the darkness. With her heart lodged halfway up her throat, she ducked down behind the island. It took a few more seconds before she screwed up enough courage to turn the flashlight back on. Washing the beam over the living room, she discovered two glowing eyes staring back at her from under one of the end tables.

"What the——" she said, switching the overhead light back on.

A gray-and-white cat sat crouched under the table looking more terrified than she was.

"You nearly gave me a coronary," she said, dropping down on one of the dining room chairs. "Where the hell did you come from?"

On the way to Emily's house, Jonah bought himself a cheeseburger from the Burger Shack. He needed to do some serious thinking and eating helped. By the time he got to her house, he'd searched his soul and had made a decision.

Trotting up the front steps, he found Mrs. Jensen and Mr. Hammond sitting on the porch swing. He did a double take when he saw that they were holding hands.

"Sorry if I'm interrupting," he said, clearing his throat to cover his embarrassment.

"No problem, son," said Mr. Hammond.

"I assume you're looking for Emily," said Mrs. Jensen.

"Um, yeah."

"She's not here, but I expect her back soon. Wendell and I were just about to head over to Ivar's Pizza for a quick bite. If you want, you can wait inside."

"Really? That would be awesome."

Mr. Hammond stood as Mrs. Jensen opened the screen door for Jonah. "Help yourself to a pop. I think there's a new six-pack of Diet Pepsi in the fridge. Maybe a Dr Pepper or two."

"Thanks," said Jonah. He entered the house and stood for a moment in the living room. It was all so familiar—the furniture, the old-fashioned TV, the pink-and-purple afghan draped across the back of the couch. The house always smelled of cinnamon—and something else he could never quite define. Maybe it was the years of wood fires in the fireplace. Or some kind of furniture polish. Whatever it was, it made him feel warm inside.

He ran his fingers along the lace-covered dining room table as he crossed into the kitchen. The light was on over the sink. Several clean glasses sat upside-down in the dish drainer. He wouldn't need one. He could just drink from the can. Popping the top, he pulled out a chair from the kitchen table and sat down. He and Emily had spent many nights here, drinking pop and talking late into the night.

Hearing the front screen creak open and then slam shut, Jonah was instantly furious at the sound of Kenny's voice. Why

261

did he have to be around all the time? All Jonah wanted was a few minutes alone with Emily.

"I'll run upstairs," came Emily's voice. "God, but I'm scared."

"Just do it," said Kenny. "I'll be here when you come down."

Jonah stepped into the kitchen doorway. "Hi," he said, feeling awkward, like he didn't belong.

"Jonah," said Emily, her eyes widening. "What are you doing here?"

"Jesus H. Christ," bellowed Kenny. "Don't you ever give up?"

"What's going on over at Fisherman's Cove?"

Emily eyes widened even more.

"I don't know what you're talking about," said Kenny.

Moving toward Jonah, her hand out, Emily said, "Let me explain."

"You think she's as pure as the driven snow?" said Kenny. "Think again."

"What's that supposed to mean?" asked Jonah.

"Nothing," said Emily.

"Whatever it is, it doesn't matter. I meant what I said the other night, Em. My love for you will never change, no matter what."

"You are such a wuss," muttered Kenny, sitting down on the footstool. "You make my brain hurt."

"I wasn't aware you had a brain," said Jonah. "Do you love me, Em?"

"I never meant to hurt you. I did it because I needed the money. I have to get out of this town before it smothers me."

"Tell me what you did."

"I helped him plant more marijuana last spring."

"And she's helping me sell it," said Kenny, chewing on a nail. "Over at Harris Lake."

Jonah stared at him. "We had a deal. We'd only grow what we could use or what we wanted to give away."

"That was never my plan."

"You promised."

"Oh, grow the hell up. Show him what's in the sack," said Kenny, a cruel smile playing at the corners of his mouth.

Jonah realized now that Emily was hiding something behind her back.

"Whatever it is, I don't need to see it."

"Oh, yes you do," said Kenny, pushing off the footstool. "You gotta take a good look at this." He grabbed the sack away from Emily, rattled it in front of Jonah's face.

"Don't," pleaded Emily, trying to snatch it back. "You said you loved me. If you do, give it back to me."

"Why should I? Romeo needs a reality check. Here." He tossed it at Jonah's chest.

"Don't open it," said Emily.

"Look at it, puke," ordered Kenny. "Unless you didn't really mean that about loving her no matter what."

Jonah parted the top and drew out a rectangular box that said "e.p.t." in black letters.

"It's an early pregnancy test," said Kenny, a sneer in his voice. "In case you can't read the fine print."

Jonah's face flushed.

"Me," shouted Kenny, ramming a thumb into his chest. "If she's pregnant, it's *my* kid."

"I gotta get out of here," he said, pushing past Kenny on his way to the front door.

"See," said Kenny, cackling with glee. "That's what you get, Em, when you hook up with a loser like him."

Jonah plunged outside into the night air, the anarchy of his own emotions nearly cutting off his breath.

"Don't bother coming back," hollered Kenny from the front porch. "Kid or no kid, Emily's mine. You got that? I ain't *never* letting her go."

30

For a Friday night, Thunderhook's lobby was unusually quiet. Jane didn't see a single soul until she approached the reception desk, hoping to talk to Jill. The manager on duty said that she'd gone home and wouldn't be back until morning.

Upstairs in her room, Jane stood for a long time, arms folded, looking out the window, watching the moon spread ribbons of light across the dark water. It was a perfect evening, the cool, liquid air ruffled occasionally by a gentle breeze off the lake. The calmness outside was at perfect odds with what she was feeling inside.

Knocking on the door between the two rooms a while later, Jane heard Cordelia's voice call, "Abandon all hope, ye who enter here."

Jane leaned against the doorframe, neither in nor out. "Are you saying this door represents the gates of hell?"

"No, just that I'm in a lousy mood." She was draped like an Ingres odalisque—one who happened to be dressed in a white terry cloth robe—across the couch, the book she'd been reading spread across her chest. "I suppose Dante *is* a bit severe. How was your walk?"

"Less than fruitful."

Picking up a highly un-odalisque-like can of Izze blackberry soda, Cordelia said, "My last hour was equally dismal. I got the word that the theater board met today and called off the play. Apparently, the ticket presales weren't particularly good, so it was an easy decision."

"You should be happy."

"Then why does the decision depress me? I've never had a show of mine cancelled before."

"It wasn't exactly yours."

"I suppose this means we can leave anytime we want."

"Not yet," said Jane.

"Yeah, we can't go when everything is still so up in the air. On the other hand, I don't know what else you think we're going to find."

Jane dug a Pepsi out of the small refrigerator. Cracking the top, she took a sip and then slipped her cell phone out of the top pocket of her jeans jacket. "I need to call Nolan, see if he's found out anything on Yvonne Stein."

"When you're done, let's go find ourselves a grunge bar and have a serious drink."

"You think we're going to find a grunge bar in Lost Lake?"

"Well, *grungy*, then. The ones I've seen all triumph in that area."

The phone rang a couple of times before Nolan picked up.

"Hey, I figured I might hear from you tonight," came his deep voice. "I have some info for you. You got a piece of paper?"

Jane removed a pad and pen from one of the pockets in her jeans jacket. "Shoot."

"Yvonne Stein served thirty-six years and seven months in

prison. The fact that she wasn't sentenced to life without parole was a miracle. The decision was made by a judge back in sixty-nine who sympathized with her cause."

"Cause?"

"The antiwar movement. What happened at the Democratic convention in Chicago in sixty-eight created a backlash. Some people thought the Chicago police stepped way over the line. Anyway, once she was out she dropped out of sight. I've been trying to chase her down ever since you called. Finally found a phone number in Bellingham, Washington, that I think might be her." He repeated the number. "Don't expect too much," he continued. "If it is her, she may not want to talk. For multiple reasons."

"I'll keep my fingers crossed," said Jane. "It's two hours earlier on the West Coast. Think I'll try her right now."

"Good luck. Will I see you soon?"

"That's the plan. I'll call before I leave. Night."

"He found her?" asked Cordelia, getting up to dig out another Izze's.

"Possibly. If you're interested, we could use the cordless to call her." She pointed to the one on the nightstand. "It has a better speakerphone than my cell. That way you could hear, too."

Cordelia retrieved it on the way back to the couch.

The line seemed to ring forever. Jane was about to give up when a low, soft voice answered, "Hello?"

"Yvonne Stein?"

"Who wants to know?"

"My name is Jane Lawless. I'm phoning from Minnesota."

"I don't talk to strangers."

Before Yvonne could hang up, she said, "I'm a friend of Sabra Briere."

The line went silent for nearly half a minute. Jane was sure she'd lost her.

Then, "What is this? How do you know Sabra?"

Tessa was lying in bed watching TV when Jill came in. Muting the sound she said, "You missed the excitement."

All the color drained from Jill's face. "What excitement?"

"Oh, honey, no, I didn't mean to scare you. Look." Tessa nodded to the gray-and-white cat curled at the end of the bed.

"Is that Freckles?"

"He was in Jonah's room. Scared the daylights out of me. Jonah probably thought he was a stray and brought him home. Except he didn't tell us." Their nephew was notorious for rescuing everything from injured chipmunks to lost pit bulls.

"Poor Mrs. Atkinson," said Jill. "We'll have to call her right away and tell her he's here."

The cat had burrowed into the cotton blankets, with no apparent interest in leaving.

Hearing the back door open and shut, Tessa called, "Jonah?"

"Yeah," came a glum voice.

"Come in here and get this cat," called Jill.

He stepped into the doorway. "Oh. Forgot to tell you about him. Sorry."

"He belongs to Betty Atkinson," said Tessa. "You know where she lives, right?"

Jonah dragged himself into the room.

"You okay?" asked Jill.

"Yeah."

"You don't sound okay," said Tessa.

He shrugged. "I've had better days. Gonna hit the sack."

"Take him over to Mrs. Atkinson first," said Jill.

"Right now? Can't I do it in the morning?"

"She's probably worried sick," said Tessa.

Without another word, Jonah picked him up and walked out of the room, shoulders drooping.

"Sweet dreams," called Tessa. She waited until she heard his footsteps recede down the stairs and then said, "Young love, I suspect."

"Was it really that hard?"

"It's always hard, young or old."

"Thanks for the compliment."

"You know what I mean."

"I need to shower," said Jill, unbuttoning her blouse. "Don't move until I get back."

For the next few minutes, Tessa watched the Duluth news. By the time the sports came on, Jill was in bed, under the covers.

"I'm taking tomorrow off," she said. "I want us to spend the entire day together."

"But it's Saturday. Your busiest day."

"You're more important."

Tessa felt for the remote under the covers and switched off the TV. "You know how long we've been together?"

"Twenty-six years," said Jill, snuggling down next to her.

"Twenty-six years, four months, and thirteen days. I'm grateful for every every hour, every minute. I wouldn't trade them for anything on earth."

They turned toward each other, arms entwined.

When they were close like this, all the tension in Tessa's muscles seemed to liquify. "I love you," she said, kissing her way from Jill's forehead to her lips. "You know that, don't you? I work with words every day, and yet I can't begin to express what's in my heart."

"I know," whispered Jill. "It's too deep."

The phone on the nightstand rang.

"Oh, Lord," groaned Jill. "I hate that thing. I wish we could throw them all away."

"And go back to carrier pigeons? Drums? We better answer it." Tessa disengaged her arm and reached over. "Yes?" she said, knowing that she sounded anything but friendly.

"Sabra?" came a whispered voice.

"Oh, Jesus. Who is this?"

"I know who you are. I have proof."

She dropped her head back and closed her eyes. "Who doesn't, these days?"

"What?"

"What do you want?"

"Fifty thousand dollars in small bills. By tomorrow afternoon."

She all but burst out laughing. "How am I supposed to accomplish that?"

"Well, ah . . . you could go to the bank?"

"Are you kidding me?"

"Okay, I'll give you until Monday. But I'm not joking If I turn what I have over to the FBI, you'll go to jail."

That sobered her. "You might have to stand in line."

"Say that again?"

"Call me on Monday. I'll see what I can do." She pressed the off button before the caller could say another word. She was sick to death of the entire subject.

"Who was that?" asked Jill.

"Nobody important."

"Are you sure?"

"I'm absolutely, one hundred percent positive," she said,

easing her arms around the woman she loved. "Now. Where were we?"

"How do I know you're not lying to me?" said Yvonne. "You could be anyone."

"I could, I suppose," conceded Jane. "But I'm not. Sabra and I have been friends for years. She's a playwright. Lives in a small town in northern Minnesota. My partner and I used to visit her quite often."

"You're gay?"

"Yes."

"Back up a minute. What did you say your name was?"

"Jane."

"Last name."

"Lawless."

"Huh. There was a guy who ran for the governor of Minnesota a few years back named Lawless."

"That was my father."

"Are you kidding me? I'm a total political junkie. I followed that race because of his stand on gay marriage. I read an interview his daughter did with one of the local papers. She owns a restaurant."

"Two," said Jane.

"My God, it's a small world. You're a friend of Sabra's?"

"She calls herself Tessa Cornell now."

"I had no way of finding her, no way to contact her. Is she okay? Healthy? Happy?"

"Yes on the first. As for happy, I'm not sure that's ever been part of her personality."

"Yeah, even back when I knew her. This is amazing, you calling out of the blue."

"It's not entirely out of the blue," said Jane. "I was hoping you could help me with something."

"Like what?" Her tone grew wary.

"I never knew about Tessa's past until last Monday, when a woman you know as Judy Clark was murdered."

"Murdered," she said, her voice hushed.

"I'm sorry."

"How did it happen?" asked Yvonne.

"She was attacked. Her throat was partially crushed and she had severe trauma to the back of her head."

"Who did it?"

"Nobody knows. A man named Steve Feigenbaumer had come to talk to both Judy and Sabra last week. In case you're wondering, he's the son of Allen James Feigenbaumer, the man you helped kill in nineteen sixty-eight."

"Shit."

"He'd been searching for Sabra and Judy most of his adult life. Two nights ago, he was found murdered. The gun used in the homicide belonged to Tessa. I mean Sabra."

"Has she been arrested?"

"Not yet. She'd lent the gun to Judy, so it was no longer in her possession on the night of the murder. But it's dicey. She's scared. So am I. Her partner asked me to help prove her innocence. In case you're wondering, I sometimes work as a PI."

"She's *with* someone?"

Jane figured this might be a touchy subject, and yet there was no way around it. "She has been for many years."

"Good. I wanted her to move on."

"You're not angry that she got away and you didn't?"

"Not for a second. I knew what I was getting into. I did it with my eyes wide open."

"I realize it must be hard for you to talk about," said Jane. "But I was hoping you could fill me in on what happened all those years ago. It might help me find the truth."

"I'm not sure how it could." She paused, apparently thinking it over. "Sabra's not a violent person, you know. Anything but."

"And yet the three of you planted a car bomb."

The sound of paper rattling and the strike of a match drifted over the speakerphone. "There," she said, "that's better. I'm a slave to these things. Can't talk without one in my hand."

Jane waited another second, and then said, "I was told the death of Allen Feigenbaumer had something to do with the antiwar movement."

"I can give you the quick down and dirty on what happened, but to really understand, I need to explain a few things first. You interested?"

"Not only am I interested," said Jane, "I'm grateful that you'd take the time."

Cordelia scooted over closer to the phone.

"Where to start. Well . . . first, I guess, you should know that Sabra and I met at an SDS meeting in Chicago in the fall of sixty-seven. We'd both been part of the civil rights movement for years, both been involved in demonstrations. I'd been arrested once. I was a couple of years older and had taken part in Freedom Summer in Mississippi in sixty-four. I worked to get African Americans registered to vote. Sabra was doing stories for an underground newspaper in Chicago by the beginning of sixty-six—the *Radical Beat*. We went out for coffee after the SDS meeting that first night. Back then, nobody was out. You think of the sixties as being sexually liberated. I suppose it was—but *heterosexually* liberated. It took Sabra and me a while to tell each other the truth. By the time we did, we were already in love. We had to hide though, even from our friends.

"Sabra had a younger brother—Jeff. He wasn't all that politically active before he entered college, although once he got there, looked around him and started to see what was happening in the world, his ideas changed. I talked to him a lot, tried my damnedest to radicalize him. After all, *his* life was on the line. He was the one who had a draft card. He began to get noticed in the ranks because he was a good speaker. He had this gentle kind of charisma that drew people to him. He was a great guy. Believe me when I tell you that he never wanted in the girlfriend department. When Judy came along, though, he fell hard. She was pretty, I guess. Knew how to get a guy's attention. She was nowhere near as political as we were. Judy was always more interested in the 'sex, drugs and rock 'n' roll' angle and in partying hard. Did she ever change?"

"I never knew her all that well. But she was married four times."

Yvonne hooted. "Doesn't surprise me. Anyway, Sabra was doing grad work at Loyola when Jeff and Judy were undergrads. I'd quit college after my first year. Just wasn't cut out for it. There was too much grassroots work to do. The fall I met Sabra I was making ends meet by working as a part-time waitress and part-time bookkeeper. We moved in together in December of sixty-seven. Honestly, I'd never been happier.

"It all came to a head in Chicago during the Democratic National Convention in August of sixty-eight. Most of the major antiwar groups were there. So were people like Allen Ginsberg and Jean Genet. We had big plans. We tried to get a permit to demonstrate in Lincoln Park, but the city denied it. They officially closed the park, and when we wouldn't leave, that's when all hell broke loose. Tear gas— and billy club—wielding pigs descended on us in droves. It was brutal, like nothing I'd ever seen before, not even in the South. Kind of changes your opinion of how power works in this country when you're in the middle of something like that. Anyway, there was this one blue-shirted Chicago cop who seemed to really be into it. He was an absolute wild man. I can still see his eyes. He came close to clubbing Sabra that day, but she ducked at just the right moment. I think Jeff was stunned by the level of violence. I remember him just standing there while others were running and shouting all around him. I think, deep down, he still believed that cops were the good guys.

"The worst day that week was Wednesday. Some people called it the Battle of Michigan Avenue. A lot of it was recorded on tape, so if you want to see it for yourself, you can find it on the Internet. Of course, you can't smell the tear gas or the terrified sweat—or feel the fear in the air. It was adrenaline-fueled rage alternating with terror, as close to pure hell as I ever want to get. We planned to march to the Convention Center. God, but I hated Johnson and his puppet, Humphrey. At some point, the cops simply went apeshit. They moved on in, started beating everyone in sight. Innocent bystanders were hurt. So were newsmen who were just there to cover the story. Their tear gas and our stink bombs got so thick that it started to drift into some of the hotels.

"That was the day it happened. Back then, the government kept trotting out this thing called the domino effect. If Vietnam went Communist, so would the rest of Southeast Asia. What happened to us was a more personal kind of domino effect. The cop we'd seen in Lincoln Park happened to be in the group that attacked us on Wednesday. Sabra, Judy, and I screamed that he was a pig, a fascist, a baby killer. He came at us with his billy club raised. Jeff saw what he was about to do and stepped in front of us. Judy ran off just as the cop began to whale on Jeff. I hopped on the guy's back, tried to make him stop, but some other cops grabbed Sabra and me and slammed us to the ground. By the time we got back to Jeff, he was out cold. We dragged him into an alley and tried to get him to wake up. The back of his head was bloody and he had scrapes and cuts all over his face and arms.

"We were finally able to lift him up and help him back to his apartment—he lived with two other guys, none of whom were home. We stripped off his clothes and tried our best, which wasn't all that good, to doctor his wounds. Thank God, nothing was broken. He was black-and-blue from head to toe. One of his knees had swelled up pretty badly. Sabra went to buy aspirin and vodka while I got him settled on the couch. We spent the rest of the day watching the news on TV. Jeff slept on and off. He'd wake up and watch for a while, then he'd drift off. We figured he was in shock. Looking back, we should have taken him to a hospital, but at the time we didn't have a dime to our names and we were afraid that if they asked how he'd been hurt, that we'd get arrested. Paranoia reigned.

"That was August. By late September, the change in Jeff was so apparent, nobody could miss it. He wasn't upbeat anymore. His gentleness had disappeared. I don't know how to say it except that he was a different guy—moody and depressed most of the time. He and Judy fought like crazy, although I'll give her this much. She hung in with him. There were days when he wouldn't even get out of bed.

"By mid-October, he'd begun locking himself in his bedroom and refusing to come out. He'd stopped bathing. Stopped going to classes. The guys he lived with tried to look the other way, but they eventually got sick of it and threw him out. He couldn't live with Judy because she had three roommates. Since he had nowhere else to go, he came to live with us. That's when the rages began. We never knew what would set him off. He'd just lose it, start throwing things, accusing us of shit we hadn't done. We kept telling him that he had to go see a counselor at Loyola. I finally extracted a promise that he'd go. He actually made the appointment, which surprised the hell out of me.

"Sabra was planning to drive him. The appointment was on a Friday afternoon. That morning, Sabra and I went shopping. We bought him a new sweater, a new pair of jeans, several new shirts, new socks, and a new belt. We climbed the four flights up to our apartment carrying the packages, feeling more hopeful than we had in months. When we came into the living room, we called for Jeff to come and look at all his presents. He didn't come, so we went looking for him.

"He wasn't in his room. His billfold was on his dresser, so we knew he hadn't gone out. We followed a cold draft into our bedroom. The window was open. I stuck my head out to look around and saw Jeff's body lying on top of a Dumpster four stories below. Sabra ran out of the room and got to him first. She was screaming that he was dead, that his neck was broken, when I made it down. I tried to cradle her in my arms, but she pushed me away. It was the single most horrible moment of my life.

"From that day on, Sabra and I had one goal. We intended to kill the cop who killed Jeff. I didn't know much about brain injuries. I read up on them while I was inside. The kind of injury Jeff sustained can change a person's entire personality. We had no idea he was suicidal, although after he was gone, we discovered a journal that he'd been keeping. He'd been thinking about little else for nearly a month. I'd never considered myself a violent person before. And yet it was all around us—part of the air we were breathing. Sabra and I didn't immediately tell Judy what we intended to do. Against our better judgement, we eventually did. She said she wanted in.

"I put out some feelers, finally found a guy who showed me how to make a bomb I could attach to the underside of a car. It would blow when the engine caught. You know the rest." She paused, drawing in her breath. "If you were to ask me if I could go back and change what I'd done, would I? The answer is yes. I'm an old woman now and I've learned that violence only begets more violence. But nobody could have convinced me of that back then. I believed what I was doing was right. I hated our government, still do for that matter. I hated the police and everything they stood for. In the end, of course, it wasn't worth it. I wasted my whole life on a principle I don't even believe in anymore. Revenge was intoxicating. So was the camaraderie, the sense that we were in a righteous war, good verses evil. And yet, I always remember that famous line. Gandhi said it: 'An eye for an eye makes the whole world blind.'"

31

Tessa woke the next morning to find Jill sitting on the bed fully dressed. "I didn't hear you leave," she said, clearing her throat. She turned over and smiled, thoughts of their lovemaking still fresh in her memory

"I couldn't sleep. I got up around two, went up to the loft to watch some TV. That's when I found this." She waited until Tessa was looking at her and then held up the black journal.

Tessa felt suddenly light-headed. "You found that . . . where?"

"In the loft. I dropped my glasses. When I bent over to pick them up, I saw it under the couch."

She didn't want to ask the next logical question, and yet there was no way around it. "Did you read it?"

"Most of it."

Shutting her eyes, Tessa placed the heels of her hands against her forehead. "I never wanted you to know any of that. God, what you must think of me." Words, once again, failed. The next thing she said simply fell out of her mouth without conscious volition. "Do you hate me?"

"Hate you?"

"For what I did?"

Jill reached for her hand. "I can't imagine what it must have been like for you, keeping this to yourself all these years."

"It was hell. But it would have been equally hellish to talk about it."

"I've always known there was something in your past that was eating at you. I thought maybe you'd been molested—or raped. I couldn't imagine why you wouldn't talk to me about it. Now I understand."

"I'm so ashamed."

"You did a terrible thing, something I never would have believed you were capable of. But that's my naïveté talking. Maybe I *am* a backcountry yokel."

"Never," said Tessa.

Jill got up and began rummaging around in the closet. She took down two of Tessa's suitcases from the top shelf and spread them open across the bottom of the bed.

"What are you doing?"

"You can't stay here. It's all going to come out. We both know that. If you stay, you'll be arrested. It might not be tomorrow, but it will come." She opened the dresser drawers and began packing up clothes. "You have to run. You did it before, you can do it again."

"But what about you?"

"I'm coming with you."

"No."

Jill's head snapped up.

"If I get stopped, you'd go to jail right alongside me. I couldn't live with that. If I go, I go alone."

Jill stared at her, her eyes filling with tears. "I'm willing to risk it."

"I'm not."

Sitting down on the edge of the bed, Jill burst out crying.

"Oh, honey, don't. When I first realized I was in love with you, I should have called it off. You deserved so much better."

"Shut up." She scraped the tears away from of her eyes.

"The night Feigenbaumer died, I did make a run for it. Fontaine happened to see me drive past the community center. He followed my Volvo in his truck. Once we got out on the highway, he laid on his horn until I stopped. I was in terrible shape. He wouldn't let me get back in the car until we'd talked things through and I'd calmed down. He offered to go with me. Said we could ditch my car somewhere, that he'd protect me, he'd get a job somewhere to support us. I almost took him up on it."

"You should have gone."

She shook her head. "I never expected that Jane would notice that my car had been driven that night. I'm sure she concluded that I'd had something to do with Feigenbaumer's murder. I wasn't home half an hour when she and Cordelia arrived to give me the news."

"She loves you, Tessa. That's why I asked her to help clear your name."

"She may love me, but she knows I've been lying. Who knows what she's told Kelli?"

"That's why you've got to leave." Without looking up, Jill returned to packing.

"I can't."

"You have to." She went to the closet and took down several sweaters from the middle shelf.

"I don't have any money."

"I went to the bank this morning, took out five thousand dollars from our joint savings."

"That won't last long."

"I realize that. You won't be able to use your credit cards or your cell phone. You'll have to figure out how to buy yourself a new identity. I doubt it's all that hard, especially if you head to the Twin Cities. I'll see what I can find out on my end."

"If I leave, I can't chance contacting you right away."

With her back to Tessa, Jill said, "Well, not for a while. You can get one of those no-name cell phones."

"You'll be watched. If we connect, they'll find out. I can't let that happen."

"Things will calm down," said Jill, crouching down to paw through Tessa's shoes.

"Jill, look at me."

"Just let me finish this."

"Stop and look at me."

Slowly, Jill turned around.

"If I go, we will never see each other again. It's the only way you'd be safe from potential prosecution. If you don't agree to those terms, I'm staying put."

"Do you *want* to go to prison?"

Tessa was terrified by the very thought. Almost as terrified as she was of leaving Jill. "Do you agree?"

"I need to get you more money. I'll figure something out and meet you later today. Say, Hill City. At the gazebo in Bear Park. Four o'clock. That will give us a few more minutes together."

Tessa could see by the look of strained resignation in Jill's eyes that she finally comprehended the full meaning of what she was suggesting.

"You really want me to go?"

"I don't want you to go anywhere. I want you to stay with

me until I breathe my last breath, but that's not in the cards. You *have* to go."

"Come here," said Tessa.

"You need to get out of here. We don't have a minute to waste."

"I'm willing to bet my life that we can waste a few."

Jonah crawled out from under his covers and sat up on the edge of his bed. His room was a perfect reflection of his psyche—a disaster. His clothes were strewn all over the room, which made him think of Kenny's basement lair. Jonah didn't much like the comparison. He vowed to clean the room up—although, not right now. He held his head in his hands for a few seconds, praying that the banging would stop and knowing it probably wouldn't. He'd stayed up late feeling sorry for himself while he finished off the bottle of Jager Kenny had given him. The hangover was bad enough, but the emotional battle inside him was even worse. How could Emily have fooled him so royally? How could she fall in love with a loser like Kenny?

Jonah pulled on a pair of jeans and slipped into a navy blue T-shirt. Under other circumstances, he wouldn't have been up before noon, except that someone had been banging around in the garage a while ago, which woke him. Even with a hangover, his stomach started to growl right on schedule. He was a machine, he thought, gazing at himself in the mirror over the dresser, running his hand over his scraggly beard. Not exactly the visage of a superhero. If he put food in his tank, he might feel better.

Staggering upstairs to grab himself a bowl of cereal, he heard sobbing. He'd figured that it was Jill who'd left the house, and yet when he entered the bedroom, he found her making the bed and crying.

"What's wrong?" he asked, stopping in the doorway.

"Nothing," she said, not looking at him.

"*Nothing* doesn't make you cry. Where's Tessa?"

"She had a doctor's appointment. Won't be home until later."

Something was wrong with this picture. "Everything okay with you two?"

She scraped the tears off her cheeks. "We're fine."

He decided to pick door number 2. "Something happen with the murder investigation?"

She shook her head. "Sometimes I just get sad."

"For no reason?"

"Cosmically sad. You've never felt that way?"

Maybe it was a woman thing. "Nope. I'm usually sad for a reason." He turned when he heard the front doorbell. "Should I get it?"

"Sure," said Jill, dabbing at her face with a tissue. "I'll be out in a sec."

Jonah found a man in a black suit standing on the deck. "Help you?" he asked.

"I'm looking for Tessa Cornell."

"Not here."

Jill appeared behind him.

"I'm Agent Eric Haas." The man held up a photo ID with a badge next to it.

"You're FBI?" asked Jonah.

He repeated, "I'm looking for Tessa Cornell. I understand she's not home. Any idea where I could find her?"

"No," said Jill. "Sorry. Is there a message?"

"Are you her sister?"

"Wife," said Jill.

That caused his eyebrows to rise.

"We were married in Thunder Bay four years ago."

"When do you expect her back?"

"Honestly, I don't know. She has a varied schedule. Can I ask what this is about?"

He handed her his card. "Tell her I'll be back."

That was ominous, thought Jonah. He closed the door and locked it and then turned around to find Jill standing in the living room, hands on the back of a chair, looking out the windows.

"You know," said Jonah, "I don't want to tell you and Tessa what to do, but maybe it's time for her to get out of Dodge."

Jill burst into tears.

Was that it? "Has she left?"

She nodded.

Jonah put his arms around her and let her cry against his shoulder. "You really love her, don't you."

"So much it hurts."

Tessa had been involved in a bombing and yet Jill still loved her. It made him feel puny, as if his love for Emily was somehow less worthy. He'd said it was deep and real, and yet when push came to shove, he'd bailed on her. He made a decision right then.

"What can I do?" asked Jonah. "You want some breakfast?"

"I can't eat."

"No. Bad idea. Some tea, maybe?"

She tried to smile as she caressed his hair. "I'll be okay, especially now that I know she's safe. You go on. I'm sure you've got things you want to do today."

"It'll work out."

"Sure it will."

"You need anything, you've got my cell number."

"Just so you know, she wanted to say good-bye to you."

"It's okay. I'll see her soon enough, right?"

Jonah ignored his stomach—something he never did—and rushed into the woods behind the cottage. Hopping on Kenny's bike, which he'd hidden under some brambles and brush, he hauled ass over to Emily's house, all the way rehearsing in his mind what he would say. It didn't matter about the stuff she'd been involved in over at Harris Lake. As far as the pregnancy, they'd figure it out. He was sure that if he told her that none of it mattered to him, that he loved her and always would, that she'd come back to him.

Sailing into the driveway beside the house, Jonah saw Emily's mom in the backyard hanging out the wash. "Hey, Mrs. Jensen," he called. Leaping off the bike, he pushed through the gate. "Is Emily here?"

Mrs. Jensen glanced around, a confused look on her face. "Am I missing something? She's on the bus. You know that, right?"

There were no buses in Lost Lake.

"On the Greyhound—on her way to the Cities."

"Oh, well, ah—" he stammered, feeling a burst of panic overwhelm him. "Yeah, right."

"She said you were meeting her down at the Conoco station to say a final good-bye. That's why she wouldn't let me come."

"I . . . I guess I got the times screwed up. Damn. What time did the bus leave?"

"Ten-fifty. Oh, honey, if you didn't make it, she's surely going to be upset."

"Upset, yeah," he said, knowing he sounded like an idiot. "Just out of curiosity, did she say anything about Kenny?"

"Kenny Moon? No. Why would she?"

"No reason." He turned and dashed back to the bike, calling, "Don't worry. I'll make everything right."

32

While Jane and Cordelia finished up a late breakfast at the Jacaranda Café, Jane felt her cell phone vibrate inside her jacket pocket.

"It's Kelli," came the now familiar voice. "I thought you'd like to know we caught a break in the case."

Jane flashed her eyes at Cordelia and mouthed Kelli's name. "Can you tell me more?"

"I got a call from a friend down at the BCA in St. Paul. They matched the DNA they found on the sock-wick that was used to torch Wendell's business with DNA found under Feigenbaumer's fingernails. The same person is responsible for both."

"Wendell."

"We'll need to get a sample of his DNA to put the dot at the end of the sentence, but yeah, I think we've got our man."

"What was the motive?"

"For the fire? That's obvious. Money. As for Feigenbaumer and Lyndie LaVasser, I'm not sure. We've got some evidence we intend to present him with. There's a connection."

"Still, you have to admit it's kind of strange that he'd hide the murder weapon in his own locker."

"It was a clever ploy. To plant the murder weapon in your own locker to make it look as if someone was framing you for a homicide seems way too clever and convoluted for him."

"It's possible he never thought anyone would find it."

"That seems more like Wendell."

"So if he did it, that lets Tessa off the hook."

"For the murders in Lost Lake, yeah. I thought you'd want to know."

"I appreciate the call. Have you phoned Tessa or Jill yet?"

"I can't really talk to them until I've got all my ducks in a row. You understand. There was another break in the case last night. I'll tell you more when I can."

"Of course."

"Gotta run."

Jane would have explained about the field of marijuana they'd found, but Kelli seemed to be in a hurry. She could tell her later. It wasn't going anywhere.

While Cordelia finished off her last Bloody Mary, Jane relayed the details of the phone call.

"If Tessa can just keep a lid on her past, she might make it through," said Cordelia, removing the white paper napkin from her cleavage and tossing it over the dregs of her breakfast.

Which begged the question of whether she should or not. Jane still felt queasy when she thought about what Tessa had done, even now, when she understood the reason. Still, she didn't want to see her go to jail.

As they made their way through the humid summer morning to the cottage, Jonah came rushing out of the woods, yelling and waving.

"Jane, stop. Cordelia? Will you help me? Please!" By the time he reached them, he was out of breath.

"What's up?" asked Jane, putting a hand on his shoulder to steady him.

"Emily. She left on the bus. I *have* to talk to her. It's life or death. I've called her cell twenty times in the last few minutes, but she won't answer."

"How are we supposed to help with that?" asked Cordelia, chewing on a toothpick, clearly not impressed by the "life or death" aspect of his plea.

"You've got a car. If we leave now, we can catch the bus. They have a little less than an hour's head start. I went over to the Conoco station, where the bus pulls in. A guy there told me it stops in Balsam and Empire, then heads down to Congress and Mobridge, and comes into Grand Rapids on Highway Two. All those stops will slow it down. I have to tell her that I love her. If I do, maybe she won't go. Will you do it? I can drive if you want."

"Wait just a minute there, buddy," said Cordelia. "It's my car. Nobody drives it but me."

His body quivering with nervous energy, Jonah tugged on her arm. "We don't have a minute to waste."

"I've had three Bloody Marys. I am in no shape to get behind the wheel."

"Why did Emily leave?" asked Jane. She figured she already had the facts on that one, but wanted know what Jonah knew.

"She had her reasons."

"Like?"

"Well, for one, she said that Lost Lake was smothering her, that she had to get out. I *have* to talk to her."

Lucky for him, Jane wanted to talk to Emily, too. "Cordelia, you can't stand in the way of true love."

"Oh, hell," she said, stifling a burp. "I'm sober enough to ride shotgun."

Unlike Jill, Tessa had never been much of a weeper. Not even at Jeff's funeral. When family and friends stood in a tear-soaked trance by the grave, she'd watched it all dry-eyed. Once upon a time it had made her feel strong. Over the years she'd come to understand that her inability to cry wasn't a strength, but a curse.

The waitress stopped at her table again to refill her coffee mug. "How were the hotcakes?"

"Okay." They were, in fact, underdone and tasteless.

"And the eggs and sausage?"

"It was all fine."

Tessa had done a lot of traveling in her life. In her opinion, breakfast was the hardest meal to completely ruin. Sure, ordering hotcakes had been a bit on the chancy side. It was the promise of maple syrup that finally seduced her, although when it came, it wasn't warm, as it said it would be on the menu, and it wasn't pure maple syrup, it was maple-flavored syrup. In her mind, the difference was a chasm. She never ordered scrambled eggs in a dump like this because they usually came homogenized and were poured directly on the griddle from a plastic bag. If you ordered two eggs over medium, at least you got the real thing. Sausage was sausage. What else could you say.

"Honey, you're sure you don't want something else?"

Tessa had been driving for less than an hour when she'd stopped at the Village Bookstore in Grand Rapids to find herself something to read. Being without a good book was like cutting off one of her five senses. She'd ended up buying an entire stack. She'd tossed in a couple of maps and a magazine and before she knew what was happening, the man behind the counter had asked her for one hundred seventy-two dollars and sixty-eight cents. She paid for it out of the cash Jill had given her. At this rate, it would be gone in a matter of days.

"Honey? Did you hear me? Want something else?"

"No," said Tessa. "And don't call me honey."

The woman glared down at her. "Aren't you a charmer."

"That's me." Once insulted, a waitress rarely returned. That's what Tessa wanted. She had no interest in pursing useless chit-chat. She'd leave the woman a good tip when she left. All would be forgiven.

Tessa wanted to think. For starters, she was skeptical about the entire concept of redemption. What were the redemptive avenues open to her? She supposed she could live a good life. She'd done that, as much as humanly possible. Her plays always dealt with moral issues, with people who had to make hard ethical choices. She liked to create the characters, put them up on a stage, and watch them behave. That was the fascinating part of writing—never knowing how it would end. Being a playwright, however, wouldn't get her very far up the redemption ladder.

The only other approved redemptive option she could think of was the church. She supposed she could ask God to forgive her. Maybe talk to a priest and receive absolution. The fact that she wasn't a Catholic might mitigate against that one. No, God wasn't the answer, mainly because the sort of God she'd been taught about since birth made no sense to her. She would gladly seek any pardon on offer, and yet it seemed rather devoid of integrity to seek something you didn't actually believe in.

An empty future loomed in front of her, a future that would erase everything that had once been good in her life. How was a sixty-five-year-old woman supposed to support herself? She would have *some* money, so theoretically, she could drive to a town, rent an apartment . . . and then what? What skills did she have?

She could type. Big deal. She could cook, although standing on her feet all day wouldn't work under the best of conditions because of the arthritis in her knees, hips, shoulders, and hands. That likely meant no well-paid construction jobs in her future. Ha ha. She supposed she could offer herself as a dramaturge at some regional theater. Except that her face was too well-known among theater folk. Scratch that. What was left? She might be able to sell an organ or two. A kidney? Wasn't life a grand adventure?

What if she couldn't find a job? That was certainly a most pressing issue. So was friendship. Did she have the energy to make new ones? A phone call with a throwaway cell phone every now and then wasn't much to hold on to. This time, there would be no angels like Jill to come along and save her.

Dropping her head against her hand, Tessa's thoughts turned to Fontaine. He'd been such a good friend. She wished now that she'd taken him up on his offer. With him along for the ride, she would've had someone to talk to—someone who might have found a job so that they could live a seminormal life. And yet, what made her think that she deserved such a sacrifice? She would be asking Fontaine to give up his life in Lost Lake and devote himself to her. Tessa's reasons for not wanting Jill to come along all revolved around getting caught. The same would be true for Fontaine. How could she even *think* of putting him in that kind of danger? It reminded her again that there was nothing like the self-centeredness of those in pain.

Checking her watch, she saw that she had three hours to spend before her meeting with Jill at Bear Park. Three whole hours. If that small amount of time seemed endless, how was she ever going to figure out what to do with the rest of her life?

Tapping the pockets of her fishing vest—she always wore one when she traveled—looking for some cash, she found an envelope instead. She'd picked it out of the morning mail before she left the cottage and then forgotten about it. It was addressed to Tessa Cornell in a crabbed hand, with no return address. The postmark was Urbana, IL.

Ripping open the top, Tessa lifted out a sheet of typing paper that had been folded into thirds. Inside was a note:

Dear Sabra Briere:

I'll get right to the point. You murdered my dad and my grandfather and you're still walking around a free woman. I want you to know that you're not going to get away with what you did. My dad may have failed in his mission to bring you to justice, but I won't. You might be out for a walk, or maybe on your way to your car some night. You won't see me or hear me. But you'll hear a click and it will be over. I don't care what this costs me, it has to be done. Honestly, I don't understand how you live with yourself. You must be a monster. You deserve so much worse than a quick death. With everything in me, I hate you and pray that God in His wisdom will provide you with the suffering I can't.

Alissa Feigenbaumer

Tessa let go of the note and watched it flutter to the table top. How did it end? How was it ever going to stop?

"With me," she whispered, sitting back in her chair with a sense of finality. "Right here. Right now."

33

Jane steered the Mercedes around a bend in the highway, hitting the dirt shoulder and kicking up a cloud of dust.

"Slow down," called Cordelia, her hands pressed against the dashboard. "I sympathize with Jonah's plight, but I don't want these to be my last moments on earth."

"No, go faster," cried Jonah from the backseat. "We're making good time."

"I feel the need for speed," said Jane, taking another curve too fast.

"I feel shaken, not stirred," said Cordelia. "If you put one tiny scratch in this car, you're history."

Jane dropped the speed to seventy.

"That's better."

They'd been on the road for exactly forty-one minutes. Jane knew because Jonah kept orally ticking off the time. In Congress, the last stop before Grand Rapids, the man at the Holiday station, where the bus pulled in, said that it had left five minutes ago. "Knowing that we're not more than a few minutes behind," said Cordelia, brushing her hair back from her face, "I don't understand why we need to pretend we're practicing for the Indy five hundred. I feel like I'm in a wind tunnel. We should have put the top up."

"Not enough time," shouted Jonah.

As they came around another bend in the road, a man on a motorcycle zoomed around them.

"No," cried Jonah, raising his arms.

"That's Kenny, right?" called Jane, the wind battering her ears.

"He's doing the same thing we are. Chasing Emily."

"Will there be others?" called Cordelia, her voice dripping sarcasm.

The back of the bus suddenly came into view. Kenny swerved into the passing lane and roared up to the front, thrusting his fist in the air and shouting something at the driver.

"He's going to get himself killed," called Cordelia.

"Couldn't happen to a nicer guy," yelled Jonah.

Emily had chosen the seat directly behind the bus driver when she got on in Lost Lake. She'd cried all the way to Empire and still felt as if she could burst into tears any second. She had wanted to leave, to make a new life for herself, but never under these conditions. She was running for her life. If she stayed in Lost Lake, she would be arrested for sure. What she needed to do was find somewhere safe, hunker down and disappear. Kenny would be angry when he found out that she'd left without talking to him. She was done arguing with him. She could never care about him the way he wanted. With every passing day he was becoming more possessive, which was why she wasn't sure how much she could trust him. Kenny had promised that he would keep his mouth shut, that if push came to shove he'd take the fall and make sure her name was kept out of it, and yet if she crossed him, if she refused his love, he could easily flip, get angry, and take it out on her. No, the only choice left was to leave quietly and never look back.

Thankfully, no one had taken the seat next to her on the bus, so her meltdown had been more-or-less private. She could see the bus driver's eyes in the mirror above his head. She'd caught him looking at her a couple of times. Not much she could do about that.

She planned to write Jonah and try to explain. Someday. Not anytime soon. Part of the problem was that she didn't entirely understand why she'd done what she'd done herself. She'd given up hope of ever being with him again. Her pregnancy—the test had shown that she was indeed pregnant—was one mistake too many.

"What the hell?" called the bus driver. "Is that guy crazy?"

Emily turned and looked out the window. She sat up straight when she realized the man on the motorcycle riding along next to the bus was Kenny. Lowering the window, she could hear him calling for the bus driver to stop, to pull over.

Emily stuck her head out and yelled, "Go home."

Kenny looked up, saw her and smiled, calling, "Hey, baby."

The bus driver shifted the bus into a lower gear.

"Leave me alone," yelled Emily.

"No can do," Kenny called back.

"Watch out!" cried the driver. He laid on his horn.

Emily stopped breathing as an SUV hurtled into the passing lane and began to pass the bus. It would have been an easy enough maneuver except that the driver didn't see Kenny. The man hit the breaks too late, colliding with the back of the cycle and sending Kenny up and over the handlebars. The cycle skittered sideways across the road and came to rest on the shoulder.

Emily gulped in air as she saw Kenny's body slam into the pavement. He didn't have on a helmet or a leather jacket. Just jeans, boots, and a white T-shirt. It was so like him—a guy who thought he was going to live forever.

The bus slowed to a crawl and finally pulled off to the side of the highway. Emily leaned halfway out the window to keep Kenny in view. He hadn't budged an inch since he hit the asphalt.

Honking the horn, the bus driver called, "That idiot up there's asleep at the wheel."

"What idiot?" Emily twisted around. A car approached from the opposite direction, closing fast. "Stop," she screamed. "Stay back!" She motioned to Kenny with one arm, waving madly at the car with the other.

At the last second, the car swerved, but the back tire clipped Kenny's torso, flipping him onto his back.

"Open the door," Emily screamed. She rushed down the steps and ran toward him. Out of the corner of her eye she saw others running, too. It took a second before she realized it was Jane, Cordelia, and Jonah.

"Someone call nine-one-one," shouted Jane, skidding to a stop next to Kenny. "Grand Rapids is probably the closest town with an EMT." She took off her jacket and laid it over his chest.

Emily knelt down beside him, pressing the back of his hand to her cheek. "Kenny, come on. Wake up."

Jane held two fingers to his neck to see if he had a pulse.

"Is he—"

"He's alive. I don't think we should move him. He could have broken bones, internal injuries."

Emily nodded, noticing Cordelia pull out her phone and move a few yards away.

"Jonah," said Jane, "try to keep everyone back. When Cordelia's done, she'll help you."

"Sure," he said, his eyes locked on Emily.

Emily didn't know what to say to him, so she returned her attention to Kenny. The right side of his face and his arm were a mass of bloody scrapes, and yet it was the tire track across his white T-shirt that caused her the most concern.

"Come on, Kenny," said Emily, smoothing back his hair. "Open your eyes. Let us know you're awake."

His face twitched.

"That's right," said Emily. "I'm here. You're going to be okay."

For the next few minutes, cars parked along the sides of the road and a crowd began to gather. Jane did her best to fend off questions. Emily kept her eyes down and refused to talk.

Seeing his face twitch again, Emily leaned over and whispered in his ear. A few seconds later his eyes fluttered and then opened.

"The fuck happened?" he groaned, trying to sit up.

"Best not to move," said Jane. "You were in an accident. The paramedics will be here any minute."

"Eee-yah. I'll . . . stay put."

"Where does it hurt?" asked Emily.

He tapped his midsection. "Hurts bad."

"Broken ribs?" said Jane.

"Dunno." Raising his eyes to Emily, he said, "Hi."

She felt tears well in her eyes. "You're crazy, you know that?"

"Certifiable." Fresh blood leaked from his nose.

"Just stay with us," said Jane.

As they waited for the paramedics to arrive, the conversation around them seemed to grow louder. The SUV was in the ditch about twenty yards away. A bald man in a business suit shouted at the driver, who continued to sit in the front seat. Another small group had gathered around the driver of the car that hit Kenny. A few were on cell phones. Some were crying.

While Emily kept Kenny awake by telling him about a visit she'd made to the hospital in Grand Rapids when she was eleven, Jane did a visual examination of Kenny's body.

"Nothing looks broken. Since he wasn't wearing a helmet, he probably has a concussion. A jacket might have helped. These harness boots are the only thing he has on that makes any sense."

Examining the boots a bit more closely, Jane did a double take.

Kenny lifted his head to watch her.

Sitting back on her heels, Jane's eyes collided with his. "You were there that night. At the theater. Your right boot. It's missing an O-ring."

"This is no time for silly questions," said Emily sharply.

Jane turned to stare at her. "You knew about it? Were you there, too?"

Everything was coming apart. A feeling of panic gripped Emily so hard that it was all she could do not to get up and run. She had to stop Kenny before he spilled everything.

"Guy had it coming," muttered Kenny.

"Don't say another word," commanded Emily.

"You shot him?" asked Jane.

"Had to."

"Kenny, no!"

"Why?"

"Guy was too ugly to live."

"Kenny, stop," demanded Emily. "Please. If you love me—"

"I do love you, babe. That's why I've gotta tell what I know. Set things right."

The look in his eyes silenced her.

"He found out about Fisherman's Cove, didn't he," said Jane. "About the marijuana, what you and Em——"

"Emily had no part in it. It was just me, got that? Me and nobody else." This time his words were clearer, with more energy behind them. "I took that guy out. Just him and me in the theater that afternoon."

By the look on Jane's face, Emily could tell she didn't believe him.

"You planted the gun in Wendell's locker," said Jane.

"Don't . . . like pussies." Kenny grinned, then grimaced, glancing up at Jonah.

"You need to rest," said Emily.

"Nah," he said. "Truth-telling . . . time. Now or never."

"Don't say that," she said. "You're catastrophizing."

"Huh?" he grunted.

"What about Lyndie?" asked Jane.

With eyes half closed, he mumbled, "Might as well tell. Nothing to lose now." He took a ragged breath. "Mr. Cop Man, he told Gran about the pot that I was selling. She threatened——" He turned on his side, doubled over, pressing a hand to his stomach. "——to . . . tell my dad. I told her not to mess with me. I never meant——" He stopped, took a couple more uneven breaths. "She called me last Monday night, told me to come to the store. I tried . . . you know . . . to reason with her, but she wouldn't listen. I got mad, grabbed her by the throat. All happened so fast. Kind of a blur, you know. She fell back against the counter. Hit her head. I was crying 'cause I couldn't get her to wake up."

"Jane," Emily pleaded, "can't you see he's in pain? He's not in his right mind."

"Mind's okay," rasped Kenny. "Rest of me's not so hot. Hold my hand again."

When she took it, it felt cold and sweaty.

Five minutes went by. Then ten. In the distance, Emily heard the faint sound of sirens approaching from the east. A few of the onlookers began to cheer, while others clapped.

When Kenny turned his head to look, blood belched from his mouth.

Emily gasped.

"Em," he said, wiping the blood away with the back of his hand. "Closer."

She hunched down.

"Ain't gonna make it."

"No—"

"Listen. That kid. You take good care of him. If he's part of you, he's the best part of me."

"Kenny, you've gotta hold on."

"Give him my name, okay. Kenneth. Don't let nobody call him Kenny."

"I promise."

"You're beautiful," he said. "We had fun. No regrets."

"Kenny—"

"No regrets," he said, closing his eyes.

34

Wendell moved unsteadily across the deck on his way to the front door. He'd had a hard time holding it together all morning. His nerves were frayed wires. He peered in one of the windows and saw Jill inside, standing behind the kitchen counter. He waved. It was a timid gesture and he despised himself for it. As he waited for her to answer the door, drops of sweat dripped down his back under his shirt.

"Wendell, hi," said Jill. "Come in."

He thought she looked awful. Frail. Thin as a stick. She tried to act all nicey-nice, though it was obvious she wasn't happy to see him. Nothing new in that. "I've just got a second," he said, stepping cautiously over the threshold, not wanting to get too far from the door. "Is Tessa home?"

"Afraid not."

"Rats. I should have phoned." His eyes darted furtively around the living room. "I've never been in here before. It's nice."

"Thanks."

Not very friendly. Tessa must have guessed who'd called her last night. Jill probably knew everything. "You see," he began, wiping the sweat off his upper lip, "I suppose Tessa told you that I was the one who called her late last night."

"You did? Why?"

"It was all a mistake," he said, refusing to look her in the eye. "I didn't mean it. Can you tell her that?"

"Mean what?"

Was it possible she didn't know? "Here," he said, shoving a manila folder at her. "Take it. It's all the information I found on Tessa—or Sabra, I guess her real name is—in Helen Merland's old papers." He looked down. "I thought I'd use it to blackmail Tessa, but I couldn't go through with it. Not so much because of Tessa. I like her okay, although I don't really know her. It's more because of Helen. What would happen if the authorities found out she'd brought two fugitives to live in Lost Lake? I don't think she has many good years left. I can't stand the idea that she might have to spend them in jail." He pressed the folder into her hands. "You've got to take this. I need you to tell Tessa that there's more. I didn't get it all. You should probably burn that. Promise me if the police come after Tessa, that she won't tell them about Helen."

Jill opened the folder and looked inside.

"Do you promise? Because if you don't—"

"I promise," said Jill, tucking the folder under her arm.

"Word of honor?"

"My word of honor."

"I better get back to the Merland house then. I told Helen I was stopping by, but that I'd be home in time to make her lunch." As he turned to go, he saw Kelli Christopher marching up the deck steps. His body went rigid. He was about to push out through the screen when Kelli put her hand on the wood frame and stopped him.

"Not so fast," she said. She motioned for a deputy to follow her up on the deck.

"I was just going," said Wendell, wishing his smile wasn't quite so forced.

"We need to talk."

"How did you know I was here?"

"I stopped by the Merland place. Helen told me. I'd like you to come down to the station."

"Why?"

"Let's not make a big deal out of this, Wendell. Just come, okay?"

"No, I won't agree to that." He stood his ground. It felt good.

"I suppose, if Jill doesn't mind, we could do it here?"

"Do what? Helen's waiting for her lunch."

"She can wait a few minutes more," said Kelli, forcing him backward into the living room. "Is this okay with you?" Kelli asked Jill.

She shrugged.

Wendell watched everyone sit down. Everyone except him. The door was like a magnet and he was a helpless iron filing.

"Sit," said Kelli.

"Don't tell me what to do." He wasn't sure why his comment should illicit a faint smile. "Tell me what you want."

"We know you set the fire that destroyed your business."

Wendell swayed sideways and nearly fell. He held on to the back of a chair for support. "That's ridiculous. A space heater caught fire in the second-floor apartment."

"That may be. But we have evidence to prove that a fire was also set on the back porch. You ignited a plastic jug of gasoline by sticking one of your socks in it, using it as a wick."

"What? No, no. I was miles away."

"We found DNA on that sock, Wendell. It matches the DNA found under Steve Feigenbaumer's fingernails."

"I didn't *do* it."

"Then who did?"

He half dropped, half fell into a chair. "I should never have listened to him."

"Listened to who?"

"He'll hurt me if I tell you."

"I'll hurt you if you don't."

The room started to spin. "This isn't me," said Wendell, a pure panic taking hold of him. "I'm not like this."

"If you hired someone to burn down your business, it is like you."

"I don't know why I let him talk me into it."

"Who?" demanded Kelli.

"Kenny Moon. Jim Moon's son." He raked a shaky hand through his hair. "I was having a beer after work one night last spring. Got to talking about my financial problems with the bartender. You know how it is. You have a drink, you get a little loose. That's when he came over and sat down next to me. Said he had a solution to all my financial woes. We took our beers over to a table in the back. He told me he could torch my business, make it look like an accident. It would be simple. When I got the insurance payoff, I was supposed to give him five thousand dollars." Wendell kept his head down, though he raised his eyes so he could watch Kelli. He could almost see the wheels turning inside her head.

"You're a real mensch, Wendell. Your wife would have been so proud."

Her words all but pulverized him. He tried to swallow but something seemed to be stuck in his throat. Perhaps, he thought, it was his misplaced principles. "I didn't murder Steve Feigen-baumer. I have no idea how the gun got in my locker."

"I might," said Kelli. "We still need to get a sample of your DNA."

"Fine. Gladly. Anything to prove my innocence."

"Oh, you're hardly innocent, Wendell. But then, I doubt that comes as a news flash."

35

Sunsets over Lost Lake were events in Tessa's life that she'd taken for granted. Fall, winter, spring, summer, they were a given, sometimes beautiful, often ordinary, occasionally breathtaking. As she stood on the cottage deck that night, watching the sun sink slowly in the western sky, she discovered in herself a new appreciation. The world could be an extraordinary place, when it wasn't approximating hell. And yet, how could a person understand the difference if they didn't exist side by side? Love and hate. Good and evil. Light and dark. She assumed humans were supposed to glean some important truth from the riddle of duality, and yet, somewhere along the line, she must have missed the point. She felt as ignorant about the meaning of the cosmos today as she had when she was a little girl, gazing up at the heavens from the field in front of her Nebraska home. Perhaps more so, in that she'd lived her whole life looking for answers.

A while later, as Tessa sat in her chair in the living room, she heard Jill's footsteps on the deck stairs. She smiled, seeing the dying rays of the sun reflect off Jill's face and turn it golden.

"I got your call. Why didn't you come to the park?"

"I couldn't leave. Not like that."

The ferocity of their kisses, their embrace, propelled them backward toward the bedroom.

"I didn't think I'd ever see you again," said Jill, holding Tessa's face in her hands. "You can't stay. An FBI agent came by this morning after you left. He said he'd be back."

Suddenly, they were on the bed, too hungry for each other to talk. They'd never made love like this before, with such urgency, every touch heightened by a sense of impending loss.

When they finally pulled apart, out of breath, Jill said, "It's not safe for you here."

"It's not safe for me anywhere." Tessa closed her eyes, breathing in the sense of comfort Jill's presence brought. "This is the way it should be. The way I want it to be. Just a normal conversation. How was your day?"

"How can we have a normal conversation at a time like this?"

"Humor me."

Laying her head against Tessa's arm, Jill said, "There are some things that happened today you don't know about. Kenny Moon's in the hospital in Grand Rapids. He was chasing Emily Jensen. I guess she decided to leave town this morning. He was on his motorcycle when he was hit by a car. Jonah's with Emily at the hospital. Cordelia and Jane are there, too. He's not expected to survive the night."

"Such a shame," said Tessa, feeling herself begin to drift.

"If he does pull through, Kelli Christopher plans to arrest him for the murder of his grandmother and Steve Feigenbaumer."

"*He* did it?" The comment pulled her back.

Jill explained what she knew. "If only that FBI agent hadn't stopped by, it might have been safe for you to come home."

"It will never be safe," said Tessa, thinking of the letter she'd received from Feigenbaumer's daughter. There was no point in telling Jill about it. Fighting a yawn, Tessa held Jill closer.

"You're tired?" asked Jill.

"There's something I need to tell you. This won't be easy, for either of us."

"What is it?" said Jill, searching Tessa's face.

"I can't run. It won't work. I found that out today, so in a way, it was time well spent. I don't have it in me to start a new life. Maybe it's my age, or maybe I've just come to the end of my rope."

"So you're going to stay and let them arrest you?"

"The police reserve the worst region of hell for cop killers. And honestly, the idea of being locked away for the rest of my life, dying alone—I can't even go there."

Jill held on tighter. "Okay, so there are no good options, but if you were in jail, at least I'd be able to write you, call you, come see you."

"It's just another form of hell."

"Why? Maybe, with the right lawyer, you could—"

"It's not going to happen."

"There are mitigating circumstances."

"I talked to a lawyer this afternoon in Grand Rapids. He walked me through what I'd be likely to face. I refuse to surrender to the legal system in this country with a false hope of leniency. Why would a judge even consider it? I didn't show Allen Feigenbaumer any."

Jill began to shiver.

"Please, honey, I need you to help me. Can you be strong, just a little while longer?"

"I can't lose you."

"I was lost the moment I planted that bomb."

"So what's the answer? What do we do?"

"I talked to another man while I was in Grand Rapids this afternoon. Remember Erasmus? Not his real name, but the one he went by. I interviewed him several years ago when I was writing that one-act play about assisted suicide."

Jill's body stiffened.

"I told him that I wanted to end my life. He gave me the new pills they're using in Europe, showed me how to use them, what to expect."

"We have to talk about this."

"I already took them. Hours ago."

Jill sat upright, her face red with fury. "How could you do that without talking to me first?"

"Would you have said to go ahead with it?"

"No. Never." She climbed out of bed and stormed out of the room.

"Where are you going?" called Tessa.

"To call the paramedics."

Summoning all her strength, Tessa followed her into the kitchen.

"This affects me, too!" screamed Jill, whirling around.

"You think I don't know that? You think I made this decision lightly, without considering all the ramifications? Listen to me. No, don't look away. I want your eyes right here." She pointed to her face. "I can't run. I refuse to go to prison. What other option do I have?"

"I don't know, but there have to be *some*."

"What do you think I've been doing all week? Sitting in that goddamned living room with my foot up? All I've done is think. I'm sick of it. You would worry about me constantly if I went to prison. You'd never have another peaceful moment. Is that what you want?"

"I want you *alive*."

"And miserable? Dealing with daily abuse? Humiliation? Worrying about you worrying about me? That's not living. Don't you get it? I made the only decision I could. Don't be angry. And even if you are, I can't change it."

Jill dug her cell phone out of her purse.

"It's too late for that."

"It's not."

"The drug is already in my system. I didn't call you until there was no turning back."

"I don't believe you!"

"It's true. I swear on my love for you."

"No!"

"Honey, please. If I could go back in time and change what I did, I would." She swayed, almost fell.

Jill rushed to her.

"Help me back to the bed."

Once she was lying down, she felt a little better. "I know this is hard, but will you stay with me? Hold me? Please," she begged. "Please."

Still crying, Jill drew her into her arms.

"Do you forgive me?"

She didn't answer.

They pulled the covers up and stayed like that, locked in each other's arms.

"I don't have long," said Tessa. She was losing track, slipping in and out. "I love you. You've been the best part of my life."

"I love you, too," whispered Jill, tenderly kissing her forehead.

"Tell Jonah . . . sorry I couldn't say good-bye. I wrote a note. Put it on his pillow. Make sure—" She swallowed, couldn't seem to finish the sentence.

"I don't know what I'll do without you," whispered Jill, her voice thick with tears.

"I'll . . . be with you, I promise. I won't leave you alone."

"I love you so much."

"We'll see each other again, I know it."

Jill squeezed her hand.

Tessa was floating now, moving further and further away. She tried to speak, but her words came out garbled.

"Say that again?" said Jill, her mouth next to Tessa's ear. "Please, sweetheart. I need to know what you're thinking."

Gathering all her all her strength, Tessa struggled to form what she'd longed to say for so many years, to finally reclaim what was lost.

"My name," she whispered, not sure if she was speaking the words or only thinking them, ". . . is Sabra."

Epilogue

With her bare feet dangling in the water, Jane relaxed on the wood dock outside her parents' cabin on Blackberry Lake, Mouse lying beside her, and watched a sailboat with a billowing white sail skim across the choppy water. It was a cloudless evening. She'd arrived back at the lodge around four and was met by a ridiculously joyful dog and a smiling Nolan. Cordelia planned to stay up north with Jill for the next week. After some hemming and hawing, she agreed to allow Jane to borrow her car so she could drive back.

The word had come down from Jill that there would be no funeral. Tessa had asked to have her body cremated and the ashes scattered in the woods behind the cottage. Jane would drive back at the end of the week for a private ceremony, just close friends and a few relatives. From what Jane had witnessed this morning before she left, Jonah had taken Tessa's death particularly hard. With Kenny's confession, the mystery of the fire and the two murders had been put to rest. Lamentably, there were still loose ends, questions that nobody would ever be able to answer. Human actions and motivations were messy, and that, of course, ate at Jane. More fodder, she supposed, for her late-night maunderings.

Kelli had come to Thunderhook to see Jane off. She invited her to come back for dinner the next time she was in town. Jane accepted the invitation gladly.

Leaving Jill was the hardest part. They'd held each other for a long time. Few words were spoken because neither of them knew what to say.

Hearing the wood deck creak behind her, Jane called, "Time for our talk?"

"Think so," said Nolan, sitting down on the other side of Mouse. He was wearing shorts and a cotton shirt. When he stuck his bare feet into the water beside hers, he sighed. "This is the life."

"You can drive up anytime you want."

"Nice to have friends with cabins. You've been lost in thought out here. Didn't want to bother you."

"I've been thinking about Emily Jensen."

"Jonah and Kenny's girlfriend?"

"I'm pretty sure she never loved Kenny. But I do think she might have been at the theater the night he shot Feigenbaumer."

"No way to prove it, though."

"Nope."

"And?"

"You think there's an and?"

"Pretty sure there is."

She laughed. "It's kind of a dark thought."

"Murder leads directly to those."

Studying the far shore, she said, "It was the way Emily reacted yesterday afternoon when I saw the O-ring missing from

Kenny's boot. It took me a while to figure it out. I believe it was guilt. I think she was there, too."

"And? You think she fired the gun? That Kenny may have been involved in a fight with the guy, but that Emily pulled the trigger."

"You're good."

"Nobody will ever know for sure."

"What a thing to have to live with."

"Kinda like your friend Tessa."

"Yeah. Kinda like." She considered it a moment more, then stretched her arms over her head. "I suppose you want an answer to your question."

He nodded. "Yes, ma'am, I do."

"It's hard, you know? I've helped a lot of friends find the truth behind crimes that affected them. When you know the people involved, when you like—or even love—some of them, it just makes it tougher."

"Well," he said, running his hand down Mouse's back. "It's never easy. Even if you don't know the people, you end up caring. It's the way of the world. Human solidarity. We don't want bad things to happen to people we like, even if they're guilty, which they often are."

She kicked her feet through the water.

"Quit stalling. A simple yes or no will do. No explanations needed."

"Here's the deal, as I see it. The reason you can take only the cases that interest you is because you have your police pension. If I sign on with you, I want the same option, which means I need the money that comes from my restaurants. Their continued success is vital to me. Being a restaurateur may not fill every up every nook and cranny of my soul, but it's a big part of who I am."

"Understood."

"This is what I'm offering. I'll do one case with you a month, as long as it doesn't take every hour of every day."

"It's not entirely what I'd hoped for, but we could make it work."

"I get to pick the case."

"I'll have to think about that one. Can we table it for the moment—unless it's a deal breaker."

"It's not."

"Then? Do we have a deal?"

They shook hands, her pale hand encompassed by his powerful brown one.

"This calls for a celebration," he said, pulling a line of fish out of the water.

"Since you caught them, it's only fair that I clean them and make us dinner."

"Sounds like the beginning of a mutually beneficial partnership to me," he said, handing her the line and grinning.